DISCIPLE OF THE DOG

SCOTT BAKKER

First published in Great Britain in 2010 by Orion Books,
an imprint of The Orion Publishing Group Ltd
Orion House, 5 Upper Saint Martin's Lane
London WC2H 9EA

An Hachette UK Company

1 3 5 7 9 10 8 6 4 2

A CIP catalogue record for this book is available from the British Library.

ISBN (Hardback) 978 0 7528 9831 5
ISBN (Trade Paperback) 978 0 7528 9832 2

Printed in Great Britain by CPI Mackays, Chatham, Kent

www.orionbooks.co.uk

For Ruby

Wow

Also by Scott Bakker

Neuropath

Writing as R. Scott Bakker

THE PRINCE OF NOTHING SERIES

The Darkness That Comes Before

The Warrior-Prophet

The Thousandfold Thought

THE ASPECT-EMPEROR SERIES

The Judging Eye

I am called a dog because I fawn on those who give, bark at those who refuse, and set my teeth in rascals.

Diogenes of Sinope

Track One

A REAL WINNER

My father always claimed I had an attitude problem. "You're too dismissive," he once told me. "Too quick to judge. Life is bigger than you know, you know."

To which I replied, "C'mon, Dad. That's just stupid talk."

That was June 13, 1981. A good day.

For some mysterious reason, maybe genetic, maybe environmental, maybe some combination of the two, I am doubtful and irreverent through and through. Show me a picture of your newborn baby and I'll ask you if you're holding it upside down. Tell me you've won the lottery and I'll give you the number of my coke dealer. Show me a flag and I see kinky sheets on a hooker's bed. I never commit, not to the big things, and certainly not to the little. It's not that I'm evil or anything, it's just that, no matter how hard I try, I never think *what I should.* Where everyone sees a Merge sign, I read Detour.

A true-blue individual—that's what I am.

You would think that would make me popular, you know, home of the brave, land of the free, all that crap. But such is not the case, alas. Truth is, the only kind of individualism Americans believe in is the one that numbs the sting of name tags, or that makes a trip to the mall an exercise in self-creation. The consumer kind.

The false kind.

And who knows? Maybe that's the way it should be.

Ignore the Merge sign long enough, and sooner or later somebody gets killed.

I'm what you would call a cynic.

This isn't to be confused with a skeptic. Skeptics don't believe in anything because they care *too much.* For them the dignity of truth is perpetually beyond the slovenly reach of humankind. We're just not qualified.

A cynic, on the other hand, doesn't believe in anything because he doesn't care *enough.* I mean, really, who gives a fuck?

You?

My name is Disciple Manning. A stupid name, I know—pretty much what you would expect from stupid-talking parents. When people ask me my name, I simply say Diss, Diss Manning. When they make funny with their faces, I lie and tell them I was named after my father, Datt Manning. I usually get a laugh out of dat. If I don't, if I still get the funny stuff, you know, the *What-fucking-planet-are-you-from* look, then I hit them, hard—unless they happen to be a cop, in which case I just keep kissing ass.

The one thing you need to remember about me is that I don't forget.

Anything.

Ever.

According to the doctors, it's driving me crazy.

And this is why I find myself sitting down and *writing.* My latest therapist thinks my problem isn't *what* I remember so much as *how.* She's a big believer in the power of *stories.* She thinks hammering my more toxic memories into narrative form will give them some kind of psychologically redemptive meaning.

Sounds foofy, I know. I've always thought writing is just what happens when we pursue our genius for justifying our scams for its own sake. But she's cute, and there's a wisdom you get after botching as many suicide attempts as I have. Putting pen to paper just doesn't seem that big a deal after putting knife to skin.

Nothing does, really. Strange knowledge, that.

Otherwise, I'm like pretty much everyone else. I used to have all these grandiose goals and ambitions, an abiding conviction that I was the master of my own destiny, blah-blah-blah. But life just kept happening, you know? And the ad hoc decisions piled up and up and up, until I found myself stranded on a mountain not of my own making. You see, it's *convenience* that drives the species, not in any grand sense but in the most squalid way you could possibly imagine. Say your wife starts coming home late on a regular basis, and you get this kind of queasy feeling in your gut, like on some parallel plane of existence you just stepped off the Tilt-A-Whirl. So what do you do? Say nothing. Follow the ruts. Keep your eyes on the habituated prize. Only ten years to go on the mortgage!

It's these kinds of decisions that define who we are, by and large. The small kind. The *lazy* kind.

And then one day you wake up, and the distance between your youthful hope and your middle-aged actuality yawns like a tiger on the wrong side of the cage. What happened? you ask yourself, but you know. It's written into the meat of you, all those little concessions to your weaker nature.

Trust me, dude, I know. I *spy on you.* I see you all the time. Gambling away your wife's savings, giving a hand job to your husband's best friend. I'm the guy who hands the envelope to your spouse so that he or she can give it to the divorce lawyer, or even worse, confront you with it. I'm the archivist of your lesser self—you know, the side of you that calls the shots between official engagements. I'm the bastard who makes your secrets real. Disciple Manning, the sole proprietor of Manning Investigations, based out of Newark, New Jersey.

That's right. I'm a private detective. A dick. The part-time security guard of the investigative world.

A real winner.

Track Two
DEAD JENNIFER

Monday ...

When Jonathan and Amanda Bonjour first came to my office, I assumed it would be yet one more missing kid gig, and I was right. When a couple comes in together, it generally has something to do with either a parent or a kid—usually the latter, but you would be surprised at how many grandmas go off the rails gambling, and how many grandpas climb *on* the rails—the snorting kind. Especially these days.

My agency lies on one of those streets where ratty sidewalk frontages from the twenties alternate with strip malls set behind lines of anemic trees. The kind of place where mom grips junior's hand a little extra tight. Pawnshops. Cut-rate pedicures and hairdressing. A bar that booms on welfare cheque day, and another bar that somehow ekes by on nothing at all—just lingers. Same-day loans. The world's most grungy IHOP.

All that's missing is a methadone clinic.

My kingdom consists of a narrow, thousand-square-foot retail slot strategically situated between a souvlaki stand and a porn shop—so when the air doesn't reek of charred lamb, it smells like cheap lubricants. My office lies at the back, next to the all-important copy-slash-smoking room. I have my desk positioned so that I can either pretend nobody's home or, with a simple crane of my neck, glimpse anyone unfortunate enough to wander in. This is precisely what I did when I heard the cowbell on my entrance cough and clunk—apparently it has a crack in it—at precisely 11:48 A.M. on Monday.

I first glimpsed the Bonjours standing side by side before my secretary, Kimberley, in the reception area, which I have shrewdly decorated with water stains and a chipped plaster ceiling. Jonathan Bonjour was heavy-set. I would have thought of him as fat, but I have this mindset where I begin flattering people mentally the instant they walk in the door. The well-practised lie always comes off the best. I knew instantly that he was a lawyer simply because his suit *fit.* Since no two people pack on weight the same way, it's pretty much impossible for fat guys to find suits that fit off the rack.

Mrs. Bonjour—Amanda—was overweight as well, but in that healthy, pear-shaped way that seems to drive death row inmates crazy. The curls of her hair shimmered violet on black in the light panning through my office's front window, and her lips were pert and poppy red, what you might expect to find on an Alabama stenographer rather than a New Jersey lawyer's wife. Her skin was real pale. Side by side, the two of them fairly shouted good genes and easy living—a testament to the American Dream.

So of course something tragic had to have happened.

I basically have two routines that I use when introducing myself to new clients. Either I play Remington, razor-sharp on the outside but warm and slippery within, or I play Columbo, a mob of yarn tangled about concealed razors. Appearances being everything, I opted for the Remington approach, sauntered out to lean against the door frame. I smiled at the couple with solemn confidence, said, "Please ... Kimberley, do show them in." I suppose the debonair image I cut jarred with the smell of baba ghanouj that happened to occupy the aromatic high ground at that particular moment, but the Bonjours seemed too freaked out to really care.

Once in my office, Jonathan Bonjour shook my hand with the inky ease of people who habitually press the flesh. His face was tanned and handsome above his jowls, and his blue eyes possessed a canniness that I immediately recognized. I've yet to meet a lawyer who wasn't a cynic of some description. You spend your life pretending to believe assholes and you're bound to start seeing shit everywhere you look. Just another hazard of the trade.

I could tell that he recognized something in my eyes as well. Weird, all these little moments that pass between people. For most everybody, they slip into oblivion, but me, I catch them like flies.

Amanda Bonjour was an entirely different story. To her, I was something out of a bad movie, yet another symptom that her life had gone from badness to madness. When I reached out to shake her hand, she almost flinched, as though instinctively loath to confirm what the greater part of her refused to believe. Everyone knows that touching something makes it real.

To spare her any embarrassment, I turned my outstretched hand into a *Please-take-a-seat* gesture. What can I say? She was a customer, and I was wearing a name tag.

She kind of plumped into the seat next to her husband's then immediately started crying. I hate to admit it, but that was the precise moment I decided to charge them my highest rate. Ugly, I know, but the doctor said this whole storytelling thing would be, and I quote, "little more than a self-aggrandizing exercise in futility" unless I'm brutally honest.

After fumbling through the introductions, Jonathan Bonjour got to the point.

"It's our daughter, Mr. Manning. She's missing."

Even though I expected he would say as much, I found myself slightly winded. I really don't know why, given that I had heard the words "She's missing" more times than somebody like you would care to remember. It's like the planes hitting the World Trade Center: you see it over and over and over, until it carries about as much punch as a movie trailer, and then one night you see it and *wham!* it steals your breath, and you sweat horror, as though part of your soul had been on that plane, and had only now remembered.

She's missing ...

"What's her name?" I asked.

"Jennifer," Mrs. Bonjour said, a wisp of reverence in her tone. She snuffled.

"Jenni," her husband added. "That's, ah ... what, ah ... what everyone calls her."

I'm not what you would call the sympathetic sort—I remember too much of my own pain to concern myself with hurts that others will eventually forget—but something cracked through Mr. Bonjour's modulated voice, something primal, and something within me answered in an empathetic rush. For an instant I could literally *feel* the teetering possibilities. I could see the empty bedroom down the hall, the door neither opened nor closed, the bar of accusing light gleaming across the hardwood floor. I could hear the silence emanating from the girlish running shoes abandoned next to the door jamb ...

The Bonjour house, I knew, was becoming a museum to "last times."

"Do you have a picture?" I asked, my voice rough enough to be embarrassing.

Amanda Bonjour immediately leaned forward, a four-by-six glossy in her hand. She stared at me intently as I lifted it.

And I could feel it, the magic of names humming up out of the photo. She would have been just another generic, beautiful face otherwise, something to focus the momentary lust of consumers. Long blond hair, straight enough to summon memories of Marcia Brady. Full lips. Straight teeth. Happiness almost shining in her sparkling blue eyes.

I knew instantly that she hadn't run away—she was too attractive. Runaways are almost always plain or downright ugly, as intent to escape the damnation of photos like these as to flee the judgment of peers, parents, what have you. Beautiful people generally lack the motive required to stage their own disappearance. On the contrary, beautiful people tend to be about *appearances.*

I should know.

"She's not a runaway," I said, looking up to meet the Bonjours' gaze. "What is she? Nineteen? Twenty in this photo?"

"Nineteen," Mrs. Bonjour said in a small voice.

"And that would make her?"

"Twenty-one." Her breath was tight, deep-sea-diver deliberate. "She's twenty-one now."

I set the photo against the base of my desk lamp so that I could reference her face and her parents with a single glance. I graced them with a sage nod, then leaned back in my chair with an open-handed gesture. "So ... what happened?"

The story they told me sounded like something cribbed from the Biography Channel. Flattering and negativity-free. You see, people always *make cases.* Always. Rather than simply describe things, they pitch them this way and that. So when the Bonjours said that Jennifer was a curious girl, an overachiever, and so on, they were literally offering evidence of the adequacy of their parenting skills, while at the same time saying, *"She wasn't the kind of girl who ..."* They wanted me to know that whatever it was that had happened to their precious daughter had precious little to do with them. And when they mentioned her "weakness for musicians," they were saying that, as perfectly as she had been raised, she exhibited a dispositional vulnerability to untoward influences—so to speak.

If I was surprised when they mentioned the cult, it was because I had expected *drugs* to be the culprit—simply because they almost always are when beautiful kids take roads not marked in their parents' road atlas. According to Mrs. Bonjour, she had found *Them* online as a high school student, first becoming, without the knowledge of Mom and Dad, a "long-distance associate," then graduating to become a "text messenger" in her first year of college. At some point she began attending weekend retreats, which cut ever more deeply into her visits home, until she dropped out of her nursing program altogether and moved into the Compound—a place just outside a Rust Belt town called Ruddick in southeastern Pennsylvania.

"What do they call themselves?" I asked. So far the Bonjours had only referred to the cult as either "They" or "Them," spoken in tones of stone-age superstition.

Both faces became pensive and sour. I half expected one of them to whisper "Voldemort" or "Sauron" or something.

"They call themselves the Framers," Amanda said.

"Never heard of them. What do they believe?"

She pulled a face. "That the world, this world, isn't really ... real."

"Isn't that religion in general?" I cracked before I could stop myself.

"You explain it," she said crossly to her husband. "Jon has a philosophy degree," she explained, saying "philosophy degree" the way others say "drinking problem."

"They're one of those New Age, human potential things," Jonathan said. "What's called a *charismatic* cult."

As I subsequently learned on the Web, this meant they had organized themselves around the revelations of a single, power-monopolizing individual—apparently a very bad sign as far as cults go.

"The leader's name," he continued, "is Xenophon Baars. He's a former philosophy professor out of Berkeley, believe it or not ..."

"You make it sound as if he should know better."

"He *should* know better."

"Maybe he does ..."

"Of course he does!" Mrs. Bonjour cried. "The whole thing is a murderous con!"

Whether it was the savagery of her interruption or the implications of that word "murderous," the outburst left an embarrassing chill in its wake.

"What my wife means," Mr. Bonjour said stiffly, "is that the cult's beliefs are too ... extreme for anyone with Baars's education to seriously entertain. We think he's simply duping these people for money and, ah ... sex."

"What do you mean by 'extreme'?"

"They think the world is about to end," he said, his tone as blank as his face.

"And?" So far the Framers were sounding pretty commonplace. The philosophy professor thing was a twist of sorts, I supposed. But otherwise? Didn't all those crazy fuckers think the end was nigh?

"Five billion years from now ..."

Fawk.

I tried hard not to smirk. "You mean, like ... when the sun swallows us up?"

"Exactly. This Baars has convinced his followers that the world is more than five billion years *older than it is.* And that it's about to end."

I rubbed my face in an attempt to wipe away a marvelling grin. I looked at them both, each desolate in a different way, gouged not only by loss but by *disbelief.* That something so absurd, so stupid ...

I nodded gravely. "I see what you mean."

I've seen more than my fair share of absurdities in my time: Christ, this job throws them at you like rotten fruit at a burlesque gone wrong. Tragedy astounds people no matter what, sure. The big things are just too heavy to be caught in human nets. But life also has a nasty habit of dishing up calamity as the punchline of a joke as well, and with a regularity that's nothing short of perverse. We keep waiting for something

Shakespearean to happen, when most of the world is just an annex to the Jerry Springer show. Squalid. Cheap. Mean-spirited.

So few people die pretty.

I glanced at the photo of Jennifer Bonjour leaning against my faux art deco lamp. An unopened bill lay askew just below it, and I glimpsed my name and the top third of my address through the plastic window. DISCIPLE MANNING, stamped across some law of perspective. The chill of sudden conviction dropped through me ... The first of many such chills, as it turned out.

I'm not sure how I knew she was dead, but somehow I did—and I suspected the grieving couple before me knew as well.

I pressed them for details of the police investigation, expecting to hear the Bonjour version of what I've come to call the Authority Rant. Most everybody who comes to me has a grudge against the authorities, either because they have something to hide or because they've been let down in some manner. When it comes to cases like the Bonjours', they almost always have a tale of official indifference, incompetence, or, if they're really mad, outright malfeasance. Personally, I had nothing against The System. I understood the kinds of limitations that cops faced: the politics, the fatigue individuals were prone to, the constraints of policy and procedure, the ways bureaucratic machinery could generate irrational outcomes.

I've worked in factories before. I know the score.

As it turned out, so did the Bonjours. The story they told was one of a local police chief who meant well but was hopelessly out of his depth when it came to this case. Caleb Nolen, his name was. Chief Caleb Nolen. From what they described, he did everything by the book, and a few things above and beyond. According to the Framers (Nolen had interviewed all twenty-seven of them), Jennifer left the Compound with another cult member named Anson Williams at around 8:30 P.M. to walk into town to a bar called Legends, where the two liked to dance. The walk was a long one, at least two and a half miles, much of it through Ruddick's largely abandoned industrial park, but apparently the two enjoyed the air, exercise, and the opportunity to talk. They were close friends but not lovers. Witnesses placed the two of them at the bar, dancing and drinking, until approximately 11:30 P.M., when the doorman said Jennifer left muted but not otherwise distraught. According to Anson, she had been nursing a headache most of the evening and finally decided to return home to sleep. He claimed that she agreed to call a cab at his insistence, but the doorman said that she left on foot, headed in the direction of the Framer Compound.

She never arrived.

According to cellphone records, Anson called her twice, once at 12:03 A.M. and again at 12:17 A.M. She didn't answer. He then called the Compound, asking whether anyone had seen her. When he learned from the doorman that she had walked, he struck out on foot after her, calling her name and searching the verges of the road. Evidently, he feared she had been hit by a passing car. He found nothing. At 1:33 A.M., Xenophon Baars himself called the police department, expressing his concern. At approximately 2 A.M., one of Nolen's deputies embarked on a cursory search of the route and the surrounding brown lands—apparently the area is mazed with abandoned steel and assembly plants, a creepy place for a young woman to be walking alone, but so familiar to the locals that they thought nothing of it. When she failed to turn up the next morning, the Chief wisely said to hell with procedure and pulled out all the missing-person stops. By mid-afternoon they had some eighty-plus volunteers combing the ruined structures and surrounding ravines. There was no sign of her. None. They tried again the next day, this time with State Police dogs. Again, nothing.

The Bonjours got the call from Nolen's office that morning, and I could see the catastrophe on their faces as they described it: the little girl they had loved, nurtured, and even suffered on occasion was missing. Gone.

They fell silent after that.

I asked them about going to the media. They said the police department had already issued a public statement, that two of the Pittsburgh television stations and the main paper, the *Pittsburgh Post-Gazette*, had aired or printed stories along with photos of their daughter—so far to no avail.

"One reporter told us they purposefully bury stories like ours," Amanda said with more than a little animus. "'JonBenét fatigue,' he called it ... But what he meant was that missing pretty white girls are out of *fashion*."

"No," Jon Bonjour said. "It's because of all the criticism the media received, you know ... for being too Hollywood."

"Hollywood?" Amanda fairly cried.

"The way they pick victims like casting directors, stories like movie prod—"

"So what are you saying, Jon? That our daughter is too blond, too beautiful? That *political correctness* is what's keeping her buried on the back page? Keeping her ... lost ..."

Lost? Was that what they really thought?

I glanced at the glossy on my desk, at the dead girl's almost smiling eyes. I could already see the crime scene photographs, the grisly before and after. Naked. The limbs bent in poses the living would find excruciating. The skin purple-grey-white. That was when I started thinking of her as "Dead Jennifer."

Sounds horrible, I know. What can I say? I'm a freak.

I shook my head and pinched my eyes. I did what I always do when my thoughts take an errant turn: I asked a question. "How would you characterize your relationship?"

"What do you mean?" Mrs. Bonjour asked.

"Your relationship with Jennifer. Was it loving or, ah ... troubled?"

"He wants to know whether the cult was just an excuse to escape us," her husband said with spousal wariness. Jonathan Bonjour, I realized at that moment, wasn't simply a lawyer, he was a good lawyer.

"Troubled," Mrs. Bonjour said stiffly. "Troubled."

"Not abusive," Mr. Bonjour interjected. "There's troubled and then there—"

Something flashed across his wife's face. "I'm sure Mr. Manning re—"

"I just didn't want him to get the wrong idea!"

They both looked to me in expectation—funny how some couples turn every third party into a marriage counsellor—so I held them in suspense for a thoughtful moment. "And what idea would that be, Mr. Bonjour?"

"Jon slapped her," Mrs. Bonjour said in a clear, broadcasting tone. "The last ... fight we had. Jon slapped ... her."

"I ... ah ..." Jon Bonjour croaked through his sinuses as though ready to spit à la NASCAR, swallowed instead. He wiped tears from his eyes with a fat thumb. "I ... I don't know what to say." These last words were pinched through a sob. His face flushed red beneath the hood of his hand.

"Jonny blames himself," Mrs. Bonjour said blankly. "He thinks all of this is his fault."

"I appreciate your honesty," I said as professionally as I could. "Most people try to doctor the story, believing they're better served if they come out looking like angels. But the only thing that serves in these situations, the only thing, is the truth." I leaned forward, placed my elbows against the desktop. Very Remington Steele. "You do understand that?"

Irritation scuttled across his fat face. "Of course," he said.

Rates, conditions, and so on are always difficult items to discuss, so you have to be opportunistic, take what chances the ebb and flow of conversation offer. I typically use money talk to doctor breakdowns in the conversation, especially if things become emotionally overwrought.

No small amount of defensiveness and aggression walks into offices like mine. But as soon as you mention money, most of the personal shit just evaporates. I could literally see Mr. and Mrs. Bonjour's heart rates slow as I discussed the terms. Few things are more dear to the human animal than simplicity, or the appearance of it anyway. And few things are more simple, more apparently superficial, than monetary transactions.

Open the wallet, close the heart—that's generally the rule.

They agreed to everything without comment or question—even the exorbitant rate. Something told me that I could have charged double, even triple, and Mr. Bonjour would have responded with precisely the same numb nod. Mrs. Bonjour, I'm sure, would have sold her liver to a Chinese penal hospital if that meant finding her daughter. I suffered that vague and momentary regret that accompanies lost opportunities. You know, *Oh well* ... I realize this isn't the kind of stuff you want to hear from your heroes. But I was juggling too many bills with too few hands—no different than you, I imagine—and Jonathan Bonjour had a big fat wallet just bursting with hands.

"I have one last question," I said, "for you specifically, Mr. Bonjour." The obvious disparity between our income brackets reminded me of an itch I'd wanted to scratch ever since I had realized that Jonathan Bonjour was a lawyer. "Your law firm regularly contracts private investigators, does it not?"

A moment of shock. He hadn't told me his profession.

"I'm not sure I understand."

"Stuff like this ... personal stuff with consequences that are, well, as big as you can imagine ... such stuff requires *trust* ..." I let him twist on that word for a second. "Why wouldn't you go to people you know?"

"This wasn't Jonny's idea," Amanda said. I had already guessed as much, but it was good to hear.

"Even still ..."

"No offence, Mr. Manning, but my opinion of your profession is rather ... jaded ..."

This was like a hooker saying she finds the company of strippers embarrassing. No offence, he says. Fucking lawyers.

"And?"

"Well, let's just say that I've come to that opinion through long experience."

"But it's not *just* that," Amanda added nervously. "You see ... Jonny's *already gone down there*, asking questions and all, and the people are ... well, *more like you.*"

"Like me?" I smiled despite myself, nodded. "You mean, like ... socio-economically disadvantaged."

I counted exactly three seconds of embarrassed silence.

"We thought that you might be able to talk their, uh, language."

Fucking rich people, man. Always riding the yo-yo of entitlement and embarrassment. The good ones, anyway.

"My ad in the Yellow Pages that bad, huh?"

Twin anxious laughs.

The conversation seemed pretty cut and dried, even though the case was anything but. Still, after-the-fact interpretation being what it is, there were enough hanging threads for me to realize this apparent simplicity would likely buckle under scrutiny, if not flip into something altogether different.

I told them I had a couple of cases pending, but that I would start right away anyway. Time is everything when it comes to missing persons. Then I did what I always do with new clients when I take a job: I gave them a list of things to do. Search her room for anything that might help: an old diary, drug paraphernalia, computer disks, or camera SD cards. Call Nolen to tell him they had hired me, that they expected him to do everything in his power to assist me. The same with

Xenophon Baars, taking care to conceal their outrage, of course. "No ego allowed," I told them, quite oblivious to any irony. "This is *not* about scoring points."

You see, the Bonjours had come to me because they were *helpless*. Sure, they'd contractually engaged my services, but emotionally they'd simply swapped one kind of helplessness for another. Who hasn't suffered a pang of impotence in the presence of a mechanic, a plumber, or (worst of all) a computer technician? My clients not only leave my office with a professionally legitimated *Don't-worry-about-a-thing* lie, they also take home a false feeling of empowerment.

A to-do list.

Makes them happy, and it makes my job easier—sometimes, anyway. Clients have a way of fucking things up.

I ushered the Bonjours to the plate glass entrance with the solemn efficiency of a funeral home director. There was an uncomfortable pause as Mrs. Bonjour knelt on the mat to retie her shoes. Mr. Bonjour simply didn't know what to say; he just copped that stiff pose that so many husbands assume when their wives interrupt otherwise economical social transactions with nitty concerns. *Why couldn't she just say fucking goodbye and be done with it?*

Meanwhile, I wrestled with the embarrassment peculiar to cracked ceilings and beaten linoleum floors. My place had that bankrupt-travel-agency feel to it—stale, grime in the creases. Real chic. I could imagine the two of them sizing it up from the soundproofed confines of their BMW, saying, "Well, it looks like a dump," with the worn-out irony of those run down to their final options.

Then I realized that Mrs. Bonjour was crying. She had knelt on one knee to tie the shoe on the opposite foot, then switched to the other and just ... hung there, her cheek pressed against her knee. Sunlight cut across her at an angle, casting arthritic shadows of her hands and wrists across the mat.

She trembled like a timid dog at the vet, keened in a baby-small voice. Her words, if there were any, were inaudible.

Fawk.

My first thought was of me: she was crying because she had been reduced to the likes of me. But that blew away like the flimsy conceit it was. It was something else—*someone* else. Suddenly I saw, not Mrs. Bonjour, but the woman my subsequent research would reveal as Mandy Bonjour née Patterson. The woman with the secrets she had never told her husband, who hoarded little mementoes that only she could decipher.

It's strange, isn't it, glimpsing the person behind the type. The feeling of inside-out recognition. The lining up of first-person perspectives. The twinge of ghosts moving *through* each other. You bat an eye and suddenly, somehow, this stranger has become a family member.

She cried for all of thirty seconds. Then, abruptly, she stood up, glared at her husband for a hateful heartbeat, then, with a cursory nod at me, pressed her way through the door into the stark world of light and shadow beyond. She strode down the street, a kind of watery walk, the laces of her left shoe kicking in front of her and trailing behind. Jonathan Bonjour wordlessly followed.

I was left with that humbling feeling of having witnessed something heroic ...

Or at least something beyond my mangy capabilities.

Track Three

ONE HUNDRED THOUSAND CIGARETTES

After the Bonjours left, I had sex with Kimberley in the copy room—or, as I had devilishly dubbed it, the copy-feely room. Kim put in about twenty or so hours a week, three hours here, four hours there, usually between 10 A.M. and 2 P.M., after which she left for her real job at a peeler joint called the Zinger Klub. She was a good kid, something of a smartass, and beautiful in that haggard, too-dolled-up way common to strippers.

The cool thing about frequenting strip bars as a small businessman is that you never need worry about employee turnover—in either sense of the term. Most strippers leap at the job, that is, until they realize a) I'm something of a prick, b) there's nothing glamorous about day planners and spreadsheets, and c) the money is for shit. But despite this, and despite the fact that I had let her dental coverage lapse, Kimberley had been game for over six months now—long enough for me to worry she might be falling in love.

Afterward we shared a reflective smoke next to the open window.

"Cancel my appointments for this afternoon," I said.

"You don't have any appointments."

Kimberley, you should know, had long ceased taking me seriously. One more happy consequence of banging your employees: they know what you look like naked. For whatever reason, it's hard to take naked men seriously. Personally, I blame the balls.

"What do you do around here, again?"

She sucked her cigarette to the nub then flicked it out the window. "The grunt work," she said, exhaling. "You know, '*Ungh. Ungh.*'"

"Har-har," I replied, tossing my butt after hers onto the gravel and cracked asphalt outside. "Into the crowd," Kimberley called it, because of the thousands of other butts out there. I stood.

"Going to Jitters?" she asked. I tried not to notice how beautiful her profile looked in the alley-choked sunlight.

"Ungh."

She gave me her trademark lopsided snort. She knew the drill.

I had to start working on Dead Jennifer.

Jitters was the name of my favourite coffee shop. It was a haunt of mine, the place where I would be whacked if the mob ever deemed me important enough to merit a hit. It was just around the corner, the kind of shop that soaked in the idle and the hurried alike, from the local bums to the professionals-on-the-run to the maternity-leave moms. Like all the businesses on the street, it had its cycles, its consumer ebb and flow. Sometimes it would be packed and stuffy, an outrage to air conditioning. Other times it would be as empty and cool as a hockey arena on a Monday morning. I was lucky enough to catch an ebb.

I complimented Ashlan on her hair on my way in, placed my order with the owner, Michelle.

"Working a case, Diss?" Ashlan asked in her hectic yet affectionate way.

The girls regarded me with the wary affection people reserve for apparently dangerous animals that have been defanged and declawed. The worst I could do was gnaw on them. "About to ..." I said.

"What is it this time?" Michelle asked, squinting at me over the rims of her glasses. "Another hooker with six toes?"

"No-no," Ashlan exclaimed. "My favourite was the guy with the ... the—what did you call it?—*pustule* on his thingy! Did he ever tell you—"

"Oh yah," Michelle laughed. "The Case of the Nine Itches ..."

From time to time I liked to scandalize the girls with stories about the more sordid cases I worked. I would give them names just to crack them up. Sir Conan Doyle meets porno.

"Nah," I said. "Gotta real one this time, girls. Respectable, like."

"And what's it called?" Ashlan asked.

After pausing a moment to consider, I said, "How about The Girl Who Died at the End of the World?"

"Hmm ..." Michelle said, frowning. "Sounds ... *serious.*"

One of the perils of constantly playing the comedian, I've found, is that when the laugh track finally pops its spool—and it always does—people don't know how to take you.

"Like I said, I got a *real* one this time."

All, you know, respectable like.

I retreated with my coffee to the place's most obscure corner, more than a little gooned by Michelle's comment. Truth is, as much as I despise all the penny-ante cases I usually work, they tend to have very little karmic overhead. I once followed this guy for two weeks because his wife had caught the distinct whiff of feces on his dick. So I take all these photos of him leaving gay clubs, show them to her, and she starts crying—get this—with *relief.* Apparently she had always suspected he was gay, had always felt proud he had stayed with her against the grain of his sexual inclinations. Her *real* fear was that he was pounding chocolate with another woman! So tell me, what are the consequences of fucking up a case like that? A better question might be, is it even *possible* to fuck up a case like that?

No consequences means no responsibilities. And that's the way I like to ride.

I mean, *look* at me. I'm what you would call a fuck-up, and if there's one thing fuck-ups know, it's that real people—you know, people who, like, *read* and shit—generally mean real trouble. Fuck-ups *fuck up*. That's what they *do*. If you fuck things up for another fuck-up, you can be damn sure that they'll fuck up as well—that, thanks to the almighty law of averages, everything will come out in the wash. This is why fuck-ups prefer hanging with other fuck-ups. Puking in Billy's car ain't so bad when Billy's already shat in your boot.

But the Bonjours, they were *real*. No car-puking. No boot-shitting. Just a wayward daughter having trouble finding her way home ...

Fawk.

I mean, I date *strippers* for Christ's sake.

So, for the first time in my oh so sketchy career, I made what my first shrink, Martin, used to call an "implementation intention."

"You *can change*, Disciple," he once chirped. "As easily as you change your underwear." He was one of those perky fuckers who continually cooked up apologies for people then called it therapy.

"But they *all* have skid marks, doc. Every pair."

"Well, then, you go commando!"

"What? And get shit on my *jeans*?"

I'm not a big believer in change, as you might imagine. Even so, I sat at my table, took a deep breath, and resolved *not* to fuck this one up. That meant doing things by the numbers.

Ever been in a car accident? If so, then you know: life is quick—too quick.

The thing to realize is that *every moment* is a car accident; it only seems otherwise because the apparent regularity of things fools us into thinking we can intervene and take some measure of control. We have this abiding *I-could-if-I-really-wanted-to* feeling. And since we're out-and-out addicted to this feeling, the true brevity of things tends to drop out of the stories we like to tell. It doesn't matter if it's the action hero's slo-mo or the anti-hero's angst-ridden reflection, everywhere you turn you see people having a hell of a lot more time than they actually have, able to scoop the gun from the gutter before the other guy squeezes the trigger, or to ponder the early days of Czech Communism between ironic barbs.

Exact same flattering conceit.

If you think about it, either we're just gabbing away on automatic or we're perpetually one step behind, fencing with the vague bewilderment of receiving change in a foreign country. The reason we think we have so much time, I'm convinced, has to do with the way we blur our after-the-fact reflections on given events into the events themselves. As soon as we zip-lock something in memory, it becomes static, something that we can run circles around. Considered from this standpoint, it really does seem that everything we do is fraught with decisions, as if every moment was a window onto thousands of future possibilities, instead of automatic and obscure.

Which is what they are—pretty much. You can sooner fish water back out of a flushing toilet.

This is why I do so much of my work *downstream*, so to speak.

As a kid, I was too cool for school—I mean this quite literally.

We had this biology teacher whom everyone seemed to love and who seemed to love everybody: Mr. Marcus. If Mr. Marcus didn't like you, it meant that there was something wrong with you—as a matter of biblical certainty. Of course, I couldn't stand him. That's me in a nutshell. The guy who hates your favourite teacher.

Marcus was prattling on about photosynthesis, and Rosie Juarez, who was a total hottie, asked him about mushrooms: "Aren't they a plant that grows without sunlight, Meester Marcoos?" The whole time, Tommy Bridgeman was wheezing and coughing in the back of the room, hacking mucus that seemed to snap like elastics in the back of his throat. I think everyone knows at least one Tommy Bridgeman. You know the type: fungal complexion, coat hangers for bones, a sheepish grin for most anything you say.

Marcus graced her with one of his eye-twinkling smiles. That was another strike against him: there's nothing I hate quite so much as twinkling eyes. Save it for the cartoons, motherfucker.

"Well, Rose," he said, "consider Bridgeman over there. He's proof positive that some forms of life flourish in the absence of sunlight. Well, maybe not flourish ..." And then he had to say it: "Coming to class doesn't make you classy."

Everyone roared with studio-audience clarity. Bridgeman just slouched his head low, wiped his nose, and grinned in a monkey-embarrassed way. Me? I was disgusted. I felt everything go smooth, the way it always does when something gets me really pissed. Suddenly, snotty little Tommy Bridgeman seemed like my kind of people, and Mr. Marcus's joke became an outrage to the Geek Nation.

"Yes, Mr. Manning?"

Without even realizing it, my hand had shot up.

"Um, Mr. Marcus, why do you think that was so funny?"

"I'm not sure what you mean, Mr. Manning."

"Well, you've said that *same thing* now, like, twenty-three times so far this semester."

I grit my teeth in joy sometimes, remembering the things I've said.

"I admit it's an old trick of mine," Mr. Marcus said—he was too cash to be anything but puzzled at this point. "But I hardly imagine I've said it *twenty-three* times. Please, Mr. Manning."

"Why?"

"Why what?"

"Why don't you think you've used it twenty-three times?"

"Because ..."—he paused ominously—"that would make me rather dull and unoriginal, don't you think?"

"That's exactly what I think," I replied cheerfully.

"*Excuse* me?"

And that's when I started, working my way backward from snotty little Tommy Bridgeman. I just hit replay in my psyche and it all came out, down to the cadences of the voices and the looks on the faces. Twenty-three of them in a row. He never interrupted me, not once, just stood there like someone mesmerized—believe me, the truth can be a big scary stick. I imagine it must have been as spooky as all hell listening to me, watching me, but the way I did it—I tell you, I *had* them. Not one of my classmates could have recalled even a fraction of what I replayed, but their other brain, their unconscious one, remembered it well enough: everyone in the class *recognized* each of the incidents I was recreating. People nodded, brandished their fists when they recognized themselves. Others shouted out the count. "*Twenty-ONE!*" The whole class roared and roared. A hundred laughs for Mr. Marcus turned into a thousand laughs *against* him.

I broke the poor bastard over my knee.

And of course got myself expelled. Apparently the administrators loved Mr. Marcus too.

That was February 22, 1982. A bad day.

But still, pretty cool.

Time. It all comes down to time. If you have a memory like a court stenographer, like I have, then you have all the time in the world to deliberate. This is probably why my romantic life reads like cover copy for a splatterpunk novel: I sit in perpetual judgment.

Not something that chicks dig particularly.

According to the doctors, I suffer from something called "hyperthymestic syndrome." You can pretty much ignore the "hyperthymestic" part—the real word to pay attention to is "syndrome." It means the doctors have no bloody clue what the hell they're talking about. Take "irritable bowel syndrome," which my father suffers from (though he always insisted that Mom and I refer to it as the more palatable "IBS"). For some unknown reason, he bloats and cramps up, then farts and shits all day long—the most wretched-smelling things, too. Demonic.

Hyperthymestic syndrome is simply irritable bowel syndrome of the head: where my dad can't dump his dumps properly, me, I can't dump my memories properly.

I retain all the crap.

Usually I grab the *USA Today* when I work at Jitters, more for appearance's sake than to read, but the paper rack was empty. So I stared into my coffee like a knob—for some reason the shining black circle ringed in white porcelain calmed and centred me. Like my dingy version of a seaside horizon.

I stared, and it all came back to me with the ease of a daydream.

"She's not a runaway," I had said, looking up to meet the Bonjours' gaze. *"What is she? Nineteen? Twenty in this photo?"*

"Nineteen," Amanda replied in a small voice.

"And that would make her?"

"Twenty-one. She's twenty-one now."

I paused to take a sip. I noticed the deliberate way her voice walked around "would be" language when she talked about her daughter. Amanda Bonjour was a woman sustaining herself through resolution, and resolution alone. She had seized hope by the throat and wrestled it to the wall.

But this struck me as obvious. If there were nuances to be drawn out, they lay elsewhere.

"They call themselves the Framers," she said.

"Never heard of them. What do they believe?"

The funny thing is that I rarely, if ever, catch the deeper nuances of my own words. I like to think that this is because I understand myself to the very bottom, but I know that this is what *everybody* thinks. After all, how can people mean things they don't mean? It sounds paradoxical, I know, and yet we do it all the bloody time: these rehearsals would be exercises in futility if this weren't the case.

"That the world," Amanda replied, "this *world, isn't really ... real."* Something in her tone suggested the eternal coincidence of stupid beliefs and stupid people.

Which was probably why my subsequent question, *"Isn't that religion in general?"* touched a raw nerve.

"You explain it," she said crossly to her husband. *"Jon has a philosophy degree ..."*

Amanda Bonjour was religious. Even more, she had spent many an infuriating evening suffering her philosopher-husband's bemused contempt. Jonathan Bonjour was not a believer. Could this have been a factor in their daughter's subsequent defection? A mother fretting over her eternal soul, a father calling her stupid in a dozen indirect ways ... Had Dead Jennifer simply been seeking the subversive in-between, the point guaranteed to maximally dismay both her parents?

"They're one of those New Age, human potential things," Jon Bonjour said. *"What's called a* charismatic *cult."*

His contemptuous incredulity seemed clear enough now.

"The leader's name," he continued, *"is Xenophon Baars."* Was there a note of personal hatred here? Had he met him on the trip to Ruddick his wife mentioned? If so, why wouldn't he say as much? Most people put a premium on personal impressions.

That's the thing about my business: everyone, but everyone, thinks they can do it themselves—until they try, that is. This isn't to say that private investigating is brain surgery, but it's more involved than your average home renovation project, if not in terms of the skills you need, then in terms of the consequences of your mistakes. Sure, most people are capable of foundation work, but if they get it wrong, the problems are nothing short of monstrous.

"What do you mean by 'extreme'?"

"They think the world is about to end," Jonathan Bonjour said.

"And?"

"Five billion years from now ..."

"You mean when the sun swallows us up?"

"Exactly. This Baars has convinced his followers that the world is more than five billion years older than it is. *And that it's about to end."*

I would have to do some research. The Bonjours' suspicions were clear enough, and for obvious reasons. Xenophon Baars was crazy—there could be no doubt about that. But what was more, he was a liar who was wholly invested in his lies. Not only did he have the capacity for murder, he could very well possess the incentive as well. Any number of scenarios suggested themselves: jealousy run rampant in the fucked-up sexual economy of the Framers' compound, a lunatic sacrificial offering to some great X-that-must-be-appeased, threats to go to the authorities over a glimpsed weapons cache, a sexual assault, a prior conviction ... These people believed the world was *five billion years older than it was*—who could say what kinds of crazy acts would fit the mad puzzle of their beliefs? Who could say what they considered sinful?

Or how they punished sinners.

Once, during a particularly nasty fight, an old biology undergrad girlfriend of mine, Sandra Ho, accused me of thinking I was the next phase in human evolution, something which has never been true, not then, not now. If anything, I think I'm an evolutionary throwback, proof positive that all humans have the *capacity* to remember most everything, a capacity that evolution has since *shut down*. Too many hominid suicides, perhaps. Either that or too many hominid arguments with hominid girlfriends—who knows? I told her as much. She accused me of lying to make her feel small. I accused her of accusing me of lying to make her feel small to make me feel small. And so it goes.

That was May 19, 1998, around 3 P.M. A bad day.

The relationship didn't last. None of them do. Could you imagine trying to argue with someone who *could actually remember* who said what when? Or who could always remember, perhaps even especially remember, all the hard things we say on the hateful fly?

There's no forgiveness without forgetting, trust me.

The fact is, the longer I know someone, the more difficult I find it to talk to them. Part of it has to do with distraction: it's bloody hard to juggle a conversation with a thousand pellets of memory.

I much prefer the company of strangers.

Or the dead, like Jennifer.

"How would you characterize your relationship?"

"What do you mean?" Amanda had asked. I could see now that this was simply a bid for time to formulate a response.

"Your relationship with Jennifer. Was it loving or, ah ... troubled?"

"He wants to know whether the cult was just an excuse to escape us," Jon Bonjour said to his wife. This time around I clearly heard a *Remember-what-we-discussed* tone. And just like that, I realized how anxious he was to police his wife's responses.

"Troubled," Amanda said. *"Troubled."*

"Not abusive," Jon Bonjour interjected. *"There's troubled and then there—"*

"I'm sure Mr. Manning re—"

I paused, trying to get a fix on her expression. It would be wrong to think of these rehearsals like video replays, because they aren't. In fact, they're almost impossible to describe. It's not like there's a little me reviewing it all in a little theatre in my head—how could there be when I'm *both* the screen and the audience? I mean, the memories are imagistic in a sense, a very fleeting sense—but they're more like a kind of raw knowledge, things I just know.

The voices, though, they almost seem like sounds.

"I just didn't want him to get the wrong idea!"

"And what idea would that be, Mr. Bonjour?"

"Jon slapped her," Amanda Bonjour said in a tone meant either to demonstrate or to humiliate. *"The last ... fight we had. Jon slapped ... her."*

Her husband snuffled. *"I ... ah ... I ... I don't know what to say ..."*

My mind always plays this trick when I recollect emotionally intense moments. A reptilian coldness soaks the scene, a kind of psychic air conditioning, one that makes me think of museums for some reason. I've never quite figured out why.

"Jonny blames himself," Amanda said blankly. *"He thinks all of this is his fault."* I had no doubt that she believed what she was saying. As far as she was concerned, nothing mattered except finding her daughter. The question was whether her husband believed what she was saying. Where her agenda came across as arrow-straight and unrelenting, his seemed decidedly bushy.

"I appreciate your honesty," I said. Though I rarely gain any self-insight from these sessions, I am often nagged by a sense of foolishness, like hearing your voice on someone else's answering machine. I've learned that no matter how thoroughly you think you've mastered the moment, everything is naïveté in retrospect. Everything. *"Most people try to doctor the story, believing they're better served if they come out looking like angels. But the only thing that serves in these situations, the only thing, is the truth."* I had leaned forward, placed my elbows against the desktop. *"You do understand that?"*

A twitch across the fat of his face. Anger, deep enough to rattle the hustings. *"Of course,"* he said. What was this? Pride? Was he simply the kind of man who resented others for witnessing his weakness? Or was there something more?

"I have one last question, for you specifically, Mr. Bonjour. Your law firm regularly contracts private investigators, does it not?"

"I'm not sure I understand." I had registered his shock the first time, the squint as he tried to remember whether he had told me he was a lawyer. What I had missed was the hunted look in his eye—the apprehension. He had come to me thinking I was a nickle-and-dime *hack*, that much was clear. But this ... this made me think he *needed* me to be a fool.

"Stuff like this ... personal stuff with consequences that are, well, as big as you can imagine ... such stuff requires trust. Why wouldn't you go to people you know?"

"This wasn't Jonny's idea," Amanda said. The fact that she was the Prime Mover would have been significant if women weren't so often the motivating force behind these visits. Men tended to bring the same macho reluctance to my office as they did to marriage counsellors. Hunting was a man's job. Avenging even more so.

"Even still ..."

Mr. Bonjour intervened—once again to explain himself. *"No offence, Mr. Manning, but my opinion of your profession is rather ... jaded ..."*

The irony was just as thick the second time. Rich.

"And?"

"Well, let's just say that I've come to that opinion through long experience." And what kind of experience would that be? Bonjour had the pudgy look of a divorce lawyer—a soft-skinned shark. Criminal attorneys tend to have more leather in their mien. They like to lean forward when they talk. Not Bonjour. He was a slumper: I suppose sucking mortgage payments out of broken marriages could do that.

"But it's not just that," Amanda added nervously. *"You see ... Jonny's* already gone down there, *asking questions and all, and the people are ... well,* more like you." Why did this bug me so much, the fact that he

had already pissed in the investigatory soup? You'd think I'd be used to cleaning up behind amateurs.

"Like me?" As was so often the case during these rehearsals, I felt my face take on my past expression: a rueful smile. Apparently this was what had sparked the several complaints Michelle had received over the years: a crazy man making faces at his coffee cup. *"You mean socio-economically disadvantaged."*

"We thought that you might be able to talk their, uh, language."

This struck me as a solid enough rationale, but there was something that nagged me—something too pat. It was as crisp as a legal brief. Even the delivery struck me as premeditated—I could almost see Bonjour coaching his wife as they circled the block looking for a place to park.

"Remember, if he asks ...

"You don't know these people like I ...

"You have to *manage* them, Mandy. Jesus! Stop being so fucking naive!

"Do you want to find Jennifer? Huh?

"Do you want to find our girl or not? Our *baby girl!*"

See, for you it's all a mush, the past. It all fades into soup. This is why you wake up every morning feeling *renewed.* Not me, ever. Waking up is more like a clerical exercise. This is why other people come to you as a haze of implicit associations, some good, some bad—we humans tend to be a mixed bag. For me, others arrive like half-unravelled balls of chronological yarn. People are never simply ... themselves.

Either that or they're more themselves than they know.

If I knew you well, I quite literally would know you better than you know yourself. I could go on for days telling you stuff that you had forgotten about yourself. And I could make you cry with my observations.

And this is the thing: where you see acts, I see repetitions, and where you see people—yourself included—I see *repeaters.* You really have no idea how much we repeat. Even when we manage to defy expectations, we're like children: unpredictable in unsurprising ways. Those repetitions you're aware of you call habits or routines, very human-sounding terms, connoting warmth and security, and in no way, shape, or form contradicting agency, the possibility of breaking free. But this is simply a trick of your limited perspective. Everything looks like insects if you pan back far enough—people included.

And you wonder why I'm cynical. I've literally "seen it all before." The truth is *we all have*, every single one of us past the age of, say, twenty-five. The only difference is that I *remember.*

This is probably why the hook set so deep—why I fell in love with Dead Jennifer. This case was unlike anything I had seen.

And like all addictive drugs, it promised something more profound than bliss ...

Forgetfulness.

I found myself staring across Jitters in a blinking stupor. Somehow ebb had become flow without me even noticing: the place was buzzing with patrons. Four old ladies next to me were laughing so hard that two of them were pawing their purses for tissue. Something sly and embarrassed in their expressions shouted *dirty joke.* I stood, squeezed past three young men who had to be Mormons—they were too squeaky clean otherwise. I felt like asking them what the trick was, believing in things that made archaeologists sigh and look to heaven.

I paused outside the entrance, imagined what the sky would look like if all you could see was bloated sun. I grabbed my Zippo, lit a cigarette. I savoured the smoke: blue slipping in, grey piling out. I wondered at that, the change in colour. I thought of the blue soaking into my lungs, swirling into my bloodstream, saturating my brain.

Beautiful blue. Like a second lens, it always had a way of drawing things into sharper focus.

Something was up. There was something slippery about Jonathan Bonjour, something that utterly eluded his wife.

I know it sounds implausible. Memory tricks aside, how could I detect something in a single sitting that Amanda Bonjour had never glimpsed in years of marriage?

It's just the way. It's not simply that familiarity blinds—and it does, catastrophically—it's a Mars–Venus thing as well. The bulk of the male and female bandwidths may overlap, but there's always a small range of gender-specific frequencies, things that only men can pick up in other men, and that only women are sensitive to in other women.

Jonathan Bonjour had something to do with his daughter's disappearance. I was almost certain of it.

Or maybe it was just an excuse to light another smoke. I slipped on my shades and began walking. It made me feel smart, wringing the blue out of the smoke.

I was just a few packs away from one hundred thousand cigarettes. Happy times.

Track Four
MONKEY CHILDREN

Tuesday ...

Some prick driving one of those big-ass SUVs cut me off about an hour or so outside of Ruddick. I had just answered a call from Kimberley, so I apologized to her and rolled down the window—one of those manual cocksuckers. The wind dragged hot and oily across my face. I leaned on the horn to secure the guy's attention—he was little more than a forehead over the rim of his passenger door—then shouted a friendly, *"Dirty-mother-fucker!"*

Now in the good old days, he would have rolled down his window and shouted back, something about my after-tax income, perhaps. Instead, he welded his eyes forward and gunned his behemoth. Anyone crazy enough to pick a road fight while driving an ancient Volkswagen Golf, he probably reasoned, had to have a gun in his glove compartment.

Which I did: an illegal Colt .45 automatic taped beneath a false bottom—a government model, no less. But still I found myself resenting the assumption.

"You're driving?" Kimberley said when I picked the cell back up. *"I*

thought you said you had stopped at a diner." Despite the roar of the road, I heard her draw on a cigarette.

"Are you smoking in the office?"

"No. I'm in the copy room."

"There's no phone in the copy room."

Another draw—nothing communicates impatience quite like a cigarette. *"I'm. In. The* copy room*,"* she repeated with *Don't-you-dare-start-with-me* obstinacy.

I didn't. I *wanted* to—I had told her precisely eleven times how alienating non-smokers found the smell of cigarettes, how she was literally driving away business. Each time she just shrugged and said, "I don't smell *anything*." Amazing really, when you think about it, how much you'll put up with for a piece of ass.

So instead I asked, "What do you want?"

Another puffing pause. *"That Chief thing-a-ma-jingi called for you."*

"Nolen called?"

"Yup."

"What did he want?"

"You. He wants you to come to his office as soon as you get into town."

The Bonjours must have gotten busy with that list I gave them. Real people are like that.

"Cool ... Love you, babe."

I tossed the cell onto the passenger seat, rubbed the bridge of my nose beneath my shades. In my mind's eye I could see the frustration in Kimberley's look, the anger and the hurt as she sat all alone in the office. Solitude weighs heavier on strippers than most. I shook away the image simply because I breeze past things I don't like. I make like everything is popcorn, knowing that few things are more powerful than a relentless good nature. I hurt people, knowing they will hide that hurt simply because the gag must go on.

Still, I knew I had to do something—and soon. She was in love with me. Like, totally.

The drive into Ruddick was interesting. The first curious thing I noticed was that the speed limit dropped about a mile or so before you would think it should. Cracked sidewalks trimmed either side of the road, and side streets divided it at intervals you would expect in a *circa*-1950s subdivision, but there were no houses, only overgrown lots staked here and there by the odd lonely tree. The place was starting to remind me of Detroit.

I saw a dead squirrel, a shiny yellow toy knotted in weeds, a kid pounding dirt with a hammer. I even saw some small-town graffiti, FUCK UP NOT DOWN, scrawled across a houseless foundation. Things I needed to forget yet would always remember. You have to be prepared for the sudden onslaught of physics while driving—I know this better than most people—and yet my eyes perpetually flick this way and that, scoping out ass and other oddities.

Part of the U.S. military's retirement package.

I passed a bustling Citgo, an abandoned GM dealership, and finally the white frame Church of the Third Resurrection before making it into the town proper.

What a dump, I thought. And I live in fucking Newark.

I took a wrong turn at some point, because I somehow found myself in the industrial park peering at all the dead factories. The first was one of those rambling windowless affairs that made me think I was looking at mismatched container boxes from a distance. The second was a stripped skeleton of rust-burned I-beams. I felt vaguely disappointed: I had been hoping for something more crowded, more bricked and rotted—more *Dickensian*—not pastel cubes in a patchwork of vast industrial lots. Fucking modernity, man. Even our decadence and decline have become generic.

I turned around on some service road, backtracked. The downtown made me feel more at home. Someday someone will eulogize the strip mall, and I for one will shed a real tear. The way I figure it, humans have always lived and worked in aesthetic abominations. The people I saw looked stupid—walking or talking or gazing with an insolence I reflexively attributed to generational inbreeding. More urban chauvinism, I know, and the fact that I think everybody looks stupid. I see people the way I imagine animals must see me: nice head of hair, ape-boy, but what the fuck happened to *your face*?

I found the police department in a building surprising for its size. Later I would learn that in its manufacturing heyday, Ruddick had been three times bigger, population-wise. This little demographic fact would figure largely in what followed, as it so happened.

Nolen was out, of course, so I hunkered down in the vestibule with nothing more than a paunchy desk sergeant to keep me company, the kind of guy who ages *watchful*, if you know what I mean. Eyes so bulbous it seemed impossible he could ever shut them—entirely. A great look for a cop, actually. He was positively freaking me out, so much so I was actually relieved when my cell twittered to the riff from "Back in Black."

"Manning," I said in lieu of a hello.

"Hey, Disciple! This is Albert. Not catching you at a bad time, am I?"

"Naw. Just aimlessly wandering the aisles of Walmart, you know ..." I winked at the glaring sergeant.

Albert Fellows was one of my bookworm buddies, a social psychologist over at New York University—one of a number of relationships I had cultivated over the years. I had called him the previous night while researching the Framers online, left a message. Since I only remembered everything people *said*, I continually sought people who could *tell* me what I needed to know. In exchange, I would score them a bag of weed here and there. You have no idea just how many academics are hard up for weed. And because they live lives so tragically insulated from crime, they tend to be almost comedically grateful.

Apparently Albert had never heard of the Framers, though he was positively giddy about the opportunity to learn more about them. He said he just wanted me to know that he was "on the case," but I could tell he had really called out of curiosity—that he just had to know what I was up to this particular lap around the track. So I filled him in—with a good dose of my own commentary.

"Come on, Albert. *Five billion years?* Could something like that be for real?" I winked at the cop once more, and *finally* the fucker looked away. "I mean, who would fall for that kind of shit?"

A long cellphone ha-ha. *"Look, Diss. The assumption is that there's gotta be something wrong with cult members. You know. Stupid. Weak-minded. What have you. But the fact is, they tend to be better educated and have higher IQs than the general population—"*

"Whatever," I interrupted. "You still gotta be crazy to believe what these guy—"

"And why's that? There's bloody good reason why psychology and psychiatry have such a hard time defining things like 'irrational beliefs.' Outside the realm of practical common sense, pretty much all human belief is irrational. All of it! *What we believe typically comes down to how the issue is framed and who gets to us first."*

I already knew this in my peculiar way. One of the big bonuses of diehard cynicism is the ability to take heart in bad news.

"We believe things willy-nilly," I said.

"Unto death, my friend. Unto death."

I hung up thinking about Dead Jennifer's photo in my wallet. I found myself blinking at the desk sergeant, who of course had resumed his slack-faced reverie from behind the desk, staring at me like I was a stain in the wallpaper. I couldn't resist.

"What? You run out of hay or oats or something?"

"Huh?"

That was when Chief Caleb Nolen came striding in.

Rule one of private investigating is to kiss official ass—you know, Bugs Bunny–style: muh-muh-muh-muh-*muh!*—unless the official happens to be female, in which case you lick boots. Contrary to what you may believe, cops generally *like* private investigators. We make them feel superior, for one, the way I imagine a rock star feels talking to a roadie—as the "be" to their "wanna." And some of us—especially the handsome, edgy ones like me—make them feel like they're in a movie, which means they choose their roles accordingly. Who would you rather be in a flick, the wry veteran or the obstructionist asshole? If there's one thing Hollywood is good at, it's giving us roles to play. Everyone loves to pretend they're in a movie, no matter where you go in the world. Good thing, too. If it wasn't movies, then it would be some psychotic legend from the Middle Ages—or worse yet, Scripture.

Even so, Nolen had this sour look on his face as I took the seat opposite his desk, as if I were the druggie cousin who kept hitting Grandma up for money. That was when I realized I was wearing my *I WOULD RATHER BE MASTURBATING* T-shirt.

Fawk.

I glanced at my chest then looked up at him helplessly. "Um ... Shit ..."

No wonder the desk sergeant couldn't stop staring. When you remember as much as I do, you end up overlooking more than a few crucial details.

"Pretty funny," Nolen said, grinning. "Actually ..."

A wave of relief washed over me. Nolen was good people, I realized. Anyone who would rather be masturbating is good people. Self-reliance is what makes this country great.

First thing I thought when seeing Nolen was that he was the kind of cop you argued traffic tickets with—which made his position as chief something of a mystery. He was fit in a gay, long-distance-runner kind of way, with hair just shaggy enough to suggest that he liked to rock out with his iPod. He had one of those soft faces where all the features seem to crowd inward—eyes, nose, and mouth packed into a space no larger than my palm—huddling as if trying to conserve expressive warmth or something. He had to be at least thirty-five, and yet his blue eyes made him seem younger, much younger. Adolescent jumpy. Adolescent eager.

Nolen began by telling me how much he liked the Bonjours, and how "this horrible Jennifer deal" had "rocked him like nobody's business."

"You try to avoid it," he said, "but you do this job long enough and you ... you start *sorting* people, you know?"

I nodded because it seemed expected. Usually—for men anyway—phrases like "you know" are a kind of verbal bondo, just something they say. They really don't give a fuck if you know or not. But this guy said it as if he *meant* it.

"My shrink," Nolen continued, "she says it's a kind of reflex mechanism, a thing people do to protect themselves. Terms like, er, you know, 'decent folk,' ah, 'low-lifes,' stuff like that ..."

Fawk. A cop who spoke openly about his shrink to a complete stranger ... The most I could do was lean back and nod. I'm not easily astonished, trust me.

"You know what I mean?" Nolen continued. "You have to crack heads in this line of work—there's no way around it. So you ... categorize ... or so she says. Dehumanize ... You know, to make it easier."

Like most cynics, I have the bad, well-nigh-irresistible habit of thinking earnest people stupid. What I wanted to ask at this point was, *Are you the mayor's retarded nephew or something?*

Instead I said, "Well ... you know ... my secretary, she called, said you wanted me to, ah, check in ..."

"Yeah. *Yeah.* So we could *coordinate.*" He leaned forward like an orphan angling for a bite of turkey dinner.

"Coordinate?"

I was afraid that the meeting would go sour. I tend to expect the worst when it comes to me and regular, decent folk, but I had no idea it would be *this* bad. There's nothing quite so ripe-smelling as excessive eagerness in an adult.

"Coordinate," he repeated. "Two heads are better than one, as they say. I just figured that a man with your expertise—"

"Expertise?"

"Exper*tise,*" he repeated, like it was a boardroom buzzword. "I've only investigated *four* missing persons in my life. Four. You could say I'm in ... well, way over my head. But I like to think I have other ... you know, gifts, that compensate for my lack of experience. I'm a puzzle man. I've always been good with puzzles."

Gifts? Puzzles? Was this guy for fucking real? One part of me wanted to tell him that the coach had lied, that it wasn't cool to brandish a little dick in the change-room shower, but the other part was actually beginning to like this guy.

"This is great. Coordination. Expertise. All great. I'll need a day or two to find my bearings on my own ... you know. Then we can get down to business."

"Sure. *Sure.*" He smiled with the daft credulity of a teenage Scout leader—or so it struck me. "Here," he said, standing to hand me a small stack of folders. "I've gathered everything I could, you know, reports, statements—some photographs of the road she used to walk along—I'm not sure why they're in there, but ..."

I hefted the phone book–sized pile with a friendly scowl. Jennifer had been missing, what, three nights? If weight translated into thoroughness, this guy was nothing short of exhaustive. At the time I failed to realize the *fear* this amount of case-overkill implied.

"All great," I said. "But would you mind if I ask you a couple of questions? I have this thing with ... you know ... talking stuff through."

The Chief grinned, placed his hands on his knees in that elbows-out, getting-to-work way. "Awesome. Me too. Talking is so much better."

Lonely, I realized. The guy was fucking lonely. He probably talked the coffee-shop regulars cross-eyed in his eagerness to brainstorm the case. Just like that I "got" Chief Caleb Nolen. He was one of those exuberant, earnest souls capable of feeling both horrified and celebratory at the same time. I had no doubt that Jennifer Bonjour's disappearance outraged him down to his deepest moral kernel. And at the same time, I knew this was the most exhilarating event in his bureaucratic life.

A real honest-to-God *mystery* ... What would we do without dead hotties?

Never one to waste an opportunity, I began by reviewing the particulars of Jennifer's disappearance, more to confirm the Bonjours' version of events than anything else. Fact was, Jon and Mandy were too invested. Invested people tend to get all the details right in the wrong way, seeing ego-friendly things like hope and vindication where there is none. Caleb, I was beginning to realize, was also too invested, but in an entirely different way.

"I think about her, you know," he said, waving his hands in a curiously frantic gesture. "Out *there* ... somewhere ... alone ..." He swallowed against cracks opening in his voice. His eyes became frail in that men-don't-cry way. "I've been doing this job for, well, about seven years now. I've even solved a murder or two—domestic stuff, though. But I've always felt more like a janitor, or custodian, I suppose. Cleaning up messes *after* they happen. But this ... I mean, this girl, *Jennifer* ... what's happening to her is happening *now.* I feel guilty just taking time out with my daughter, or reading the paper. I feel guilty for being ... well, you know, a small-fry cop in a small-fry town. I feel like she needs a comic book hero or something ..."

I had this friend growing up, Joey Sobotka, who always told me that I had superpowers, that I would grow up to be someone important, envied and admired. A real-life superhero. He was killed in a train derailment somewhere out in Montana, of all places. Who dies in a train derailment?

And what kind of superhero lets his friends die?

"The world's a toilet, Chief. Janitors are the only superheroes that matter."

Apparently he didn't know what to make of that. He just stared down at the fan of documents across his desk like a kid wondering how he was going to explain his latest D to his pop.

"Did you know her?" I asked on impulse. "Personally, that is ..."

He blinked and frowned. "Yeah. She was the Framers' representative at these community policing things we put together."

"What was she like?"

"An angel," he said. He laughed and scratched the back of his neck. "I would always get this ... this ... weird *urge* whenever I saw her ..." He must have glimpsed what I was thinking on my face because he fairly tumbled over himself to explain. "No. *No.* Nothing like that. No. This urge to get her ... well, a *gas mask.*"

"A gas mask, huh."

"I know how it sounds. But you live here long enough and you begin to take a dim view of things, you know? There was just something about her that made you think she was, well, *in danger.* Like she was an endangered species or something."

"She is, Chief. She is."

I continued reviewing the details as the Bonjours had provided them. Not forgetting anything has made me quite the effective interrogator over the years. In a matter of several minutes I was satisfied that the Bonjour version was in fact the *official* version—though, given the peculiarities of Nolen's character, it suddenly didn't seem all that "official" at all. More like just one more dude's take.

I then asked the standard questions, about known sex offenders, whether any recent events could possibly be related. No, not in Ruddick. None. Then I moved on to the question that had been burning a hole in my curiosity pocket.

"So I gotta ask: what do *you* make of the Framers?"

Nolen hesitated.

"Drive up to the Compound yourself," he eventually said, chewing the inside of his bottom lip. "I wouldn't go so far as to say the Framers are *good* people, you know, but they are, ah ... co-operative."

Part of me wanted to say, *But do they have any expertise?*

"What about the locals? What do they think of them?"

A lick-lipping pause.

"The thing you need to understand about Ruddick, Mr. Manning—"

"Disciple," I interrupted. "Call me Disciple."

"Sure ... er, Disciple, then," he replied with an embarrassed *How-could-that-be-a-name* look.

The urge to hit him passed quickly, and not simply because he was a cop. You know the saying: bloody a cop's nose, break your future's neck. He was too ... well-meaning.

"Well, Ruddick has seen better days. Pretty much *anyone* is welcome in our community, if you know what I mean ..."

Ruddick was open for business. I could almost see him sitting with a bunch of Chamber of Commerce fat-asses strategizing around a bucket of KFC. Hell, even cult members make the odd run to the Sam's Club for toiletries and whatnot. The Enlightened wipe their asses at least as much as the Saved, probably more, given all that hummus.

"But, you know, people ..." he added uncomfortably.

"No one much likes them."

"This is God-fearing country, Disciple."

He spoke my name as though warming to it, as though realizing it would spike the tedium of his coffee-shop stories.

"And the Framers?" I prompted.

A curious shrug. A *guilty* shrug. "Well, you know. I don't want to, you know, *stereotype* ..."

Of course not. That would contradict the police code of honour.

Fawk.

"Not decent folk, huh?"

Nolen grimaced. "Well ... Not to sound, ah, er ... *bigoted* or anything, but they *are* a cult. They have a way of making you forget as much when you're up there and all ... but still ..."

I couldn't resist a winning grin. "They gotta be crazy somehow."

Another thoughtful pause. "You tell me."

I never did. Nor would I ever. What Albert had told me less than an hour previously about irrational belief had simply confirmed something I had suspected all along. "Crazy" is simply a numbers game. If there were only twenty-seven Roman Catholics in the world, *they* would be the crazy-ass cult, and people would be wagging their heads about how their symbol is simply an ancient electric chair, or how they pretend to be cannibal vampires once a week, washing down their Maker's flesh with a gulp of his blood.

Nolen escorted me to the front door, pausing at an office to introduce me to his deputy chief, a dour old law enforcement lifer named Jeff Hamilton. He had the kind of face you see on banknotes from some obscure European country. Shrewd eyes. Buzzed grey hair. Flapjack jowls. He stood, nodded, smiled, and shook my hand with a banker's choreographed cheer. But something in his look, a kind of Slavic intensity, told me that he *disapproved*—of me, of Nolen, of his subordinates—that pretty much everything except his wife's lasagna fell short of his expectations. His office even reeked of cheese.

I would have bet my expenses that he had some kind of contemptuous nickname for Nolen.

I sparked a joint while still parked in the station lot, sat back, and began to review this latest conversation. One statement in particular kept floating back to the harried centre of my attention: *"Well, Ruddick has seen better days. Pretty much anyone is welcome in our community, if you know what I mean ..."* Something about the way Nolen had said "anyone"—a kind of grimace in an otherwise avid, even eager expression ...

Was it *fear*? Had the Framers got to him somehow?

Truth was, earnest people had been freaking me out since at least the second grade, when I announced to the entire class that there was no such thing as Santa Claus, that it was all another social control mechanism. Little Phil Barnes told me—with a conviction that would have made a suicide bomber blush—that not believing in Santa was *naughty*, and that *everyone* knew what *that* meant.

He had this list, you see.

I was out-and-out bawling by the time I got home, convinced I had been blacklisted by the fucking fatman. I've suffered an irrational fear of Santa ever since. And a deep distrust of honesty.

Decent folk like Phil.

As a cynic, the problem you face with earnest people is pretty much the same problem the British faced with Gandhi. All of our schemes are corrupt in some manner; gaming the system is inked in our DN-fucking-A. And a certain ability to ignore the disconnect between our rhetoric and our actions is all it takes to keep the show running, an instinctive tolerance of ambient hypocrisy. One honest idiot is all it takes to bring it all crashing down—which is why so many honest idiots end up at the bottom of the river, metaphorically or otherwise. Finding strength in your convictions may be good when it comes to independence from colonial rule, but when it comes to the weave of interpersonal schemes that holds offices and families together, it's nothing short of disastrous.

In a world of funhouse mirrors, it's the straight reflection that deforms.

"Pretty much anyone is welcome in our community ..."

Nolen was going to be a problem. I could feel it in my bones.

I peered across the world beyond my windshield, the world of Ruddick, PA, my thoughts crusting about the rim of innumerable memories. The sun was still high, so that the people I could see had only shadows beneath their brows—no eyes that could be seen. Something about them and the surrounding collection of little buildings, scrubby trees, and cracked sidewalks made me smile.

Fucking small towns, man. You gotta love them. Big enough to pretend. Too small to *be.*

I cranked the key, listened to my poor old Vee-Dub rattle to diesel life. As I pulled onto Kane Street, one last fragment of my conversation came floating back to awareness.

"No. No. *Nothing like that. No. This urge to get her ... well, a* gas mask."

"A gas mask, huh."

Gas mask, indeed. It was time to meet the Framers.

Track Five

THE LAW OF SOCIAL GRAVITATION

I'm guessing that when you pass a woman laughing with a clutch of children on the sidewalk, your heart smiles—or something like that. The sun abruptly shines, and your next breath feels like a lucky pull at the slots. This is because you see people as surfaces. Not me. For me, people are always the latest instance of a history. So where you see a smile hanging in the blank blue of now, I see a smile superimposed on a snarl, shriek, laugh, sneer—you get the picture.

I never see people—I see crazed bundles. Battered suitcases, stuffed to overflowing, cinched shut with belts and frayed twine.

An old girlfriend of mine, a visual artist named Darla Blackmore, once tried to convince me that the exact opposite was the case, that given the rarity of my condition I was likely *the only person on the planet* who saw "people." Everybody else, she claimed, saw only thin slices of people, which they then mistook for the whole thing. They saw *types*, she said, not tokens. Apparently this was a big distinction among the philosophy majors she hung out with.

Now, I should have been flattered, but instead I was irritated. Not all repetitions are equal. Some, like sex for instance, never get stale, no matter how high I stack the pile. Sex is one of those things you always do for the first time, perfect recall or not. But others grate, and when I say grate, I mean *grate.*

Like when people call this curse of mine a fucking gift—as if it were a superpower or something.

So I told Darla that if people were in fact tokens, they would be better off being types, because what I see is ugly beyond redemption.

To which she replied, "Is that how you see *me*?"

I should have seen it coming. Maybe that's what made me so angry—angry enough to speak the truth, which is to say, *too* angry. I told her she was a chorus of Darlas, a cacophony of lyrics sung simultaneously, with only one sweet note to redeem her.

"And what note is that?"

Of course I had to be honest a second disastrous time. "Your—"

That was October 26, 1993. Another bad day.

The Framer Compound was an old horse farm a mile or so outside of downtown—on the edge of a largely abandoned industrial park. It's funny the way movies fuck up your imagination. You begin to see Drama everywhere you look, little particles of it waiting to be taken up in this or that narrative arc. Everything I glimpsed while driving became a crime scene. A series of concrete cylinders, beached among thronging sumac and grasses: that's where Jennifer was assaulted, where she screamed her last breath. A collapsed outbuilding, its aluminum siding buckled like discarded clothes: that's where *he* watched and waited, holding his binoculars with one hand while rubbing his cock with the other. A swath of open ground, brown and ragged, where the toxic buildup prevented everything but the hardiest weeds from taking root: that was where she ran, trying to scream past sobs of exhaustion and terror. And the dead factories themselves, bland and imperturbable save where missing panels afforded glimpses of pitch interiors: that's where she tried to hide, tripping through the whooping dark, gasping air that smelled of rust and residual hydrocarbons.

On and on, everywhere I looked ...

A million and one places to hide a Dead Jennifer.

The Compound had that well-heeled rural manse look, everything prim and oh so agricultural, only with an inward Waco air. Us against the world—you know. The iron gates stood ajar. I clattered down the lane in my old Vee-Dub, craning my head this way and that to get a sense of things. Gravel popped loud through my open window. Two monstrous willows swayed their skirts in the summer breeze—a whiff of paradise in that, I suppose. The original farmhouse towered grand over a series of white-brick additions. Despite the obvious age of the original structure, everything about it had that tight, buttoned look—like new windows nailed down. Wood chip gardens sprawled around the foundations, bright with flowers. The lane hooked around, opening onto a lot hedged on two sides by long, low barns that had been renovated to house human livestock. The place was *huge*, I realized. At least thirty thousand labyrinthine square feet. Maybe more.

Just another factory, I told myself.

A guy appeared from behind a sun-flashing glass door. He looked like someone out of a pharmaceutical commercial—you know, middle-class good looks and an unflinching hope-for-the-future smile, only with crooked teeth. He wore a uniform—a white suit of some kind with no collar on the jacket.

Not a good sign. A belief system with its own outfits. Fawk.

He timed his stride to reach me the instant I slammed my car door. He shook my hand in a firm, dry grip, introduced himself as Stevie. I found him instantly irritating.

I gave him my card, and while he struggled to read the print along the bottom of the giant iris and pupil I used as my logo (I fucking told Kimberley that nobody could read the print, but apparently I was the only one with vision problems), I explained that the Bonjours had sent me to investigate the disappearance of their daughter, Jennifer. Stevie nodded sagely, returned the card.

"How can I help you?" he asked.

"I was hoping to talk to Baars ..."

"The Counsellor? He's teaching a class."

"Cool. Would it be okay for me to sit in?"

He blinked and smiled—like a Buddha listening to a child.

"Have you crossed the Lacuna?"

"Lacuna?"

The fucker knew I had no clue as to what the Lacuna was, and yet he baited me with the question anyway.

"Sorry. You'll have to wait in the Clink."

For a second I pondered smacking him. Everything about the guy made me bristle. I understood immediately that he was one of those smug little pricks who could only laugh *to* himself—you know, laugh that insipid self-congratulatory laugh, either because he thought he had said something witty or because he thought himself clever for getting something witty said by someone else. Stevie. Cult member.

What a fucking loser.

All these people organizing their lives around an invisible world. I had an uncle who was a missionary, who would always probe me about my relationship with Jesus in warm, gentle tones, like I was the world's last orphan or something. Then, late at night, I would hear him screaming at my mom, telling her I was damned to blister in hell.

So I learned early on that when you're with people, you're never really with people—not simply, anyway. Not only do they tow their histories around with them, they carry their ideologies with them as well. You can't serve pork chops to just anyone, you know.

But then, this assumes it's possible to organize your life in any other way. If you think about it, there really isn't that much *practical* difference between things like Wall Street and Paradise: You believe that certain numbers in certain circuits will grant you life after labour—retirement—simply because you've diligently attended to these numbers. Because you're one of the righteous.

Not knowing shit and yet acting in all ways as if you do: this is the essence of human civilization.

They've even invented a name for it.

Trust.

Either way, I was having none of it.

The Clink, it turned out, was simply their nickname for the Compound's waiting room. I was at once surprised and more than a little relieved that the Framers had some kind of sense of humour. Strange when you think about it, the antipathy between religion and humour, worship and ridicule. Ruthless ears on the one side, ruthless voices on the other.

The Clink ran parallel to the south end of the parking lot, a long room with tinted plate glass along one wall and floor-to-ceiling mirrors across the other. Of course Stevie-boy planted me in a seat opposite the mirrored wall. I'm pretty easy on the eyes—dark with those avian features that so many women find irresistible—so that wasn't a problem. But being *stuck* with your reflection is something altogether different. There's the whole *Taxi Driver* thing, the slippage between being and posturing. Otherwise, there's just something damn creepy about watching yourself watching yourself ... Something wrong about seeing the guy *behind* the seeing.

And confusing. I mean, really, just *who* was that good-looking, two-dimensional man?

We may never know.

My cell crunched out the riff to "Back in Black." It was Kimberley, of course.

"Where are you?" she asked in a higher than usual tone. I knew instantly that something was wrong.

"At the hotel, checking in."

"Look ..." A moment of cigarette-inhaling silence.

"Look what?"

I winced at my tone, as well as at the crash of recollections that followed. I have more than a few bad habits when it comes to managing women and their fears and expectations.

"I just need to know what you meant when you said ..." Another draw on her cigarette, then a dead-air pause. *"What you said."*

I shot a questioning look at the guy in the mirror. He shrugged.

"Said what?"

I could feel the anger balling into fists on the other end.

"You know ... 'Love *you, babe ...'"*

Fawk.

A head-scratching squint from the dude in the mirror.

"Just an expression, honey," I said. "You know, 'Love you, baby!' My way of saying, 'Good work!'"

"Good work," she repeated in the voice of the undead. I've heard people talk about STDs with more enthusiasm.

"Yeah ... you know ..."

But the phone was already dead.

Shiyit.

"Mr. Manning!" someone called across the tiled foyer.

Xenophon Baars.

The guy was a physically impressive specimen: tall in that angular, Honest Abe kind of way, with a slight stoop that paradoxically suggested strength rather than infirmity. His face had a boyish air that no amount of aging could dispel, one accentuated by the long-banged unruliness of his hair. His eyes looked sharp behind the reflections gliding across the lenses of his glasses. He wore a white suit identical to Stevie's in every respect save that it sported a red collar. Nice touch, that, I thought.

Real *Star Treky*.

"So what do you think of our place?" he asked.

"Looks like a juvenile detention centre."

Not very diplomatic, I suppose, but something about the guy suggested that my peculiar brand of cynical honesty would be appreciated. He was a former philosophy professor, and I have enough egghead friends to know that cynicism is their favourite way of hiding hypocrisy in plain view.

We spent a couple of minutes commiserating about Jennifer before he led me deeper into the Compound. She was well loved and sorely missed and all that ya-ya crap. I got the sense that her room, wherever it was in this labyrinth, had already been "repurposed." Baars himself, at least, didn't seem all that sentimental. I found myself thinking of Amanda Bonjour crying while she tied her shoes. The inaudible tap-tap of tears across cracked and raised lineoleum.

"I suppose," he said, his manner as brisk as his pace, "that you want to ask all the usual questions. Who sleeps with who. Who despi—"

"To be honest, this whole cult thing is kind of a curveball. I like to start from the outside and work my way in. I think I need to understand *you* first."

He turned to me with an appreciative look. "Perhaps we should begin with a tour—you think?"

"Sure," I replied.

Obviously the guy had a script he wanted to follow.

So we toured the Compound, my eyes darting this way and that as he described the history of the Framers from their beginnings in southern California to the purchase and renovation of the buildings around me. The place was a veritable maze, possessing, in addition to the seminar rooms and the dormitories, a small gym, a library, a games room that he called the "activity centre," and even an indoor garden. Despite the thoroughness of the renovations, a kind of spiritual lurch and jar haunted the structure, inexplicable steps, zigzag halls, the ceilings claustrophobic one moment, agoraphobic the next—what you typically find when an architect imposes drastic new uses across ancient floor plans, only writ large.

Bad as the human brain.

"At first we considered buying one of the abandoned factories you passed on your way out here," Baars explained, "but we ran into considerable ... *resistance*, you might say, from city council."

"Hard to zone silly," I replied.

He smiled as if I were the kind of asshole he could appreciate.

We had come to a corridor with doors set at hotel intervals. Without warning or explanation, Baars pressed one open, gestured for me to join him. Several seconds passed before I realized I was looking into Jennifer's room.

"The police have already been through—as you can see."

Tossed or *ransacked* would have better described it. Either that or Jennifer Bonjour was a pathological slob.

The room was larger than I expected, with a double bed and night table crowded in one corner, and a small sectional arranged opposite an entertainment centre in the other. Despite the mess—strewn books and magazines, cushions piled like rubble, blankets balled like cabbage—it all seemed so *suburban* in a consumer credit kind of way. I guess I was expecting something more monastic. Say what you will about the Framers, self-denial was certainly not part of their creed.

I had rooted through the rooms of several missing persons by this time, so I was accustomed to the sense of spookiness. But her room troubled me more than usual for some reason. It was almost as if Jennifer's sheer *normalcy*—down to the bloody *Twilight* books and DVDs—made her disappearance all the more tragic.

But in investigative terms, this was little more than a sneak preview—for me, anyway. In the movies, the dick always roots around and finds a decisive clue. Either a bona fide lead, like a pack of matches with a water-damaged phone number. Or a cipher, something that initially makes no sense whatsoever, like a gob of chewing gum in a condom, say, but eventually unlocks the entire case. But these are just narrative conceits. In reality, everything can mean anything—abject ambiguity is the rule, and if you go in blind, you will sure as shit read things wrong.

Jennifer's room was what you would call a primary text, and I was just getting started on the secondary sources. Going in now would be like deciphering hieroglyphics using a tourist phrase book.

I needed to learn the grammar of the situation.

At least that was what I told myself at the time.

I turned from the entrance into his quizzical gaze. "Is there someplace we can talk?"

Baars smiled and nodded as if I had slipped the noose of one pet theory only to confirm a second.

He led me back into the maze, yapping the whole way.

His tale was a familiar one: boy meets New Age revelation; boy builds end-of-the-world bunker. I could tell he had told it many times before, and that he never tired of repeating it. And why not, when it made him the Moses of the Modern Age? Conviction, whether religious or otherwise, requires a certain hunger for repetition. And flattery makes everything taste sweeter.

"It's taken a lot of commitment," he said, "and even more hard work, but the Framers are here to stay ..."

"Until the world blows up."

A patient smile. "Do you really think we're that simple, Mr. Manning?"

"Define 'simple.'"

Baars laughed like a teacher finding evidence of his genius reflected in a pupil. "'Simple,'" he said, "is to follow the path of least social resistance, to go with the flow and believe what most everyone believes. In that sense, Mr. Manning, we Framers believe *against* the law of social gravitation."

After so many smartass girlfriends, I knew this game. "But what if gravity is simply *belief in general* instead of this or that dogma? What if real courage consists in resisting belief altogether?"

Baars simply laughed harder. "Spoken like a true ironist!" He turned and fixed me with a look I found far too canny. "I imagine cynicism is a hazard of your trade—yes? The crazy parade of crazy people, everyone bent on justifying this or that petty transgression. It would be difficult not to take a dim view of people and their beliefs."

"Ironist ..." I said. The fucker was trying to turn the verbal tables. "Huh?"

"You think you wander a world filled with self-righteous morons, don't you? Conceit. Vanity. Envy. Greed. You've seen it all, so now that's all you see. But don't you worry, Mr. Manning? I mean, 'moron' is simply a version of 'sinner,' isn't it? A word we use to make ourselves feel superior. What if cynicism and self-righteousness were one and the same thing?"

Condescending prick. This is generally what I think of people who say things that fly over my head.

"But I *do* wander a world filled with self-righteous morons."

Exactly, the man's smile replied.

Usually, I feel sorry for ultra-self-conscious people—people like Xen Baars. They just spend so much of their time *pretending*. They sit in coffee shops forcing the kinds of conversations they think people like them should have. They laugh from the top of their lungs. And in the seams of their patchwork timing, you can always glimpse panic, like drummers too sober to keep the beat. Living is *work* for these people. An endless tour of performances with no spectacular failures to redeem them.

But this guy had taken the pantomime to an entirely different level. Inventing worlds behind worlds to redeem the artificiality of his existence. What could be more spectacular than that?

Without explanation, Baars turned to press open a heavy oak door to our right. He ushered me from the sun-bright hall into a low, dim room that reeked of bedpans and astringent. I grinned as my eyes sorted shapes in the gloom: because I remember everything people say, I have a bad habit of cracking myself up while others are talking. Obnoxious, I know.

But what I saw slapped the grin off my face. A hospital bed, illuminated by a single reading light, set in a semicircle of gleaming devices and spectral readouts. And a woman, impossibly frail, swaddled by blankets, wired into so many tubes that it seemed she would hang suspended if the bed were kicked away. She was more than old, she was *ancient*, withered not only by time but by some deep, internal trauma. Her mouth hung half open, as if her lower jaw were slowly shrinking into her neck. Her eyes were little more than black perforations at the bottoms of her sockets.

Then the reek hit me. Indescribable, really, like death in diapers.

"Her name is Agatha," Baars said from beside me. "She suffered a mid-cerebral arterial stroke some five weeks ago. Since she's one of ours, we decided to let her die here, among us."

I tried not to breathe, swallowed out of some reflex. Fawk. It seemed I could actually *taste* her dying.

"Hello ... uh, Agatha."

What was he up to?

"Something wrong, Mr. Manning?"

"No ..." I lied, knowing (without knowing) that this was exactly what Baars hoped I would do. The scene reeked of unwelcome object lessons.

"Troubling, isn't it? To turn a corner and find all your concerns breaking about some fact of tragedy."

I shot him a hard look. "*Your* concerns seem pretty intact."

"Yes," he said, glancing down to his shining toes then out to Agatha dying in her pale pool of light. "But then that's the point."

This was when the disgust hit me. Unlike you, I remember all the little ways in which I've been manipulated, verbally or otherwise. I simply gazed at him in my flat-faced way.

"I'm sure the Bonjours told you that we seemed ... relatively ... unconcerned with Jennifer's fate."

"On the contrary. They said you had been very co-operative. They hate you, of course. They think all of this ... is, well ... some kind of monstrous con, but ..."

I let my voice trail into the sound of Agatha drawing a mechanical breath. I felt vaguely nauseous.

"You need to *understand* us, Mr. Manning, really understand us, because if you don't, you will *suspect* us. And if you suspect us, you will waste time and resources investigating us, time and resources that I fear Jennifer Bonjour desperately needs."

I wasn't buying any of it. Rule one of all private investigating is that everyone, but everyone, is full of shit. You know that niggling instinct you have to nip and tuck your reality when describing this or that aspect of your life? Add an inch to your dick here, shave a year off your Corolla there? That temptation pretty much rules the roost when you have something *real* to hide.

I grinned as best I could manage. Shrugged. "Blame the weirdo, huh? Is that what you think I'll do?"

"Why not? People can't help themselves, Mr. Manning."

"Don't I know it."

A canny look and smile. "This is why I wanted to introduce you to Agatha ... to help you understand how something so obviously tragic from your frame of reference could be *cause for celebration* from ours."

This was where I got that sinking feeling ... like finding a crack pipe in your nephew's rucksack.

"Cause for celebration, huh."

"I know how it sounds," Baars said, gesturing for me to leave the room. "But I suspect you, Mr. Manning, know precisely what I'm talking about ..."

"And what would that be, Professor?"

"Not feeling what others think you should."

Owich. I was beginning to appreciate the fucker's power, I give you that. If he could give *me* the itch, cynical cocksucker that I am, then his followers need not be the morons I had assumed they would be. Albert had told me as much already, I suppose.

"Imagine," Baars said, leading me down the hall. "Imagine a society that has evolved beyond things like meaning and purpose, where nothing matters because anything can be done. Imagine a society that treats the modalities of human experience, everything from the extremes of rape and murder to the tedious mainstays of snoozing and shitting, the same way a gourmand regards items on a restaurant menu ..." He pressed open a glass door that led onto a small terrace with a single table. "As things to be consumed."

"Consumed?"

I took the seat he offered—an iron-and-wicker thing. We were in another small courtyard, this one completely shaded save for an oblong of brilliance across the spikes and hostas. The air smelled of mint and earth cooling in the evening. Gleaming porcelain crowded the table: apparently we were about to have some tea—or as I like to call it, coffee with the balls cut off.

"Did you ever read *Dick and Jane* in public school?" Baars asked as he poured out two dainty cups of tea.

"Nah. For me it was *Mr. Mugs*."

Another enigmatic smile. "Do you ever go back to reread *Mr. Mugs*?"

"Of course not," I replied.

"Why?"

More games. "Because it's *stupid.* Only retards and little kids can appreciate it."

"Exactly!" Baars exclaimed.

The guy was baiting me. Usually this makes me ornery, toxic even, but like I said earlier, these people had organized their lives around an invisible world. At the moment, Baars was my only flashlight.

"I'm not following you ..."

He smiled. "Some forms of understanding require ignorance."

"I'm *still* not following you."

"Our *lives*, Mr. Manning. Our lives are like *Mr. Mugs* or *Dick and Jane*. They can only be appreciated from the standpoint of *not knowing certain things*, not seeing ..."

"So what are you saying?" I asked.

"That this, *all of this*, is ... not quite real."

"You mean like the Matrix?"

I must have used my *here-we-go* tone, because Baars roared with laughter. "No, not a simulation. Not quite. More like *theatre*, where the world is a prop, and the actors forget their identities to better inhabit their roles. We all have roles to play, Mr. Manning. Even you."

I grinned in a heroic effort to twist hilarity into oh-ya admiration. "Like method acting taken to the absolute ..."

"Trust me, Mr. Manning, I know full well how mad I sound."

This seemed as good a moment as any to sip my tea. "There's a difference between knowing a thing and appreciating it."

He grinned in eye-twinkling admission. "But really, if you think about it, I'm not actually saying anything new: only that there's a world beyond what our eyes can see, a world *more fundamental.* So you tell me, honestly, what's the difference between what I'm saying and what Christians or Jews or Hindus or Muslims or Buddhists say? If I sound mad, it's simply because the beyond I describe has no tradition, no mass consensus, and therefore no social sanction."

Fucking philosophy professors. There oughta be a law ...

"That's what you mean by the 'Frame,' isn't it?"

He nodded. "Indeed. The 'Occluded Frame' is simply the name we give our more fundamental world."

"So what you're saying is that you're just another religious nut."

Even as I said this, I knew it couldn't be the case. He was saying that life—the very existence you and I are enduring this very moment—was wall to wall, top to bottom, a kind of ride at Disney World, only one where we had our memories wiped so that we wouldn't *know* it was a ride.

Not all that religious when you think about it.

"Yes!" Baars cackled. I was really starting to hate the man's laughter: it made me feel like a developmentally challenged kid hamming it up in life skills class. "Exactly!"

"So then what makes you *special*?"

That knocked some seriousness into him. "Because *I've been there*, Mr. Manning. I've crossed the Lacuna. I have literally walked the Frame."

Is that where he got his slogans? *Johnny Cash* tunes?

"Like I said, what makes you special?"

A long, appraising stare. No matter how much noise a man makes about being open-minded, a part of him will always out-and-out *despise* contradiction. "Nothing," he admitted with a shrug. "I could be insane, like you think. I admit that possibility. I've even visited neurologists to investigate the possibility." He tapped his temple, grinning. "No tumours, I assure you. So when it comes to *your* judgment and my *experience*, Mr. Manning, I will err on the side of my experience every time. Wouldn't you?"

"Fawk, no. Are you kidding me? I *know* that I'm an idiot."

Baars smiled a knowing smile, the kind of smile that says, *Liar*, not as an accusation but as a bemused observation. A classic *not-so-different-than-me* smile.

"Like a good skeptic, huh?"

I shook my head with mock seriousness. "Not at all. A skeptic suspends judgment. A cynic just doesn't care."

"A perilously fine distinction, wouldn't you say?"

I shrugged my shoulders. "Whatever."

Once again, Xenophon Baars roared with laughter, a minute-long *ho-ho-he-fucking-he-he* that forced him to take off his glasses and wipe the tears from his eyes. Say what you will about the guy, he definitely dug my brand of humour. "The story is absurd, I admit, Mr. Manning. Claiming that the world is five billion years older than it appears, that our lives are a kind of spectator sport for an inhuman generation. Madness! It has to be. But if you *think*, if you really honestly consider, you'll see that we're not saying anything surprising at all. Only that we're the ignorant children of ourselves, Mr. Manning."

I couldn't resist. "Cool name for a band."

"Excuse me?"

"Ignorant Children of Ourselves."

I could even see the album cover: *I-C-O* in giant golden letters across the top. Three angels smoking a joint below. A bag of weed leaning against a sandalled toe.

Because of the link between memory and sleep, my memory shrink sent me to this sleep researcher, Philip Ryle, who wanted to see whether there were any significant differences in the way you and I dream. Apparently not. But the guy was definitely one of the more interesting eggheads ever to stick pasties to my head.

You see, the thing about dreams is that they pretty much prove that the outside world is *all in our heads*. We have a "world generator" in our brain, which, when we're both awake and sane, is anchored to the *world*-world through our senses. But when you fall asleep, your brain draws anchor, and your world generator drifts through time, place, and possibility. You dream the crazy-ass shit you're afraid to tell your wife in the morning.

Ryle was always going on about how this meant dreams and waking life were of a piece—two versions of the same thing. He was a big fan of something called lucid dreaming—you know, where you wake up in your dream, realize that your dream *is* a dream, then take control. One of his grad students told me Ryle had this Playboy Mansion dream that he was able to replay at will. The kid could have been joking, but I was inclined to believe him. I've never met anyone who loved his sleep quite as much as Ryle.

But Ryle was also a believer in what he called *lucid living*. In the same way you could develop "metacognitive awareness" of your dreams and take control of them, you could also develop metacognitive awareness of your waking life—and so take control of it. This, he liked to say, was pretty much what meditation and "enlightenment" were all about. Unlike dreams, you couldn't control *what* happens, but you could control *how* things happen, and, more importantly, *whom they happen to.*

He liked to claim that he could dissolve his "self" at will, and simply become the "raw space of existence." Sometimes he would say crazy things like, "Yeah, sorry, Diss, I'm not here right now."

I always wondered what it was like for all those dream Bunnies screwing a "raw space of existence." I suspected it felt an awful lot like banging a dirty old man.

What Baars was saying was that the world generators in our heads had been hijacked to make it *appear* as though we were living in the early twenty-first century, when in fact we were living in some absurdly distant future. And in a curious sense, he was advocating a kind of lucid living not so different from the one recommended by crazy old Philip Ryle. Like the song said, we needed to party like it was 1999—give or take five billion years.

Either way, I could give a flying fuck. Here and now, baby. Dream or not, *this* is where the bad stuff happens. This is where beautiful young women like Jennifer Bonjour vanish, and this is where they are found.

Besides, I got the feeling my paycheque would bounce in the Frame.

I drained the last of my tea. "I gotta ask ... You don't think that Jennifer, you know, has ... *crossed over*, or something ... do you?"

"That depends," Baars replied, his eyes troubled beneath the glare of his glasses.

"Depends?" Something told me he wasn't talking about my favourite brand of diapers.

"On whether she's dead, Mr. Manning."

Thanks to Baars's little explanation, I now knew the Framers were every bit as crazy as they seemed. But thanks to Albert and his phone call, I knew this meant jack shit, simply because *everybody* believed in some kind of madness. Except me, of course.

Convinced I had a handle on the kooky dogma, I walked the Professor through the wonky events the night Jennifer vanished. He claimed he knew something was wrong the instant Stevie told him that Anson had called to check on Jennifer.

"I never approved of their forays," he said. "The dancing I understood. She was ... young. Very young. But they insisted on *walking* for some reason. I always told them it wasn't safe ..."

I could hear it in his voice, the *let's-move-on* hesitancy. Even though Baars wielded absolute authority, he was still accountable to his past. He couldn't make it up as he went along—at least not the way I did. Power turns on legitimacy, and legitimacy—to the chagrin of more than a few tyrants—turns on consistency.

What could he say, really? It was all a *simulation*, wasn't it? Dead factories. Abductions. Rapes. How could the almighty Xenophon Baars tell anyone to be afraid of "worldly" things?

Perhaps this was the motive for her recklessness. Perhaps she had resented Baars's domination even as she surrendered to it. Perhaps making him worry was one among a dozen ways to get even ...

Perhaps Baars had had enough.

When I asked him whether she was sexually involved with anybody in the Compound, he said, "Yes," without missing a beat. "Jennifer and I were lovers."

A clipped response, and the one I expected. Perhaps Jennifer's dancing—and not the walking—had been his real concern all along. A cult leader is one thing. But a *jealous* cult leader? The first thing this business teaches you is that there's nothing more murderous than ambitious genes.

"Another undergrad infatuation, huh?"

"On the contrary," he said. For the first time he looked almost offended, which was amazing considering the number of zingers I'd laid on him so far. "I'm quite convinced that ... that this level of me, at least, is in love with her ... Yes. Quite in love."

Fawk ... This *level* of me?

Mad as a fucking hatter. What would it be like to be at once in love and to look at that love as a kind of gift shop curiosity—like a snow bubble from Montreal or something?

I have to admit, I was getting excited, not in the woody way, though given who I am and what I suffer, it would have been more than understandable. This was utterly—almost over-the-top—*new*. Totally unlike any case I had ever worked. So even though I was shocked, even bewildered, by what Baars had said, I sat there smiling my *fucking-bootiful* smile. You couldn't make this shit up if you tried!

"Tell me, Dr. Baars. Does anyone get ... you know, *impatient*?"

"I don't follow."

"You know. Like the Jains in India. Or the Cathars in medieval France. When you make death a virtue, when you make this world some kind of perversion, moral or whatever, you have an *incentive* to die, don't you?

Take you guys. For the Framers, death is a kind of waking, a supreme form of enlightenment, isn't it?"

A hard look. "Are you suggesting she committed suicide?"

I wagged my head in a big *naw*. "Look. I'm big on *circumstances*, on the ways they warp the stakes of things. I don't think about bad apples so much as bruising bushels. The fact is, Dr. Baars, at a basic level there's precious little that distinguishes your lot from the rest of the planet. You guys are at least as fucked up as the rest of us—at *least*. Add to that the fact that death doesn't carry the same cold water for you as it does for someone like, say"—I shot him a big cheesy grin—"me."

A long sour look, followed by a quick glance at his gold watch. I think I'm kind of like Lenny Bruce that way: my routine tends to wear down even the most expansive sense of humour.

"Sorry, Mr. Manning," he said, recovering something of his original charm. "I have another seminar coming up in a few minutes." A glum, *c'est dommage* smile. "I'm certain we'll find time to speak again ..." He stood in that way that suggested I should stand and follow him—crazy, when you think about it, the haze of monkey-see imperatives that surrounds even our simplest actions. "But in the meantime, when you find yourself thinking that it's always the crazy lover behind these sorts of things, please keep in mind that Ruddick is a ... complicated town."

What do you make of a conversation like that? I mean, fucking really.

The guy simply *had* to be crazy. And the creepy thing was that he seemed to *know* it. I've known quite a few genuinely crazy motherfuckers in my day—I've even been told what it *feels* like to have wings crack and snap out of the bones of your arms. And almost without exception, crazy motherfuckers are convinced they are as sane as sane can be, as well adjusted as the First Lady. But Baars. He seemed to know he was crazy—worse, he seemed to *revel* in it, as if it were another stage on his quest to blow the great spirit load.

The more I thought about him, the scarier he became.

And if that wasn't enough, he seemed *happy*. Happy people make me sick, especially when their lovers have gone missing.

He escorted me back to my car, careful to fill the silence with more observations on their recent renovations. Oak banisters and all that bourgeois bullshit. Everything was local artisan this and local artisan that—leading me to remark that Ruddick must have quite a cool flea market scene.

Even though he said nothing, his smile was pure fuck-you.

Once in my car, I cranked back my seat and sparked another joint—a pinner this time. Though I remember the transcript perfectly, I find that the circumstantial details don't ... decompose, you might say, at the same rate if I run through a conversation immediately after having it.

I gazed out the windshield, saw poor Agatha crumpled in her hospital bed.

"Something wrong, Mr. Manning?"

"No ..."

The Agatha stuff, I decided, was far more than the object lesson Baars made it out to be. He wanted me to understand him and his beliefs, sure, how they might lead outsiders to mistake their complacency for guilt. Baars knew that he would have to fess up to a sexual relationship with Jennifer, knew that this would automatically make him the primary suspect—especially once you factored in his bizarre, detached attitude. Agatha was his way of throwing a towel over the alarm bell just before the fire drill.

But it was also an example of how Baars went about *recruiting*: confront emotionally vulnerable people with troubling things, disturbing things; get them telling small lies to conceal their discomfort—like I had—then use this as a way to pry them open to his ideological freak show. This guy didn't simply believe the world was five billion years older than it was, he had managed to *convince* a group of otherwise intelligent people of the same thing. Something to remember ...

He was, like, an evil mastermind or something.

I leaned back, puffing my joint, savoured the oily burn across my tongue. I closed my eyes to better allow my subconscious to present its case. You notice so many things without noticing—you have no idea. I saw steaming tea and sun-sharp porcelain across the backs of my eyelids.

"Do you ever go back to reread Mr. Mugs*?"* Baars asked.

"Of course not," I replied.

"Why?"

"Because it's stupid. *Because only retards and little kids can appreciate it."*

"Exactly!" Baars cried.

This was his primary tactic, I decided: leading you by the nose to answers only he understood. I wondered whether this was a charismatic cult leader thing or whether it was peculiar to Baars.

"I'm not following you, Mr. Baars ..."

He smiled—of course, given that this confession was what he had been fishing for all along. *"Some forms of appreciation require* ignorance.*"*

"I'm still *not following you."*

"Our lives, *Mr. Manning. Our lives are like* Mr. Mugs *or* Dick and Jane. *They can only be appreciated from the standpoint of* not knowing certain things, *not seeing ..."*

"So what are you saying?"

"That this, all of this, *is ... not quite real."*

Fawk.

I pinched the joint between thumb and index finger, sucked smoke through kissy lips. At the same time, I sat on a wrought iron chair in the Compound courtyard, fixing Baars with a bemused stare.

"That's what you mean by the 'Frame,' isn't it?"

There was something wary about his nod, I decided. Up to this point

I had come across as merely clever, a good practice partner for the verbal sparring he so obviously loved ...

Anything but a threat.

"Indeed," he replied. *"The 'Occluded Frame' is simply the name we give to our more fundamental world."*

There it was. The shift in intonations. The narrowing of his gaze.

"So what you're saying is that you're just another religious nut."

"Yes!" Baars cackled. But the laughter was forced. I was certain of it. *"Exactly!"*

"So then what makes you special*?"*

"Because I've been there, *Mr. Manning. I've crossed the Lacuna. I have literally* walked *the Frame."*

"Like I said ..."

So I worried him. It could mean he was involved in Jennifer's disappearance, but it could also mean that I had tweaked him with my snide remarks—I have this way of snapping people's elastics. In the Compound, he was *both* king and pope, and here I come waltzing in, challenging, questioning, dismissing ...

And most importantly, *reminding.* That the borders of his fiefdom were small-small-small. That he was just another me-me-me dope like the rest of us.

I leaned back in my seat, blinked while soaking in the stone. At the same time I strolled with Baars down a hardwood hall, Agatha and her humming apparatus behind me.

"Imagine," Baars was saying. *"Imagine a society that has evolved beyond things like meaning and purpose, where nothing matters because anything can be done. Imagine a society that treats the modalities of human experience, everything from the extremes of rape and murder to the tedious mainstays of snoozing and shitting, the same way a gourmand regards items on a restaurant menu ... As things to be consumed."*

Of all his monologues, only this one really tingled ... but for reasons that had precious little to do with the case. I replayed it in my imagination again and again, mooned over it like a kid with a nudie picture.

A number of questions to ask during the follow-up interview occurred to me. I was especially interested in the details of this Crossing the Lacuna thing. Just what did they use to induce their hallucinations? Did it involve drugs of some kind? Baars had some kind of Timothy Leary thing going—like, totally.

A cloud passed over the sun, and in the momentary gloom I suddenly glimpsed the room—an office of some kind—beyond the plate glass window opposite my car. I saw Stevie sitting behind a grand and paperless desk, leaning back in ergonomic repose, watching me with the intensity of a starving owl.

The evil henchman.

Matching his gaze, I sucked my roach to the nub then flicked it out the window. I started the Golf, then, grinning, shot the guy a quick finger.

Prick.

Track Six
ONE POTATO CHIP AT A TIME

She stepped into the restaurant and I saw the whole porno.

Her name was Molly, Molly Modano, and she did not belong. California girl—immediately and obviously, even in an age when geographical identity claims have been pretty much scrambled into white noise. I would have bet my Volkswagen on it.

It was early evening, and I had risked the roaring four-lane traffic to try out the small diner across from my motel. Hard to look cool scrambling across a busy road—almost as hard as looking tough queued up for airport security. The diner sported the name Odd-Jobs in lightless neon tubing across the front, but it was the Day-Glo quip on the port-a-sign that caught my attention: *Eat or be eaten.* I was just sitting at a booth, pretending to study the menu, swirling my coffee with a clinking spoon, and then there she was, tits on a stick.

Just so you know, there's *always* a girl with me. You could say I'm like Hollywood that way. Always hunting for a fresher face.

I didn't waste time—I never do. I was standing up just as she was sitting down. The key, I've found, is to beat the waitress to the punch ... Or maybe that's just a superstition of mine.

"Mind if I join you?"

She looked up as if startled and simply said, *"Eew."*

"Eew?" I exclaimed. "I haven't even unbuttoned my trenchcoat yet!"

All hotties have routines specifically designed for contingencies like me. Some just tell you to go fuck yourself, literally. Others, the ones who are genuinely evil or who just desperately want to be nice, find more creative ways to tell you to go fuck yourself. I actually had one chick offer me change like I was a bum or something!

Molly desperately wanted to be nice. "Sorry, but ... I don't even *know* you."

"Apparently you know me well enough to be grossed out."

"I just got this thing about first impressions."

I certainly wasn't complaining from my end: narrow hips and a flat abdomen. High breasts beneath a largely ceremonial bra. A boyish athleticism rounded into feminine allure, like a red-headed Mia Farrow or Gwyneth Paltrow—which simply made it seem all the more appropriate, given that I was a combination of Brad Pitt and the Devil.

"Here I thought first impressions were the only thing I was good at."

Believe me when I tell you that I have a winning grin, the kind that can shrug away even the most determined ill-willing. She looked at me as though assessing my planetary credentials, then laughed a girlish in-spite-of-her-better-judgment laugh ...

"A martyr, huh?"

"Depends on the cause," I said, sliding into the seat opposite.

Just so you know, I've been called a sexist pig exactly sixty-nine times. Coincidence? I think not.

The fact is, I *am* a sexist, in the sense that someone who plays cello all the time is called a cellist. I. Love. Sex. All things being equal, I will choose getting laid pretty much every time. And just so you know, when I say "love," I don't mean the snuggle-with-your-wife-on-the-couch variety but the *real* deal—you know, the kind only crackheads and junkies can know.

The love that keeps you coming back.

An old girlfriend of mine laid it all out for me once. She was a systems analyst named Joyce Pennington, but everyone used to call her Jimmy for some reason. No fewer than 7 of those 69 accusations belong to her—a whopping 11 percent. (She's also responsible for 9 out of the 19 times I've been called a narcissist, but that's another story.) The first four times she called me a sexist I just shrugged it off—prick a guy with the same insult long enough and he becomes numb. But the *fifth* time I blew my stack for some reason. So in the calm voice I use to package all my outrage, I gave her the little spiel I gave you above. It was fucking *biology*, for chrissakes. Was hunger a sin? How about shitting? Was voiding my bowel yet another fascistic exercise?

"And murder isn't biological?" she replied. I swear her laugh lopped two inches off my dick. You know, that cruel feminine chuckle you hear so often on *Sex and the City*, the one that says (with pious charity) that, sure, men are all half retarded, but we love them anyway, don't we? The kind of laugh that men reserve for Labrador retrievers. Bad boy. *Bad.*

"Oh, Diss," she continued. "How can you treat women equally if you see them as accessories to your dick?"

I stared at her wordlessly.

"Well?"

So I told her my dick was the only thing I was proud of ... that for as long as I could remember I used my sexual prowess as a crutch, a way to limp around the fact that I was too much of a loser for anyone to love. Nobody *lubs* me. Boo-hoo.

Whatever it takes to get laid.

She figured it out eventually, of course. 2002. On the fourth of July, no less. Jimmy was one smart chick.

Patriotic too.

See, the thing is, I score *large*. Since I was fourteen, I have slept with at least 558 different women, probably more if you count the nights I've blacked out from drinking. I think this is pretty impressive, given that I'm not a rock star. So this is my dilemma: how can I stop seeing women as accessories to my dick when so many of them so obviously *want to be*?

Seriously.

Look, I know it's a problem, a *vice* even. I know it shuts down the possibility of a mature relationship with a certain percentage of the world's population: the hottie demographic. I know the older I get, the more debauched and pathetic I become. If I were completely honest, I would admit that when the Bonjours handed me that photo of Dead Jennifer, my first thoughts were almost entirely carnal—that when I trolled her Facebook page on the Web afterward, I secretly hoped to find photos of some drunken lingerie party.

But I can't help myself. Even my second therapist said I have bigger fish to fry.

Like the fact that I think nobody loves me.

So we talked, Molly and me.

She had this narrow, birdlike intensity, with a look that avoided yours with push-pin concentration, as though you were part of her game world but perpetually fixed just to the right of the cursor. It was a strange tick, one of those little wrinkles that never gets ironed out of a personality, like hiding your teeth when you smile.

I found it intensely erotic.

She was a journalist with the *Pittsburgh Post-Gazette*, or the "PG" as she continually referred to it. Well, she was actually more of a stringer than a real journalist, and she was hoping to break into the biz by writing an in-depth story on—you guessed it—the disappearance of Jennifer Bonjour.

Score. So much meaningless shit happens that coincidences are bound to abound. Sometimes the world is so small it can only be grand.

"Opportunity of a lifetime," I said.

She made a pained face. "It's horrible, I know. But I figure it can't be all that bad if I *help* ... you know, find her ..." She trailed as though unconvinced.

"The dead don't sweat," I said, grinning. "Neither should you."

There's such mystery in meeting a woman for the first time. I knew she had a life, that behind her scenes there were scads of people—friends, family, lovers—and to be honest, I didn't really give a fuck. I know that sounds bad, like banging her was all I cared about. But the fact of the matter is probably worse.

Remember, I don't forget. This makes me pretty much impossible to get along with, simply because the longer I know a person, the less they seem a person. Remember, I see all the ways you people repeat.

This makes falling in love pretty much radioactive. The pain is stacked high enough as it is, and with me it never, ever goes away. So the way I see it, this means either I become celibate like a priest or I womanize like a hound dog. What would you choose?

"And you?" Molly asked. "What brings you to the booming metropolis of Ruddick?"

I shot her my best whisky-ad grin: rueful, infinitely assured. The kind that says, *Oh, yes, I will be laid tonight.* Teeth are a window on our genes, and my pearly-whites positively gleamed.

"An opportunity of a lifetime."

If my ragged good looks were the hook, then Dead Jennifer was the bait. I knew it the instant I finished describing the Bonjours and their piteous request: I was Molly Modano's first break. Her initial *Oh-no-not-another-one* wariness dissolved into avid interest. After about five minutes of relentless questioning I began to wonder who was catching whom. I also realized that I almost certainly wasn't going to score that night. In Molly's eyes I had made the miraculous transition from being another asshole to being a possible night of fun in the sack to being a *resource*, something that required cultivation and rationing. I cursed myself for not lying at the outset, certain that somewhere in some journalism textbook stuffed in the back of her closet there was a rule that said, "Do not, *under any circumstances*, bang your sources."

Codes of professional conduct. Fawk.

I felt my eyes glazing. "Woo," I said, expelling a lungful of specious air. "I. Am. Bagged."

"What time you think you'll be up for breakfast?" she asked.

Knocks on my motel room door always unnerve me. The great thing about motel versus hotel rooms is the way they open up onto the world—like home. But this also means they're *exposed*—like home. Hotels give you a controlled environment within a controlled environment. The really good ones make you feel like you're in a Fabergé egg or something. The world is reduced to soundless motion behind tinted glass.

Just one more gorilla exhibit.

I thought about grabbing my gun from my overnight bag, but decided against it. I knew who it was.

"Hi, Molly," I said, pulling open the door. The light across the motel frontage was haphazard at best, so that my room light provided her only illumination. Her face stared up at me, bright and warm. My shadow fell across her body. Then I noticed ...

There were *tears* in her eyes.

Fawk.

"Look," she said hesitantly. "I know ... I know how this works ..."

"How what works?" The lack of interest in my voice shocked me.

She swallowed and blinked. She wiped the tear that fell from her left eye so fast that it almost seemed like a magic trick. Sean O'May, my old hand-to-hand trainer, among other things, would have been impressed.

"I mean, I know ... know what you were ... expecting, and um ..." Her eyes were bouncing all over the place, but I could tell they had glimpsed my bed.

"What's wrong, Molly?"

She tilted her head to the weight of her hair, flashed the kind of embarrassed smile that had duped me into thinking I was in love more than once.

"The funny thing is that I probably *would have*, you know? I mean, you're ..." She swallowed once again. "... handsome enough. And it's been ... well ... a long time, you know? And I—"

"Molly," I said on the edge of forceful and gentle. Kind of like the way I am in the sack.

"So *now*," she continued babbling, "now I'm like ... like—"

"Molly."

"What?"

"Would you like to, ah, accompany me tomorrow?"

Any deal you strike with the media is going to be Faustian through and through—something I learned during the war. Good in the short term, disastrous in the long run. You see, if you're successful, you get the whole circus except the ringmaster, hundreds of very clever and generally unscrupulous (because let's face it, nothing justifies fucking people over quite so conveniently as the truth) journalists all feverishly working their own manic angles. It'll tear you apart, even if you don't give a rat's ass about things like honour and reputation or have a career that's remotely political. Media attention incites mobs, and mobs have the bad habit of looking for goats.

And the sad fact is, just about anyone will do.

Molly made a show of scrutinizing me—as if any con man worth fearing had ever been sussed out in a single glance. Finally she gave me one of those phony shrugs and said, "Sure," in a little sister's voice.

I began closing the door, leaning forward so that my face remained squarely in the gap. "I'll meet you for breakfast at ten ..."

I never was a morning person.

That night I dreamed. Generally I smoke too much dope to dream: though the Lord's Leaf is in no way neurotoxic, it does change the way blood flows through your bean, and this, apparently, affects a chronic user's sleep patterns. A welcome side effect, in my case.

What made this dream positively kooky was that I woke up convinced I was as awake and as alert as a goaltender in overtime. I bolted from my pillow and *there he was*, watching me through a haze of cigarette smoke, my old war buddy, my mentor in all things violent: Sean O'May.

I'll save his story for another therapy session.

He sat in the chair next to my room's small table, slumped back, with his snakeskin boots kicked out, one to either side of a black hockey bag. His hair was dyed orange and slicked back like the old days. His eyes were sharp as always, so small they glittered perpetual black. His trademark cigarette hung from his trademark Mickey Rourke grin. For as long as I knew him, he was loath to reveal his teeth—probably because they were so freakishly small, like baby teeth.

"Soooo ..." he drawled. "What are you saying, there, Disciple?"

I sat blinking at the sheer impossibility of him.

"You're dead," I finally managed to cough.

He snorted through his nose, sucked his cigarette bright. "Yah," he rasped, raising two fingers to pull his smoke from his mouth. "Well, you know how it is ..."

"How *what* is?"

That was when I noticed his cigarette was glowing from *both* ends. I watched with a kind of blank wonder as he closed his lips about the burning inner tip. It seemed I could smell his lips sizzle.

"There's dead for me," he said, "and then there's dead *for you.*"

I sat paralyzed while he watched me with those fucking *he-he* eyes of his.

"What's that?" I finally asked, looking down at the hockey bag.

"Good question." He leaned forward, smiling at me, squinting against the smoke of his cigarette as he grabbed the zipper and tore it open. He peered into the dark maw, shook his head with a Southerner's slow-motion disgust. Sean had grown up in Chattanooga, Tennessee, where he had started drinking Jack Daniel's (where his father worked) at the age of nine.

"Aw, hell," he said, shaking his head in a blue-stringed haze of smoke. "She's all busted up."

"She ..." I repeated in horror.

"Shiyit. What a nasty piece of work."

"Who?" I cried.

He had this way of frowning, as if wincing at a pain that was all yours.

"Yah, you know. Dead Jennifer."

Her name still comes up in my dreams, rare as they are. Dreams of doom—as bad as anything from the war. Without exception I bolt from my blankets, grope the night table to palm my Zippo and cigarettes. I smoke in the dark, watching that orange jewel hover above the shadow of my hand.

And I wonder what it would be like, burning the world from both ends.

Wednesday ...

Pretty much everyone loves spring, except those winter-loving mutants who are generally too cheerful not to die of cancer at some point. I love spring as well, but for reasons peculiar to me. Most people love the retreat of the snow and cold, the dawning of things green and alive. Me,

I love the way the thaw exposes all the hidden garbage, from soggy coffee cups to pockets of dog shit.

Winter is a season of forgetfulness. Spring is a kind of remembering, in all its splendid ugliness.

And so spring reminds me of me—the one thing guaranteed to bring a smile to my face.

What does this have to do with Ruddick in the dry height of summer? Because for me, anyway, the town was locked in wintry silence. It needed to be thawed.

My breakfast with Molly was uneventful. She tried to strike up conversation, but I'm too much of a prick in the mornings to trust myself with small talk. Coffee-coffee-coffee—need I say more?

I didn't so much explain my MO to Molly as demonstrate it. I had her feed me directions from my town map as I rattled around in my Vee-Dub diesel. Once I got a feel for the communities adjacent to the Framer Compound, I began canvassing. I grabbed the flyers that Kimberley had printed for me using the photo of Dead Jennifer that the Bonjours had provided. I parked on a strategic corner, then, with the quizzical redhead in tow, began going door to door with an official-looking clipboard and envelope held like an accountant's ledger in my arms.

"Hi, ma'am. Sorry to trouble you. I'm going round town to take up a collection for the Bonjour family, to help pay for a private investigator to look into their daughter's disappearance."

"Oh. Oh my. Yes, I saw that on the news ... *Horrible.*"

And then I did what I always did: I struck up conversations.

My version of a spring thaw.

"What are you doing?" Molly finally cried in a shrill *Enough-is-fucking-enough* voice.

She had seemed placid enough sitting there in the passenger seat, watching me empty the cash from the envelope and load up my otherwise lean wallet.

"Read between the lines," I said, enumerating my take: 174 bucks. Not bad for a morning's work. "You've heard that before, haven't you?"

"What? *What?* That doesn't even make fucking sense!"

"Not to you, obviously."

She made this face.

Because I have this problem when it comes to forgetting, I carve the world along different joints. I literally see things you would call ephemera as *objects unto themselves*, so to speak. So passing expressions that you simply notice then forget have an existence all of their own for me—to the point where it sometimes seems like it's the person who's ephemeral.

In Molly's case it was Classic Feminine Disgust: a subtle yet heady blend of exasperation, frustration, and a kind of *why-me* outrage, as if the problem wasn't so much men as the fact that they couldn't stop loving them—us. As it so happened, Classic Feminine Disgust was an old friend of mine, so much so I caught myself saying, "How you doing?"

But she was gone, replaced with Atypical Bewildered Fury—another old friend. She almost rolled her eyes back into her head, made a mouth that said *Hide the knives, honey.*

"How am I doing?" she cried. "How am I *doing*? I'm stranded with a psychopath who's conned me into being an accessory to fraud. *How the fuck do you think I'm doing?*"

Redheads. Sheesh.

"Fraud? This is how I work all my missing persons."

"I suppose you call this 'fact-finding.' Is that it?" The sarcasm she poured into her air quotes stung for some reason. I'm never surprised when I'm misunderstood—Christ, I'm rarely surprised *period.* But the resentment never seems to go away.

"Fact-finding. Sure. Good a name as any."

"So where's your tape recorder? Huh? Where are your notes?"

I shot her a nose-crinkling look, pointed to my bean.

"Please," she said. She had the air of someone realizing they've been conned *after* signing the papers.

"Seriously. I *remember* things."

"Oh yah," she said in that *Whatever-you-lying-son-of-a-bitch* voice.

I shook my head, reached back to pull a joint from my rucksack. With so many old friends dropping by, I figured we should turn it into a party. I sparked the thing while she watched in horror, took a deep and most gratifying haul.

"You don't believe me," I said in that voice tokers use to keep their cough pinned to the mat. I offered her the joint, but her look was a lethal *Get-that-shit-out-of-my-face.* Up. Tight. Oh well, more for me. I really needed to be stoned at that instant. I mean *really* really ...

"No, Disciple. I do *not* believe you."

And so, my brain soaking in sweet-leaf lubricant, I showed her. It's remarkable when you think about it. I mean, if people can *recognize* a thing like a conversation, it means it has to be *all in there somewhere,* doesn't it? Which begs the question: where does it all go, our intelligence? I gave her names and addresses, then a verbatim recital of what was said. I even mimicked the way old Mrs. Toews raised a self-conscious finger to cover her old-maid-stache, or how Big John Recchi always wagged his head no as he was agreeing with you.

I'm not sure *dumbfounded* is a heavy enough word to describe the expression on her face.

I grinned my best *Übermensch* grin, tapped my temple with a witty-witty finger. "Wait till you see my dick," I told her. I wasn't kidding.

But she laughed anyway—laughed *hard.* She kind of sounded like a horse, but it was intoxicating all the same. I decided that I liked Molly Modano.

She had good taste in men.

* * *

Molly had a million questions. They always do. She had this way of rolling her head as she talked, kind of like an animated holding pattern, neither a nod nor a shake, but endless prepping in the in-between. Her eyes flashed green and blue.

There were several *You-mean-absolutely-everything?*s. A couple of *God-my-brain-is-such-a-sieve*s. And of course the inevitable *Too-cool*s.

To which I eventually replied, "Not really."

Then suddenly she said, "Ohmigod. You've heard all this shit *before*, haven't you? Like a million times—*only you don't forget*, do you? It must sound so ... so *stale* ..."

And there it was, another old friend staring out from her face, just as female as all the others: Pure Feminine Compassion.

"No wonder," she said, turning to gaze out the passenger window. "No fucking wonder."

I simply stared at the street, signalled and turned, signalled and turned.

Some friends demand silence.

I always expect most of the doors to be dead when I do this on a weekday. But the fact is, a tremendous number of people actually stay at home all day long. How they make their living is a mystery to me—one of the government's infinite entitlements, I suppose. Disability. Unemployment. Social Security. Alimony. Cyber-crime. You would expect them to be rude, treat door-to-door cold-callers with the contempt they deserve, but a substantial proportion of them actually seem to be pleased. It gets pretty lonely scratching your balls on the couch all day, I guess.

They all squint: this is universal. Almost all of them clear their throats—the sludge of not talking. Most are wearing something comfy and informal, though you would be surprised how many people get dolled up to do nothing. Lots of stubble on lots of chins. A couple of hairy female armpits. The odd whiff of reefer. The glimpse of Nintendo on pause in the living room. Some are pleasant. Some are gruff. Some are indifferent, while others are actively hostile. One guy actually had his rifle hugged to his chest, which was alarming in its own right. When combined with his *Are-you-an-earthling?* peer, it was nothing short of terrifying.

The next time you drive through your neighbourhood, take a look around, remind yourself of all the fucking lunatics living in your midst. Seriously. Unlike that cocksucker Baars, I have no clue whatsoever what we humans are up to as a species. I only know what we *aren't.*

Like healthy, for instance.

Molly was particularly surprised by how many people had heard nothing whatsoever about Jennifer Bonjour. I had expected it. I'd learned from earlier expeditions—different people missing in different ways—that a good proportion of the population pay no attention whatsoever to what happens locally. If they crawl out of their video-game-soap-opera-horror-movie world at all, they typically sit vegging to Fox or CNN, soaking up abstract enormities to the exclusion of the struggles next door.

Same as me, actually.

She seemed scandalized, whereas I was *torn*—well, not torn (I would have to give a shit for that), but "of two minds," let's say. Speaking to them was a waste of time, of course, but they did tend to make larger than average "contributions," and I had expenses to cover, like the ten skins I had lost in Atlantic City a couple of weeks previously, not to mention my long-standing massage parlour addiction. Fucking vampires.

Tragic news is kind of like Twinkies that way: better fresh.

I imagine someone like Molly would say that you "meet all types" or some such after doing this for a while. Not me. The thing that always strikes me is just how *alike* people are—variations on a theme, no different than their yards and their houses. I know there seems to be an enormous difference between a morbidly obese housewife, her jowls caked with cover-up, and a string-bean teenager with a fading hard-on, but only if you can conveniently forget all the transitional species in between—which I cannot. I tend to see people with the eye I imagine a dog breeder must take to canines: sharp enough to discriminate the fine-grain differences, broad enough to see them as expressions of the same basic set of genes.

Humans. Fawk. Whether it's the environment or a hand-washing OCD, their concerns pretty much all amount to the same thing: saving their asses.

The only people I spent any length of time talking to were those who claimed to have seen Dead Jennifer before she went missing. There was this cashier at the local Kroger who checked her groceries several times when the Framers came in for their once-a-week communal shop. "To be honest, I always thought she had, you know, airs about her." There was the rickety old Jehovah's Witness who had tried to save her soul one morning at the Waffle House. "You know what she told me?" the stingy old bitch said, handing me a quarter that gleamed a sinister digestive-tract green. "She told me man had outgrown salvation. *Outgrown!*" There was the war vet who used to ogle her at the wheelchair-accessible library. "I like to think if I had a daughter ..." Several of them in all, and no matter how much they *tsk-tsked*, you couldn't shake the feeling that they were secretly thrilled to have landed a glancing blow on a real honest-to-God mystery.

Small towns. You gotta love them.

Just about everyone asked me about the investigation. I uniformly lied through my teeth, told them I knew next to nothing except that everyone seemed to suspect the Framers. The responses were predictable, ranging from "Yeah ... What is it they believe again?" indifference to bald-faced declarations of bigotry. This one guy, Phil "the Pill" Conroy of 93 Inkerman Street, asked me if I had heard of *pogroms* before. "I tell ya," he pronounced in a liquored grunt, "*that's* what we need—what *this country* needs. Some kinda reckoning."

The prick didn't give me a dime, of course.

The consensus seemed to be that the Framers were a symptom of things gone wrong, a disease of the body social, as if America had rolled out of bed one morning to find boils marring its clear white skin. Where was the ideological Clearasil? Fawk. There was also the implication that we had lost our *nerve* more than our way. Of course, not one of them could tell me what the Framers actually believed—only that they *believed wrong*. And even though I knew that these kinds of judgments were simply the brain's version of the gag reflex, something compulsive and inevitable, I found myself nodding and then nodding some more.

Siding with the simple and the confused.

Suddenly I understood why Baars had taken me to see old Agatha. He knew full well what he was up against. He knew he would be swimming against the tribal tide.

Heretics are doomed to be burned. In the fires of the imagination, if not otherwise.

Molly fairly radiated disapproval: she was put off by all fraud, apparently, even when as petty and as ingenious as mine. But I could tell she had been chastised by my earlier demonstration. There was more to me than could be easily scavenged by her journalistic eye. I could even glimpse it every once in a while, shining in her wayward looks ...

Respect.

We discussed our day at the diner that evening, weary and footsore. Exhaustion tends to clear the workbench of communication, at least when it doesn't clear everything away altogether. You can sit and talk like Vulcans, always on topic, always moving forward, without the baggage of lust and hurt. We had our pious moments, sure, where we congratulated ourselves for being thin or urban or intelligent—but then that's simply par for the human course, being better than everybody else.

"So what do you think?" I asked while still blinking at the fluorescent lighting.

"Creepy."

"Creepy? How so?"

"I kept pricking my ears at, like, every house we went to, thinking I would hear a moan or a ... a cry or something. I kept telling myself that she had to be in *someone's* basement somewhere. Every place. It was like a compulsion or something. I just couldn't stop."

What she described sounded like a typical reaction, a natural way for an average imagination to screw with a normal head. Since insults were the rule when I encountered natural, average, normal things, I kept my mouth shut.

"What about that Phil the Pill guy?" she asked after an awkward moment. "What did you think of him?"

"Besides the pictures of Rush Limbaugh taped to his underwear?"

She graced me with a weary grin. "You know what I mean. *Pogroms?* Please. A guy who believes in rounding up whole populations is certainly capable of rounding up a lone woman, especially one, you know ..."

I knew what she was talking about. I had a couple of memories from the Gulf War that I would pay good money to scrub if I could. This one guy in our crew—Wendeez we called him, because he always smelled like hamburger—took the "forces" in Special Forces a little too literally, way back when. Funny how the young and the pretty so often find themselves singled out for punishment.

"Naw," I said, doing my best to blink the memories away. "I don't think Phil's a concern. Any time a dude *tells* you his nickname, you can be pretty certain he's insecure. Whoever grabbed Jennifer—if that's what in fact happened—you can be reasonably certain he has some kind of ice in his veins. Goofballs like him just don't have what it takes."

"Some do, Disciple. Trust me."

This had the smell of a college sob story.

"Besides," I said, "you're looking at this the wrong way ..."

"How so?"

"The point of canvassing, at least the way I do it, isn't to find your suspects, Molls. Suspects are rare creatures, not easily found. All we're trying to do is get a sense of his natural habitat."

That earned me a long, appreciative look, but little else.

We parted ways with the awkward sense of unresolved matters. I caught a glimpse of pale abdomen as she raised her arms in a faux yawn, noted the twining of green rising from the rim of her blue jeans: barbed wire.

I thought about the way tattoos seem to peek from every feminine hemline: the plunging décolletage, the sagging sock, the T-shirt tag, and of course the hip-riding orbit of their pants and shorts. Little mementoes to mysteries unseen. Bruises to a glimpse. Invitations to a gaze.

If men were going to stare—and let's face it, they were going to stare—then you might as well give them something to read. The best candy comes with labels—all the rest is bulk.

"Good night, Molly."

"Night."

I've heard people say their brains are stuck between radio stations enough to know that it's a popular metaphor for the kind of mental static the Forgetful are prone to when they're stressed or burned out. The feeling I get—or I should say, the feeling I *live* with—is nowhere near as linear. It's more like being stuck between *all* channels simultaneously, cable and satellite, military and commercial. I've been asked by friends and researchers whether it gets worse as I get older and the reel of my memory gets fatter and fatter, and I want to say, "Yes, definitely," but the fact is, I really don't know. It's kind of like treading water in the middle of the ocean that keeps getting deeper and deeper—more and more abyssal. You have this sense of drowning depths yawning ever more profoundly below you, but still, there you are, bobbing like a cork, peering this way and that, trying not to hum the theme to *Jaws.*

Anyway, one of the things I love about my post-conversation reveries is the way they silence the multi-dimensional rumble. In my case, the best way to avoid drowning is to flee the dappled surface and swim down, down into the cerulean dark.

Follow the sparks of the past as they dwell within me.

I was never meant for the Now—I know that much. I sometimes think I'm a creature of the Ages, shoehorned into the slot you call waking life. As mangled and twisted as oversized mail.

Amazing, really, the way they're all still in there, *in me*, the voices and the people. More than a little spooky, the way they never stop talking, saying what they said over and over and over and over and over ... Makes me feel like a cannibal, sometimes, the eater of momentary souls.

Lying on my bed, I sorted through channels looking for a baseball game. Baseball, I find, is far and away the best sport to *not* watch on TV. Since pretty much nothing happens outside what you see on *SportsCenter*, you can be an expert without seeing a single game. The ability to pass judgment without work or research has got to be the coolest consumer good since the invention of philosophy.

I closed my eyes while a vacuum-tube voice recited statistics—when everything's slo-mo, you have plenty of time to measure and tally. The world somehow faded away without really going anywhere. I was stretched out, my clothes soaking up the air-conditioned cool, and I was standing on yet another porch in Legoland, raising an arm to wipe the sweat from my cheek and brow ...

"Yeah-yeah. We heard about that. We're brand spanking new."

This was Jill Morrow speaking at around 2:38 P.M. She was an attractive-ish woman in her mid-thirties who lived at 371 Edgeware Street—a white-brick bungalow with a real estate sign swaying in the hot-sun breeze. I really wasn't surprised that she had found her way to the front of the queue. I had already decided I would call Nolen later that night, suggest he drive out to interview her.

She and her husband Eddie had moved to Ruddick just a couple of weeks previously, something which, what with the empty boxes, the bare walls, and my estimable powers of deduction, I had failed to realize until she told me. The thing was, when I handed her the flyer with Dead Jennifer's image in the top left corner, she *recognized* her.

This marked Molly's one and only verbal intervention. *"Really? From where?"*

This was when it dawned on me how much it had helped having her tag along. I don't sleep well, so I generally have this perpetual brooding, strung-out look. And even when I dress like a prep, there's something about me that just doesn't wear Christian clothes well. If I were a television show, I would sport a transparent box in the corner containing *L N V D.* Language, Nudity, Violence, Disturbing content—you name it.

Molly, on the other hand, was pure PG.

Not only had Jill and Eddie seen Dead Jennifer before, they had seen her *the night she disappeared,* walking down Highway 3, the road that led out of Ruddick proper, through the industrial park, toward the Framer Compound—sometime around twelve, she thought. Apparently they were coming back from seeing old work friends in Pittsburgh: Eddie Morrow was a former program component designer—which meant he got paid to jerk off to internet porn, or so I assumed. Jill had taken a job as a high school administrator in Ruddick, which was why they had moved.

She became progressively more anxious the longer we talked, especially after I told her that she needed to talk to the Chief. The time had come to go.

"What did you do after?" I asked her on a whim as Molly and I retreated from her foyer.

"My husband dropped me off."

"Ah, where did he go?"

A momentary hesitation, pretty much inexplicable when you considered how forthcoming Jill had been otherwise.

"He's at a conference in Pitt. Software design thing."

"No, I mean after he dropped you off."

Blank look.

"To grab some cigarettes from the Kwik-Pik." A nervous shrug. *"Smoker ... You know."*

I could tell I had pushed too far with my questions. The last thing you want to do, I've learned, is ask people questions they themselves have buried. No one likes the living dead. Wives especially. There's a reason they always decide to go to bed when the zombie movie starts.

"Sorry," I said. *"I can be a nosy prick sometimes."*

Then I was back in my room, blinking to the noise of the baseball game. Crowds roaring. Some guy with a massive ass had just belted a home run. With thighs that thick, I imagined his dick must look small.

Eddie, I thought. I needed to dust the snow off Eddie Morrow.

If I were to be terribly honest, which I rarely am, I would have to say that *I prefer* talking to people this way—after the fact, in the humid terrarium of my mind. There's a *power* to it that sometimes strikes me as almost authorial, the way I can freeze-frame and fast-forward, pause and replay things like the juicy bits of a porno. It's a kind of TiVo, only without the monthly fees. TV you can really crawl into.

Of course, I can't change anything that gets said, but I can lance it with angle after interpretative angle, squeeze it until it gets inflamed with multiple meanings or dries up and heals.

And then there's those 558 women ... All beautiful, even the ugly ones.

The harem that is my soul. Every curse has its upside, I suppose.

The second person in the memory queue was Tim Dutchysen. He was the kind of kid I had seen in the mirror a thousand times before the army muscled me up and straightened me out. Twenty-two or so. Skinny, possessed of a kind of bodily insecurity, limbs devoid of a resting position. Eyes that bounced like India rubber, especially when he was agreeing with something. Good teeth. A grin too clownish not to be 110 percent sincere. Even when he stood absolutely still, he seemed to be moving—as if he were too thin not to be running from fat all the time.

And he was a real talker, the kind of guy who was always more honest than he planned, especially when he was full of shit.

"The guys all call me Dutchie."

"Dutchie it is then, Tim."

He worked at the local Kwik-Pik—an assistant manager, no less. Not only had he been at Legends the night of Jennifer's disappearance, he openly admitted to watching her with his friends ...

"Oh, man, you have no idea how hot she was. The way she danced with that black guy. And the way she dressed ... Jeezus! *I mean, no offence, but I bet you there's a bunch of us who only went to Legends because of her. I mean, when she went missing and all, don't get me wrong, I actually volunteered to go searching for her, and not just because everybody in our church did. I had, like, the biggest crush on her. I mean, you should have seen her. But I always thought she needed to be, you know, more ... more, like, careful. I mean, I appreciated the way she did herself up and all, but the way it got everyone talking. What with, you know, all the orgies and shit they get up to at their Compound. That's just a rumour, I know, and I'm not someone who goes spreading rumours, but the others, even guys from my church, they kind of get carried away sometimes, you know? In what they say, I mean. There's no one*

I know who would actually do anything—I mean, we all stared at our beers whenever she looked in our direction! Jeezus, I think I forgot how to walk a couple times when she passed me!"

Molly shot me a covert *ding-a-ling-a-ling* look at the height of this monologue. I imagine she understood that men are pigs in a general sense, most women do, but thanks to the daily subterfuge that polite society forces upon the homelier sex, she lacked the ability to discriminate between men who truly are sexually troubled and kids like Tim, whose horndoggery plum got the best of his manners now and again.

"What's your church, Tim?"

This was actually a significant question. Because rape had always been the unspoken assumption, and because Ruddick seemed peculiarly devoid of known sex offenders, I had hoped to find someone like Tim all along, someone who could steer me toward the local pervs and abusers—many of whom like to hide in the shadow of Jesus.

"Church of the Third Resurrection."

"Oh ya. I remember passing it. The white frame place, right?"

"We're having a pig roast this Saturday aft, if you're interested. Everyone's welcome!"

This was the conversation that marked Molly's conversion, the moment when she finally grasped the genius behind my kooky MO. Striking up relationships with people is as easy as can be, especially people who harbour a secret loneliness, like Tim or Jill. All you really need is a pretext. Once you're attached, it's simply a matter of creeping out along their six degrees of separation.

Like selling life insurance.

Friends, as Sean would say, beget enemies. And that's what every good case needs.

A bad guy.

"Oh ... One last thing, Tim—er, Dutchie. What time does the Kwik-Pik close on Saturdays?"

"Midnight ... Why?"

I tapped the pack of Winstons in my cargo pants. *"Smoker ... You know."*

"Nasty habit," he said, raising two nicotine-stained fingers in a peace symbol.

I called Nolen shortly afterward, around 9 P.M.

"What are you doing?" he asked after our mutual hellos. He was chewing something, and I could hear a television droning in the background. I saw this image of him and his family hunkered down in their living room, their faces blank and blue, their eyes reflecting some televised atrocity.

"I'm at the library, going through microfilm," I lied.

"Library? What time is it?"

"I'm in Pittsburgh. Researching the Framers."

"Oh," he replied with a shamefaced laugh. *"No rest for the wicked, huh?"*

I snuggled back into my pillow, blew a stream of pungent smoke at the idle ceiling fan. "No rest for the wicked."

I told him about the Morrows' encounter with Jennifer the night of her disappearance. "My gut tells me there's probably nothing to worry about, but I got the sense that you were a man who minded his Ps and Qs."

"That I am," he said with daft pride. *"Thanks for this, Disciple."*

More crunching on his end—chewing. Some people, I've noticed, keep their eyes glued on the screen while watching the tube and talking on the phone. Others look down and out, to better concentrate on what is being said. Nolen was obviously the former.

"Not a problem."

A crunching, crackling pause while he chewed. The bugger had used my reply to sneak another chip into his yap.

"We're going to do this, aren't we?" He swallowed, then added, *"We're going to save this girl."*

Sure, I thought.

One potato chip at a time.

Track Seven

YOU PEOPLE

Thursday ...

The thing that kills me about you people—and by that I mean everyone but me—is how you've built the world to compensate for your shortcomings. Everything, but everything, has to always be the same. Same Exxon. Same Kwik-Pik. Carbon-copy brands in carbon-copy stores on carbon-copy streets in carbon-copy towns. As bad as an old Deputy Dawg cartoon.

Sure, you complain about this too. And yet you keep queuing up, keep ordering your Chicken McNuggets with two too many sweet-and-sour packets—just to be safe. You talk a good game when it comes to the unexpected, and yet you keep paying for more of the same. One of the great gifts of forgetting, it seems to me, is that it absolves you of the need for any consistency between your words and your wallet, not to mention your Scripture and your porn collection.

It all comes down to the bottom line, doesn't it? You childproof your existence to better secure your illusion of control, and so continue gliding on autopilot while you focus on your appetites and your vanities. All of it—the mass-production franchises, the shake-and-bake blockbusters, the commercial-jingle pop songs, the seen-one-seen-them-all subdivisions—is simply an extension of your sloth and your amnesia. Stretchy pants for the fat ass of your soul.

Did I tell you I was a cynic?

I say this because I want you to understand why I was sick of Ruddick before I had even arrived—and why I found walking from door to door, across lawn after neat, orderly lawn, so *painful.*

Fawk.

Why sometimes simply breathing bored me to the point of contemplating suicide. And why the hairy tongue of my soul had been numbed beyond the ability to taste, let alone to crave or appreciate. The contents of the world are like words: repeat them enough and they lose all significance.

Even Molly, as young as a college diploma, as fresh as only a wannabe can be—even she was beginning to bore me. She brought her laptop with her to breakfast, eager to show me her small capsule story the *Post-Gazette* had printed for that day's edition. "Page A13," she said with a shrug, "beneath a story about a mad cow hoax in Amish country." She bounced her head back and forth with a grin. "Imagine being beat out by a cow."

"My sister was quite the heifer," I replied with a *What-are-you-going-to-do?* squint.

She laughed in that way women use to tell you you're being mean and they love it. "Here," she said, sliding her laptop around. "Check it out."

Cult Member Still Missing

Ruddick, PA—Jennifer Bonjour, a 21-year-old member of a small New Age cult called the Framers, went missing last Saturday. She was last seen leaving a local bar at approximately 11:30 P.M. Despite extensive searches of the surrounding brownlands, authorities report no leads. Anyone possessing information regarding her whereabouts should contact the Ruddick Police Department.

"Huh ..." I said.

"Not much," she admitted, crinkling her nose. "I fairly screamed at Cynthia, my editor, to include the term 'female' in the header, but she pooh-poohed the idea. They usually hate it when hacks try to upsell their stories."

"It would have been better if they'd run a larger photo," I said, "one that showed her wearing a tank or something like that. But it's the cult stuff that's the real hook. Trust me, they'll be back for more."

Molly pressed a sheepish face into her forearm. "God, I hope so ..."

For whatever reason, door after door went unanswered that day—as if we had stumbled upon the gainfully employed subdivision or something. It was pretty much a waste of time, as the ever-helpful Molly pointed out on more than one occasion. I had resolved to return to the Framer Compound, of course, but I wanted to steep myself in the town that encircled them first. Like I explained to Molly, it's hard to figure out a fish when it's flopping around on the dock of your assumptions. You gotta get wet.

I was also waiting for Albert to get back to me with his research.

Because so many doors ended up being duds, the two of us had ample opportunity to talk, about Dead Jennifer some, but more about ourselves and our "aspirations."

Molly possessed an optimism that could only be called young. Had she been in her thirties, I would have said stupid—or maybe naive if I happened to be in a forgiving mood. But she was still smoking the bong of possibilities, and had yet to hit the hard bottle of fact. She wanted, wanted, wanted. Prizes. Fame. Ultimately she hoped to work for none other than *The New York Times*, the newspaper of selective record. To live in Manhattan, where the beautiful go to enjoy the labour of the ugly.

Otherwise, she was pretty much the product of what you might expect. She had a west coast education to correct her east coast reserve. Her siblings lacked her vision. Her friends were, like, the coolest ever. Her parents sunburned easily.

Every once in a while she even said "Daddy."

She admitted that her motives were probably as crass as could be when it came to Dead Jennifer. A cousin of hers who worked as a trainer for the Pittsburgh Penguins had caught wind of the story for some reason, and she had thought, "Eureka!" Jennifer Bonjour had all the elements that made news *news*, which is to say, a missing blond hottie, a crazy cult leader, and no relevance whatsoever to the lives of those who would be interested.

Her rationale was that she could only help.

To which I replied, "Really."

"I'm helping you, aren't I?"

"Nip down to the doughnut shop and get me a coffee, will ya?"

She laughed as if I had been joking.

All in all, we got along pretty well. After I had bludgeoned her finer scruples to death with a barrage of clever crudities, she even began to laugh. I only genuinely pissed her off once, when I bailed between radio stations in the middle of this incredibly sappy tune.

"So let me guess," she said, her eyes fluttering in irritation. "You hate Kelly Clarkson too."

"Not at all," I replied. "She makes me want to light some candles, draw a steaming bath, and shave my vagina."

That earned me several minutes of fuming silence. But I'm pretty sure I caught a head-shaking smile reflected in the passenger window.

Now, a career counsellor would tell you that a job like mine is "soft-skill intensive," which is just a fancy way of saying you need to be a "people person" of some description to do it well. As you might have surmised, I am *not* a people person. I tend to hate people, as a rule. What I am good at is disarming people, getting them to say things they might not otherwise say. I have a gift for manipulation, or so Dr. Ken Shelton told me on June 11, 1999.

I mention this because the more people I asked about the Framers, the more troubled I found myself. You see, by this point I was pretty much sucking on the *idea* of the Framers like oxygen. Like I said, I had never worked a cult member's disappearance before, and I fell on the novelty of it all like a homeless guy on a half-smoked cigarette.

This probably made me a little more sympathetic to their cause than I should have been. Surround a guy with enough smiles and he'll prize the first angry asshole he meets—sure as shit. So I found myself poking the unsuspecting citizens of Ruddick with the fact of the Framers, mentioning them the way I might note a strange-looking mole on their skin—you know, with that *You-should-get-that-checked-out* tone—just to see what kind of reaction I would get.

And I discovered that for a goodly number of the good inhabitants of Ruddick, the Framers were a matter of rote, reflex—as simple as simple could be. Guilty, probably. Symptom of some social malaise, certainly. Otherwise, they were a bunch of dangerous fools.

Of course, this made me think they were harmless.

Only Xenophon Baars kept me guessing ...

The day was pretty much a strikeout as far as Dead Jennifer was concerned. Sure, there was old Dane Ferrence, who insisted that God was simply trying to tell the Framers to turn to Jesus. And there was sixteen-year-old Sky Armstrong, who had taken swimming lessons with Jennifer at the local YMCA the previous summer. "She was weird," she said in that tone people reserve for declarations of peer-group solidarity. Then immediately contradicted herself by saying, "She was really normal, though."

But otherwise, nobody knew nothing.

Rather than return to our rooms, Molly and I drove directly to Odd-Jobs—to spare me the embarrassment of dodging traffic on foot as much as anything. For a time we just stared at our menus in that witless way, soaking in the damp hum of summer exhaustion. The tailings of what counted as rush-hour traffic in Ruddick roared up and down the road beyond our window. Nolen walked in almost the instant after we had placed our order: the turkey surprise for Molly and a BLT for me.

He looked like a man run ragged, too skinny for his police shirt, too fat for his uniform pants. But true to type, he smiled and laughed at nothing when I hailed him. I introduced him to Molly, whom he thought he recognized. He sidled in beside her without a wisp of embarrassment: he was used to being welcome, I could tell.

"What's that I smell on your breath?" he said, fixing me with a smiling frown. He must have caught me exhaling or something. Either that or he was just fucking with me, which would mean he was more clever than I had credited.

I shrugged and said, "Mint?"

He had this way of laughing, hands held close yet flared out like a magician, and a stiff-necked backward lean. Adolescent self-consciousness hardened into adult habit.

"So you talked to the Morrows?" I asked.

"Yeah ... But first I have to ask you something."

"Shoot."

"What's this I hear about you, um, taking a, ah, *collection*?"

I could feel Molly's eyes boring into my profile. Funny the way their stares cut so much deeper *before* you've slept with them.

"Just part of the cover, Caleb."

His frown made him look like a mascot for some kind of mattress or furniture company.

"Look," I added quickly, "you know how people get ..." I had already accumulated around nine hundred bucks, thanks to Dead Jennifer. When it came to missing persons, pretty chicks were almost as lucrative as blond children. A couple more and I would have a good chunk of my Bally's Visa paid off, and I could go back to playing craps *for real.* Cover my odds instead of rolling naked. "There's a big difference between what they say when they think everything is off the cuff as opposed to, you know, all *official.*" I made a *Who-likes-that-crap?* face for emphasis.

"Well ..."

I grinned and waved dismissively. "Don't worry, Caleb. We're keeping close track of who gave us what. It'll be all returned." I turned to prod some expression of affirmation from Molls. "Even the nickels and dimes."

Nolen laughed at that. I think an excuse to laugh it off was all he really wanted.

I steered the conversation back to what mattered and away from the dope on my breath and the dough stuffed in my pocket by asking him how things went with Jill and Eddie Morrow. I couldn't resist a *you-people* grin at Molly when he pulled out his notebook. I could have hung silver dollars from his forehead, his frown lines were so deep. Pressing the thing flat like a Gideon on the table, he gave me the rundown on his interview, responding to each of my successive questions with what seemed more and more anxiety. He was one of those guys who became more nervous the more he heard the sound of his own voice. Molly watched with the look of patient boredom women often get while waiting for men to confirm their mutual intelligence.

"So neither of them said anything about Eddie going out after dropping Jill off?" This was a rhetorical question: Nolen had already told me that he interviewed the two together, and I had gathered enough from my short conversation with Jill to know this was something both would be keen to paper over with silence. This is the glue that holds most relationships together: things unspoken and wilfully overlooked.

"No ... I mean, *yeah,* that's right. You mentioned something about that, didn't you?"

Do you see why I feel like I've been stranded in a life skills class for the developmentally challenged? Don't laugh. The whole world rides the short bus, you included.

"Let *me* look into it," I said.

Okay, just because I score large with the ladies doesn't mean I *understand* them. They always seem to come at me sideways. Here I think we're taking a pleasant stroll in the park heading toward soft pillows and cool sheets and suddenly, click—

I'm standing on a land mine.

Nolen beat an awkward retreat partway through our dinner. Neither of us said much—just munched in that silent too-much-fun-in-the-sun way. It seemed a joke, driving the car across the street to the motel. It happened too fast for me to pick up on any telltale signs. In all honesty, I was doing cartwheels of joy inside, the way she simply followed me to my door after we got out of the Vee-Dub.

Naked time, I thought as I ushered her in. I could almost feel the soft skin of her ass.

"Us?" she cried the instant the door clicked shut. *"Us?"*

The thing about carnal fantasies, I find anyway, is their *stickiness.* Typical daydreams wink into nothingness at the first sign of trouble. Spike them with the promise of sex and they get as hard to flick as boogers or gum.

So I could only stare at her, trying to blink her clothes back on. Fawk.

"Don't play stupid, Disciple. You're not stupid."

That was when I realized she was talking about my collection scam.

"Well, technically, you *are* standing next to me when they break open their wallets."

Now I know you know *exactly* the kind of bewildered gaze she shot me, either because you've weathered it a thousand times, like I have, or because you've *looked* it just as many.

"Are you a sociopath, Disciple? Are you a *fucking lunatic*?"

"No, babe. Just stupid."

"Ah!" she cried. "Fucking *aaaah!*"

"Molly ... C'mon."

But she was laughing to herself—rarely a good sign. "You know, Disciple, I fucking knew this would happen. I glanced at you on my way in and said to myself, 'Now that guy, Molly my girl, is *bad fucking news.*'"

I was actually relieved to hear this, vain prick that I am. Here all along I'd worried she had said "Eew" because of my age.

"Well there you go," I said with a grin. "News is news. You had no choice but to cover me ..."

The shadow of a smile.

"This routine of yours actually work?"

I tugged her closer by the hands. Maybe I could turn this around after all.

"Only on intelligent, sensitive, highly educated nymphomaniacs."

"Nymphomaniacs?" she cried. "Is that word even, like, *legal* anymore?"

She laughed aloud this time, and I really thought I had clinched things—I really did. But she abruptly pushed back against my chest, backed away looking down, shaking her head with four fingers held to her forehead.

"No ..." she said, her eyes fluttering. "No. I'm not going to let you charm your way into my pants. This is serious, Disciple. I have a *fucking career* I'm trying to build here. A fucking career! And not to mention poor fucking Jennifer Bonjour! But does Disciple Manning give a shit? Noooo. Apparently Disciple thinks—"

She was on one of those finding-her-way-back-to-her-anger rolls. I remember it all word for word, of course, but I suspect you've pretty much heard the whole thing before. The important thing, the crucial thing, was that she had mentioned Dead Jennifer, who had become, without me realizing it, a *trigger* of some kind.

And a strange one.

You know that feeling you have when you're fighting with your husband or your wife, that aimless disgust which seems to blanket the world corner to corner? It has no bottom, believe me.

"The whole thing is a murderous con!" Mandy Bonjour cried.

"And if you suspect us," Xenophon Baars said, *"you will waste time and resources investigating us, time and resources that I fear Jennifer Bonjour desperately needs."*

"We're going to do this, aren't we?" Caleb Nolen asked around a mouthful of potato chips. *"We're going to save this girl."*

There was too much crosstalk for me to recognize, let alone solve, the problem fuming before me. "I have some Xanax," I heard myself say, not so much as an insult but because I knew that was where I was headed.

She glared at me in horror.

("You want some Xanax? You could probably use it more than I could.")

She stormed out, leaving my door swinging, then slammed the door to her room (which was immediately adjacent) so hard that the goofy floral prints hanging on my wall rattled. I thought that was uncalled for.

"Drama queen!" I bellowed. But all I could hear through the wall was her TV cranking out the theme song to *Jeopardy*.

Can you believe that? Fucking *Jeopardy* ...

Women like that make me happy to be banging my secretary.

* * *

Now I *know* her sociopath comment has got you thinking. My army therapist used to tell me I have nothing to worry about, that unlike true sociopaths I actually have the neural machinery for "social emotions," as the eggheads like to call them: guilt, shame, compassion—all that bullshit. The only way I can explain it is this: think of your worst long-term relationship, the way it just got to a point where you just couldn't feel anymore, the crap was piled so high. Well, that's pretty much how I feel all the bloody time.

Burnt out, not emotionless.

But still, I worry sometimes. It seems to me that even though I'm not a sociopath per se, I am kind of one, you know, for all practical and romantic purposes. I mean, when I think about all those people forking over their cash to help the Bonjours hire me to find their dead daughter when they had, like, *already* hired me, I know I should feel guilty ... But then I think about Vegas and hookers and Jimmy Beam and I smile.

Circus Circus, baby. Where the cheapskates go to win.

Perhaps I am a kind of "as if" sociopath, pretty much indistinguishable from the real deal—except, of course, for the odd times when all that unfelt remorse comes crashing back in and I try to kill myself.

I continued mentally arguing with Molly as I drove into downtown Ruddick, looking this way and that for the bar, Legends, where Dead Jennifer was last seen alive. I pretty much kicked her verbal ass—same as you, I always win the fights in my head. I was about to land the argumentative death blow, some comment about her mother (whom I knew nothing about), when I sighted the joint on the corner of Talbot and Ross. Chapped paint. Covered windows. Half the sign's neon had died, so that *LEG   S* was all that glowed.

All in all, it struck me as my kind of place. Like school in July: no class.

A smart-ass-opath, I decided. That's what I am. Fawk.

* * *

This is something I do quite often, pretend that I'm working a case when I'm actually looking for a way to get blotto. I'm a huge fan of booze, always have been, always will be, simply because I'm not a big fan of feelings.

Feelings fuck you up.

The irony, of course, is that booze turns you into an emotional slob. Drinking generally points you in the right direction—good times, baby—but things always turn, and like any rock tossed skyward, you end landing in the same dirt. Only harder.

So why do it? Why go toe-to-toe with the law of psychological gravity? Why hide in a bottle when that's where the floodlights are certain to find you?

I could just as easily ask why you waste your money on lottery tickets. The laws of probability are just as ironclad, pretty much.

But you never know, do you? You *could* be a winner. I drink for the exact same reason. Someday I might find that perfect bottle of Jack or Johnnie or CC and blast myself into orbit.

Good times forever.

That, and because it's less addictive than crack.

So there I was, Legends, pretending to be working the case, wanting to get wasted, scoping the dance floor for poon. The place was gloomy in that bricked-in way. It smelled like an old houseboat, dank, like the underwear you peel from the bottom of the hamper. An asthmatic's nightmare.

I had expected as much, but I had also expected to see a fair number of people, freshly showered and showing off the latest rural fashions. John Deere caps and bling and leather jackets—that kind of shit. What I had forgotten was that this was a weeknight in a small town. Christ, the place was as dead as Jennifer.

So I kind of stood there like an idiot—the way everyone does when they wander into an empty restaurant or bar. I stood there and blinked at the gloom, and felt kind of sorry for myself ... for being alone in a lonely place, I suppose.

Lights flashed across a mostly bare dance floor. Two dolled-up fat-bottoms swayed to the ponderous beat, their eyes clicking across various upward angles, anywhere they could avoid the gazes of the shadowy men who sat hunched here and there through the darkness. There were no shouts, no squeals or laughter. Just a living room filled with nervous strangers.

The last place Jennifer was seen alive.

And the perfect place to get drunk, I decided. Normally, when you get drunk alone, you want your surroundings to be noisy enough that you can at least pretend to be "partying." Put enough losers in a pile and soon you have a heap of winners—such is the human contradiction. But the pathetic ambience of the place resonated with my hard-done-by mood. Legends had become Exhibit A, if not in the disappearance of Jennifer Bonjour then in how the world was out to get me.

I ambled toward a stool at the bar. I'm something of a talker, if you haven't noticed, and I had an overriding need to pepper someone (I didn't really care who, though a sense of humour would help) with various cynical observations, mostly about how everyone is so full of shit. You know, play the Philosopher Dick.

Of course, the whole time I would tell myself that I was working the bartender or whoever it was for information. But really, deep down, I was just trying to look smart—distinguish myself from the run-of-the-mill losers who get drunk alone on weeknights.

Then I heard: "Disciple! Hey! How's it hanging, man?"

It was Tim Dutchysen, or, as he liked to be called, Dutchie. I had walked by his table without even noticing him.

"Same as always," I said. "Nine parts bullshit, one part air freshener."

Maybe I would accomplish something after all.

I joined him at his table, where he'd been sitting alone. He claimed to be waiting for some friends—just finished his shift at the Kwik-Pik, he said—but I didn't believe him. Unlike me, he hadn't come here to get drunk alone, he had come hoping to bump into somebody, anybody to fill the verbal void of another night alone. He would keep an eye out for chicks, of course, but I could tell he had encountered too much rejection to take search-and-inseminate missions all that seriously anymore. Besides, my guess was he had learned to make do with internet porn. The chicks were hotter.

He asked me about the fundraising and the state of the investigation. I quizzed him about the Framers, using a *What-the-fuck-is-up-with-that* tone to cover the systematic nature of my questions. He did little more than parrot several of their more outrageous claims—refracted through the lens of rumour—in the funny singsong voice people use to report the other, offending half of an argument: you know, the "and then *she* said, 'mew-mew-mew-mew-mew'" bullshit, where people use mocking tones to make others look stupid.

"We laugh at them, sure," he said. "Hard not to. The Reverend says they're a *sign.*"

"Sign? Like for handicap parking?"

He had a strange laugh, like his sense of humour had never developed past the age of five. In a bizarre way it actually made me feel, well ... protective.

"No-no! A *sign*, you know, for the end of days—*Armageddon.*"

I found this boggling. A religion using an end-of-the-world cult as proof the world was about to end? The World Court really needed to start prosecuting crimes against irony.

"Has anyone from your church tried to convert them?"

I had a hard time keeping a straight face asking that one. Baars may have been crazy as a shithouse rat, but I could see him giving Tim's reverend the intellectual equivalent of a body-cavity search. Then saying something like, *"So sorry, my friend, but there's nothing up your ass but more ass."*

Tim shrugged. "Not us. No use talking to crazies. But they used to recruit all the time, handing out flyers and whatnot. Apparently there were quite a few arguments ..." He trailed off to take a long drink. He had that look people get when talking about something they're not sure they *should* be talking about, not because they've been told to keep it quiet, but because they've suddenly realized they've never heard anyone else discussing the matter. Nothing quite so spontaneous as small-town conspiracies. "Then the Reverend went out to visit that Baars guy and they agreed to, you know, split the difference. They agreed to leave us alone, *Ruddick* alone, and we agreed not to burn their Compound to the fucking ground ..."

I took a moment to absorb what he had said. He was still young enough to marble his talk with kick-ass bravado, so I chalked the burning comment up to that. The idea of a gang war between a cult and a church was just too rich.

"I was still in high school back then," Tim nervously added. "So this is all, you know, hear-talk ... or whatever it's called."

"Hearsay," I said.

I drank three beers, all the while pining for whisky. I really didn't think that hard about what was said, knowing that I could sift through it all afterward anyway. Wasn't in the mood.

Besides, the kid was starting to reek of dead ends. I meet a lot of mouthpieces in my line of work, people who desperately *want* to contribute and yet have nothing whatsoever to add. It pays to be able to identify them early, otherwise they suck the time right out of you.

"You should come out to the barbecue day after tomorrow," he said. "Really."

"Church, huh?"

He grinned, as if unconsciously sensing my rekindled interest. "Yeah. Our annual pig roast."

I crinkled my nose.

"Not a church guy, huh?"

This is always a touchy question, no matter who happens to be asking it. It could be a little old lady with a baby's daft smile and you could find yourself wiping spit off your face in seconds flat. One wrong word is all it takes. So all I said was, "Nope."

"C'mon. You gotta believe in *something*." The implication being, of course, that *everybody* believed in something, which meant that most everybody *believed wrong*, given that everybody believed so many contradictory things. But I wasn't about to say as much. I said something worse instead ...

"Too easy to be fooled."

"How do you mean?"

I shrugged, took a long draw on my Bud. "A guy pulls a gun in a convenience store," I said. "What is he?"

Tim jerked his head back like a turkey. "What?"

"Play along with me for a sec. *A guy pulls a gun in a convenience store.* What is he?"

A big, gum-revealing grin. Tim was one of those kids who was so gratified to be included in whatever that he was pretty much game for whatever.

"A robber," he said. "What else?"

"Yeah, but he's got a badge."

Tim laughed as if he had suddenly seized the entire point. "Okay. So he's a *cop*."

"There's a Brinks truck parked out front."

Now he frowned. "So he's a security guard?"

"Yeah, but there's two men in their underwear bound and gagged in the back of the Brinks truck."

He rolled his eyes in what I had already pegged as a characteristic Tim expression. "He *is* a robber, then! Like I said."

I raised my shoulders, shot him a look of heavy-lidded skepticism. "Yeah, but there's a camera crew next to the canned goods, filming him."

Now the kid was thoroughly perplexed. "So he's an actor?"

"But what about the News 7 van parked behind the Brinks truck?"

"Then I was right in the first place! He's a robber!"

"Yeah, but he has a beard, and he's wearing a vest stuffed with explosives."

"You mean he's a terrorist?"

I let him hang for a moment—watching people intellectually squirm is one of the few genuine pleasures life offers me. The fact that I never finished high school makes it particularly gratifying. "Do you get my point, Tim? This isn't about what the guy 'really is,' it's about you—about the traps everybody falls into when hearing or reading language. At each stage it seemed pretty clear, didn't it—what the gunman was? But each time I complicated the background, he suddenly became something different."

"So?"

"So, it demonstrates two things. First, that what words mean depends on the background we bring to them, *contexts*—and contexts can potentially go on forever. Second, that people are prone to jump to conclusions. You can't see what you don't see, so you simply assume that what you do see is *all there is*. That it's simple, clear as day. The guy's a robber."

"But he *is* a robber, isn't he?"

Uncertainty had wired him, I could see that much. But whether he was freaked because he understood what I was saying or because he didn't have the slightest clue, I couldn't tell.

I looked away to the dance floor. Some old sunglass-wearing drunk had taken the place of the two heifers, smiling with rotten pride, dancing with his arms held out—to some Ozzy tune whose title I couldn't remember because I had only read it. "Suicide Solution," I think.

"So what?" Tim finally said. "You don't believe *anything*?"

"I believe plenty."

"Like what?"

"That you and I are sitting in a bar drinking beer, for one."

A scowl furrowed his narrow face. He was taking our conversation seriously—dreadfully so. "No, I mean, like, you know, the *big picture*."

I shrugged. "Big picture? Well, I believe that humans are survival machines, and that pretty much everything else is plumage."

"What's plumage?"

"Something for show," I said in the quick way you use to dismiss a conversation. "You know what? I think I *will* take you up on the church pig roast thing. Check it out ..." I made a show of rubbing the back of my neck. "I've been feeling a little, I dunno ... *hollow* lately."

It would be a free meal at least, and at most it would allow me to further penetrate Ruddick's social marrow. Fucking church pig roast—hilarious. When you remember as many things as I do, you really come to appreciate little gems like that.

"Awesome!" he exclaimed. "You could hit the Reverend with that whole-whole context thing—let him sort it out."

I winced at that, realizing that Tim was more than just a little naive. Everyone, but everyone, makes noises about being critical and open-minded—even extreme believers like Baars. But confirmation is really the only thing they're interested in. People are as allergic to contradiction as they are to complexity and uncertainty—and none more so than those who devote their *lives* to bullshit.

I already knew how to get to the Church of the Third Resurrection, but Tim seemed to take so much pride in his knowledge of the town that

I listened like someone oblivious. I used my cigarettes as an excuse to bail after that. I kind of felt bad leaving him alone there drinking, but then I kind of felt jealous as well.

Truth was, I had completely slipped back into a working mindset. According to my cell, it was almost ten, which struck me as a likely hour for a high school administrator to go to sleep on a work night.

As good a time as any to stake out Eddie Morrow.

I parked about twenty yards or so down from the Morrows', in front of a house too dark not to be filled with sound sleepers. I spend quite a bit of my time in my old Golf, watching this or that residence—primarily waiting for husbands. Typically, I kill the time either banging my head to heavy metal (during the day) or arguing with my memories (during the night).

Talking to yourself doesn't necessarily amount to anything. You can do it for years without experiencing any personal growth or cognitive decline. *Listen* to yourself long enough, however, and you eventually become a comedian, whether you want to or not. It's the only way to stay interested.

Eddie Morrow slipped out his door at exactly 11:13. No porch light, as expected. A quiet tug to close the Saturn door, as expected. He had backed into his driveway so he could slip out without bathing the front of the house with light. Somehow I knew he wouldn't back in when he returned. I found myself wondering whether Jill ever noticed that the car had done a magical one-eighty while they were asleep. I'd witnessed enough of these capers to grasp their furtive Gestalt. This was my eighty-seventh, to be exact.

But then, none of them had ever involved a missing cult member before.

I fired up the Vee-Dub, winced the way I always wince at its tractor roar and rattle, then began following him at a discreet distance. Ruddick was small enough that I didn't have to follow him far.

He turned down an unkempt street, Omeemee, where every other house seemed abandoned—yet one more demographic relic of better days. Idling at the intersection, I watched his Saturn cruise through the glow of its lights, slow, then park before a low brick bungalow—a place that had an un-illuminated sign of some kind posted out front. I waited until he had disappeared into the building before turning to follow.

I did a cursory drive-by, caught enough of the sign in my headlights to read

> **MASSAGE-BY-JENNY**
>
> Registered Physiotherapist

Then I turned around and parked along the curb opposite the house. I rolled down the window, sparked a J, absorbed that magical combination of boarded windows and sixty-year-old trees. To tell the truth, it almost felt like home sitting there, periodically glancing at the hooded picture window, pondering the sordid shenanigans behind the drapes. Summer darkness surrounding an orange-glowing world.

Ah, Eddie ... Did you lie awake in shame? Cringe from the enormity of your petty crimes? Think *Oh-my-god-if-Jill-ever-found-out ...*

Or were you a different animal altogether? Had your appetites slipped their leash, compelled you to commit atrocities? To do things that convinced our ancestors we needed hell?

What about Jennifer, Eddie? Did you hurt her? Hide her?

Eddie was definitely more relaxed leaving 113 Omeemee than he was 371 Edgeware. I heard feminine laughter as he bantered back and forth with someone at the side door. The fear didn't climb back into his face until he climbed behind the wheel of his car. He pulled farther down the street, turned around in someone else's driveway, then passed within spitting distance of me on his way back home. He had the clutched look of someone running through worst-case scenarios.

I cracked open my door, crossed the street, walked the narrow slot between the brick wall and the Ford F-150 parked in the driveway. I came to a screen door, which I knocked on because its wood companion was already ajar. I could see linoleum and half a kitchen hutch in dim light through the screen. Moths and gnats tapped at the light above me.

After a moment, a woman answered the door dressed in a tank and panties. Jenny—obviously and immediately. She was too petite to be a model, and she had a friendly, farm-girl face, but I found her horribly attractive. Eddie was making more sense to me with every passing moment.

"Do you take walk-ins?" I asked.

She looked me up and down, smiled, and rubbed her cheek into her shoulder like a kitten. *When they look like you*, her eyes said. But her voice asked, "Sore shoulders, honey?"

"Like I'm carrying the weight of the world."

She welcomed me in with a swing of her arm—clipped enough to tell me she was sober. I really hadn't known what to expect from the sex trade industry out here in the backwoods. A part of me had expected rotten teeth and hilly-billy diction—but Jenny seemed all right. The house was tidy, nary a single dirty dish on the ceramic countertop. The floors were slightly bowed: old houses tend to sag in the middle—kind of like people that way. The furniture was newish—veneer, but hey, who the hell was I to judge? Two massage tables dominated the living room; they almost looked like gurneys with the white sheets that had been draped over them. The couch, the flat screen, and the coffee table pushed beneath the picture window suggested that Jenny broke the tables down during the day and used the space the same way civilians did: to rot in front of the tube.

"So what can I do you for, handsome?"

"The works," I said, fishing out the wad of fives and tens I'd scored over the course of the day. What can I say? Sex is just one of those horses I ride backward. "That ... and ... some questions."

She did her best not to roll her eyes. Hookers generally don't like guys—guilt-ridden nerds, mostly—who ask a lot of questions. All the questioners want is to get fucked, and yet they go through all the motions of "empathizing with the plight" of the women they're fucking as a way of servicing their moral debt. I actually knew this one hooker who had *CASH ONLY* tattooed above her shaved pussy. "Read the sign," was the only answer she would give to questions. "Money ain't the only thing that talks," she told me once, "un-fucking-fortunately."

"Well, really, I only have one question."

Jenny had already grabbed my hand and pulled me into the living room gloom. "Shoot."

"You know that guy who was just here?"

"Yeah, sure," she said, undoing my belt and tearing open my button fly. "Brad."

I smiled. "*Brad.* Exactly."

"What about him?" She said this while palming the crotch of my boxers. The auto-tease. Most hookers are as mechanical as a car wash.

"Did he swing by here last Saturday night, say around midnight?"

She stopped, took a confused step back, which was kind of embarrassing because she had peeled my jeans down to my knees. "You mean when that girl went missing ..." she said. "The other Jennifer."

"Yeah."

"Are you a cop or something?"

"Hell no. Just a private dick. Her parents hired me to assist the police."

I could tell she had already guessed as much. It was pretty obvious that the two of us had come from the same side of the tracks, even though I was urban and she was country. The side that called cops "pigs."

"Do you think they'll find her?" she asked.

The way she said this told me she had been following the story closely. I supposed it was unnerving having someone with your name vanish in a town this small—especially doing what Jenny did for a living.

"No," I said with a *what-can-you-do* shrug. "Not in one piece, anyway."

"I think so too," she said, her look wandering from sharp to vague to sharp again. "I just have this feeling, you know?"

Fucking feelings. Only do you any good in the movies.

"So what about Brad?" I pressed. Otherwise known as Edward Morrow.

"Brad? Oh. Yeah-yeah. He was here last Saturday around then, you know ..." A fatalistic hitch of the shoulders. "Balling me."

"I figured as much," I said with a sly glance at my dropped drawers. "Just needed to be sure, you know?"

She sidled back up to me with a husky chuckle, pulled my jeans to my ankles with the palm of her right foot. "So they hired you, huh? Her parents?"

"Yeah," I replied, pressing my boy against her midriff. "I'm famous."

Afterward, I quizzed her more generally, knowing that she, more than anyone, would know who the town freaks were. We had pushed the two massage tables together for the purposes of our transaction. She answered me with her chin on my chest. Periodically her hand would crawl down to my groin to tweak and twiddle. I chalked it up to force of habit.

When she had heard about Jennifer—or "the other Jennifer" as she called her—the same questions had occurred to her. Some of her clients liked the rough stuff, but they tended to be the ones she thought the least likely to do anything "wonky," as she put it.

"No one much fucks with me," she said, tossing a negligent thumb in the direction of the hall that led off the kitchen—to the bedrooms, I suppose.

"Why's that?"

"Because my brother's always out back, playing his video games."

"Brother?"

"Well, stepbrother. Jerome. Nobody fucks with Jerome."

"Could you introduce me to him?"

"Not unless you want to fuck wi—"

That was when the riff from "Back in Black" began wailing in miniature from my pants where they lay crumpled. My cellphone.

"Sorry," I said, peeling myself from Jenny's sweaty side. "I'm on the clock, you know."

She just snorted. "Me too."

God, I love hookers. Almost as much as I love the drugs that make them hook. It was making my skin itch just knowing that somewhere near, beneath the couch or in a cupboard or drawer, there was a bag of goodies.

According to the display, it was Molly. "Yep," I said into the phone.

"Disciple. Disciple! Where are you?"

"At a rub-and-tug," I answered in a querulous *Where-else-would-I-be* tone.

"A rub and what?"

"A rub-and-*tug*. You know, a jack shack."

"Spare me the bullshit, Disciple," she snapped, all, like, time-is-money and shit. *"You need to meet me at the corner of Inkerman and Kane."*

"What? Why?"

"Nolen. He's found a severed finger."

A classic pan-in-zoom-out moment. Molly, it turned out, owned a police scanner, an item I had thought about getting several times but had just never seemed to muster the scratch for. Bad dice and the odd Jenny will do that to you, I suppose. Apparently while I was out busy investigating my vices, she was in her room watching *CSI* reruns and keeping tabs on what the state-sanctioned professionals were doing.

"Wait," she snapped. *"Wait!"*

I could hear her scanner squawking in the background ...

"Shit-shit-shit," she gasped, her voice taut with genuine fear.

"What? What's going on?"

"Another one," she exclaimed. Frantic. She was genuinely frantic. *"They found another finger just a couple of blocks away!"*

"How?" I asked, hopping with one leg in my jeans. Jenny's laughter told me I had forgotten to put on my boxers. Bouncing around, my dick flopping like a tassel. Fuck it, I would go commando. "Did they say anything about *how*?"

"I can't talk now, Disciple," she called over my stream of muttered curses. *"I gotta be out there. I'm going. I'll meet you, 'kay?"*

"Molls!" was all I managed before the line went dead.

It's strange. I had no bonus arrangement with the Bonjours, so it really didn't matter whether I was instrumental to what happened or not—I would get paid no matter what. And yet, beneath the move-move-move urgency, there was this crushing sense of *failure* ...

I had known that she was dead all along, hadn't I?

I kissed Jenny full on the lips, left her standing naked with the full roll of bills in her left hand and my boxers hanging from her right. I suffered a pang of remorse driving away. I had really liked those boxer shorts: a National Geographic number depicting The Whales of the World. They even sported a blue whale arching across the fly, boding the appearance of the purple.

Forgotten gauchies. As good an excuse as any, I supposed, to find my way back to 113 Omeemee.

My phone began riffing literally the second I shut the car door. It was Albert—and about fucking time.

"Heeeey!" he cried over the sound of music and voices. *"Disciple, he-heee ... Didn't think I would catch you. What you doing so late, man?"*

He was more than a little drunk, I could tell.

"Jerking off to *War and Peace.* I always get wood when the French are defeated. You?"

Breathless laughter. *Great,* I thought. Albert was one of those guys who became cool on a blood alcohol gradient. His cat's-ass tone told me he thought he was pretty much the coolest thing going, which meant he'd hiked a good distance up shit-face hill.

"Impromptu grad party," he said. *"Talking bullshit. Scoping hotties—you know how it is ..."*

"So what di—"

"Smoked the last of that green," he interrupted. *"If you know what I mean."*

A mental frown. "I'm sure I can hook you up."

"Bonus! You put the Weeeee! into weed, you know that?"

He found this pretty funny. Over his laugh I heard a young feminine voice say, *"Is that your guy? Is that your guy?"* in the background. *"He's a riot!"* I heard Albert reply.

"And you put the *Hurray!* in shut-the-fuck-up," I said, not at all comfortable with being Albert's "guy." "Have you been telling people about our little arrangement?"

Another guffaw, as if I had been joking. *"Seriously, though. Dude. I meant to call earlier, but I fucking forgot ... so I thought, heeey! I'll just leave him a message! You're my favourite round-eye bad-ass, you know that?"*

"And you're my favourite gook-geek. What did you find out, Albert?"

"Yah-yah-yah, sorry. I called this old buddy of mine who did a philosophy post-doc at Berkeley. Baars was already gone by then, but apparently he was still big news ..."

Like most drunks, Albert overestimated the drama of his stories, and so kept decent people hanging with trivia.

"And?" I said.

"Brilliant. Eccentric. Divorced ..."

His tone told me he was saving the juicy bits. "And?"

"Rumour was he knocked up one of his sophomores ..."

That was interesting, at least. But I knew there was more. "C'mon, Albert. Cut me a fucking break over here. What else?"

"Well, it seems he taught a course on cults ... Cults, *Disciple!"*

He fairly shouted this, so I knew *he* thought it was significant, at least. "So?"

"Soooo, think about it, dude! The guy knows *..."*

"Knows what?"

"All of it. The psychology. The sociology. The history. Which means he knows how to act, how to organize, what kind of claims to make ..." Music and droning voices swelled to fill the silence. *"There's just no way, Disciple."*

"No way what? For him to believe his own guff?"

"Sure, there's that. But there's also no way for him to not be manipulating these people. It's at least as bad as L. Ron Hubbard. Worse!"

I drove in a state of blank absorption. It made a kind of dreadful sense, to be sure.

"Hey ... about the weed," he said, signalling super-cool, drunk Albert's return. *"You wouldn't happen to have a ... you know, a number I could call or anything?"*

"Try Kimmy," I said, knowing I needed to shrink-wrap this latest twist, save it for some future lull. "She should be getting off about now ... I'll text you her number."

I found Molly looking smart and forlorn on the corner of an intersection that seemed surprisingly urban. Three Ruddick cruisers blocked the street at angles, bathing the bricked-in spaces with rolling lights. A thin crowd of onlookers had gathered in clutches here and there on the sidewalks. But otherwise things seemed surprisingly sedate. Only one uniform was visible.

The first words out of her lips were, "Jack shack, huh?"

"I's got needs," I said.

"Why do you *do* that? Why do you always lie when people ask you where you are?"

"Keeps me sharp," I replied, surprised that she would have anything other than this latest twist on her mind. "Reminds me I'm a captive of the facts as the world presents them."

"Weird, you know that?" she said, shaking her head. "You gotta be the strangest man I've ever known."

"We should all be so lucky," I said. Then, intentionally shifting gears, I added, "So which fingers are we talking about?"

"The index and bird fingers," she said.

"*Bird* finger?"

"Yeah. You know." She flipped me the bird.

I sometimes have this fear that the women I'm interested in are actually psychic, that they can see the truth of me all the way down to the grimy bottom but just play along because they like the attention. The superstition struck me like a bolt right then.

Molly filled me in on the rest of the details. The first finger had been found just a couple of blocks over, in the backyard of an old amputee—a Vietnam vet or something. Apparently by sheer dint of coincidence, the second had been called in less than an hour after, found by a bunch of high school kids who had "wandered into" the abandoned warehouse looming before us, "looking for a lost dog."

One of Nolen's men—a guy so tired he had to have been dragged off the day shift—barred the way, and refused to even discuss the matter with us, let alone let us past. So we just stood there, every bit as tired, cooling our heels. I studied the small crowd of onlookers, knowing the chances were good that our perp would be keen to survey the social consequences of his handiwork first-hand. I described the males to Molly in a low murmur, just to be sure they would stick ...

"Skinhead dude with forehead wrinkled like scrotum ...

"Soccer coach dreaming of teenage ass ...

"Punk who should sell me whatever it is he's smoking ...

"Guy who looks like BO ... *Yeesh*, that fucker is ugly."

It didn't take much to get Molly laughing. Always makes me feel smug, killing two birds with one stone.

When Nolen finally came out, he looked ragged and more than a little shell-shocked. Dust feathered his left shoulder, and he seemed to have lost his cap. "The fingers are bagged," he said, holding a hand out to pre-empt our questions. "We're sending them to Pitt to get them DNA typed—just to be sure they belong to Jennifer. We also need to know whether they were cut from her while she was, ah, you know, alive ... But the doctor ..." Something caught in his throat, something that demanded to be swallowed. "Um, he seems to think the cuts were, ah ... well, post-mortem."

This occasioned a moment of silence. Laughter warbled from a group of kids assembled on a nearby corner.

"What about the scenes?" Molly pressed. "Could you let us check out the scenes?"

"Scenes? You mean where we found the fingers?"

"Of *course*," she said, with enough exasperation to earn a gentle elbow in the ribs from me. You have to be careful with people like Nolen, I had learned, not because they could be prickly, but because they were *unlikely* to take offence. Some people are so dispositionally agreeable that the urge to take liberties is well-nigh irresistible. The sad fact is that people primarily harass others not because the others deserve to be harassed but because they *can*. The easier a guy is to bully, the more likely we are to invent reasons why he *needs* to be bullied. Often our fuse is long or short depending on what we unconsciously think we can get away with.

"Not much anything to see," he said, scratching the back of his head.

"So no notes?" Molly asked.

"Notes?"

"Yeah." Again the telltale impatience. "You know, like ransom demands or anything."

"'Fraid not. Just fingers in these queer little cages."

"Cages?" Molly asked in a ragged voice. Things were just beginning to sink in for her, I could tell.

Nolen shrugged. "Yeah. You know, like to keep them from getting snatched by wildlife or something."

"To make sure they would be found," I said.

Fawk.

Guitars crunched from my pants pocket. Another call. Kimberley this time, probably calling to bitch me out for telling Albert she could hook him up. I didn't answer. As it was, Molly was all over me about leaning on Nolen to let us check out the two places—as bad as an ex-wife carping about child support.

"Get used to it," I said. "This is the way it works for people like you and me. Most of the time you're stuck on the outside looking in."

"But what if there's any, you know, *clues*?"

The thing about popular misconceptions, I've found, is that they typically involve people knowing *more* rather than less. We always know less than we think. We always control less than we hope. Even forensics is so hit-and-miss that there's a real question as to whether it should be called a science.

"You were watching *CSI* again tonight, weren't you?"

I took the fact that she said nothing as a big fat yes.

A moment of silence passed between us, one that seemed to cement the fact that we were stranded on a cracked sidewalk, walled in by dead brick buildings. Funny, the way you can just sense things, like how late it is by how cool the cement is ... I felt a distinct absence of daytime heat.

"What are the chances?" she asked in a numb voice I had never heard before. My second therapist once told me that this was why I womanized—not because I was carrying out some ancient evolutionary program to spread the sperm, but because I could only love women when they were *new.*

I found myself gazing at Molly, arrested by her profile in the oscillation of red and blue lights. "Chances?" I repeated.

"Yeah," she said, blinking tears before turning to me. "You know ... that the fingers belong to Jennifer."

"You're serious?" I asked. I managed a sombre shrug even though I wanted to laugh. "A town this size? ... Things ain't looking so good, Molls."

"So she's ... she's ..."

"Of course she is."

We were *dog*-tired by the time we got back to the motel. Call me weird, but I found the act of driving with her in separate cars powerfully erotic—like road rage turned on its head. Road lust. My heart muscled through the seconds we spent saying nothing while standing in the gap between our motel room doors. I couldn't resist grinning *yippee!* when she followed me ...

She made an act of it, as though she were just too goddamned tired to resist my relentless advances. But the fact was, she wanted it, maybe even *needed* it. Who's to say? Most of the time I'm just stumped when it comes to the reasons women—especially beautiful ones like Molly—condescend to sleep with me. Whatever it is, it certainly doesn't have any staying power.

We kissed, in that long way that makes magic of fumbling hands and fingers. There's glory in feminine yielding, in the shyness of a woman still unnerved by her desire. We flopped like two tangled ropes across the bed. I pressed her onto her back, snuggled my pelvis between her legs, and without warning she gasped, "Wait-wait! What's your favourite band?"

"Um ... huh?"

"You can tell a lot about a man," she sighed.

Believe it or not, I was utterly unsurprised. It could have been the exhaustion, I suppose, but the fact was I had been asked plenty of things by plenty of women the moment before first contact. Loopy things.

"Monster Magnet," I said.

"Never heard of them. What's their thing?"

"I dunno. Comic books and metaphysics ..."

She frowned in a *This-feels-too-too-good* way. "I'm ... I'm not sure ... What's your second favourite band?"

"Tool."

"Tool? Eew. I ... ah ... hate ..."

I was grinding against her now, slow and languorous.

"But Tool loves you," I said, grinning like a cat pinning a budgie. "Tool loves you long time, baby."

She laughed, groaned. "You idiot ... How can you ..."

She exhaled, like I was a birthday candle or something.

Score.

I woke up in the middle of the night, the way I always seem to do. Molly lay tangled in the sheets, splayed like her parachute had failed to open. I clicked on the TV with the volume muted, scrounged my bag of weed. I sat upright in the surgical light, watching the drip of soundless images across the screen while rolling a fat one.

Her voice startled me.

"What's it like?"

Her face was still squashed into her pillow. For all the world I had thought she was sleeping.

"Sticky," I said, spinning the doob into a perfect cylinder. "Skunky ... Everything weed should be."

The pillow scrunched her smile into her cheek. "No ..." she said, rolling onto her back. She brushed her hair from her face with a groggy hand. "What's it like *being you*?"

I inhaled. Like cigarettes, joints buy you several seconds to cook something up when a chick asks you a hard question. Time I squandered for some reason.

"Hard ... sometimes."

"Why?" she asked, staring at the ceiling. Televised colours danced across the cheap stucco swirls.

I exhaled a ghostly horn of smoke across our legs, shrugged. "You know the radio, how they play the same hit parade over and over?"

"Sure. That's why I got satellite in my rental."

"Well, I have a hit parade all my own."

She turned to gaze at my profile. "Memories," she said. "You mean memories."

"The thing is, it's the *bad ones* that stick. And I don't mean like a hazy flash of images, but moments of ... of *reliving*, I guess. With the smells, the surge of emotion ... like a miniature dream or something."

"Can you give me an example?"

I was afraid she was going to ask that.

"Like ... well ... your eyes, they remind me of my mother, so sometimes when I look at you, I'm *also* sitting in my folks' kitchen, and my mom, she's at the sink grabbing me some tea. And there's this fly walking across the window's reflection in the counter, you know, like it's pacing out a treasure map in fast motion, fifteen paces this way, stop, twenty paces that way, stop. And *Mom*, she's smiling—she always had a sunny disposition, my mom, always giving me the gears about being negative—well, she's smiling and looking out the window, and I notice there's tears in her eyes. So I say, 'Whazzup, Mom?' and she turns to me, blinks a couple of diamonds, grins her best *You're-such-a-good-boy* grin, and says, 'I have cancer, Disciple. They say I have only a few months.'"

"Oh gawd ..." Molly whispered.

"And that's one of the love songs."

Track Eight
SHRINKAGE

Friday ...

Breakfast was tasty and numb. Circumstances have caught me being glib or flip too many times for this latest twist to rattle me all that much. A go-figure attitude was about as chastised as I could get.

Besides, like I told you, I already knew that Jennifer Bonjour was dead.

But Molly seemed about a pubic hair away from devastation. That's the thing about youth: your hopes fly high when you lack the ballast of experience. Life has a way of stuffing our pockets with sand. Of course she had her catechism of low expectations like the rest of us, that sense of superstitious doom that prevents people from celebrating the purchase of lottery tickets. But at some profound level she had thought that everything *ruly-truly would* unfold according to fantastic plan. That Jennifer Bonjour would be found bruised and dehydrated, that some unassuming villain would be apprehended, and that her hair-raising story would vault Molly Modano into the heights of print celebrity. Yet one more Barbie-doll Ordeal welded into the public imagination.

Now here she was: ambition meets the mortician.

"How could the doctor tell?" she asked.

"Tell what?"

"That her fingers had been cut from her *after* she was dead."

"Not sure. Something to do with the way the tissue sheers? I know that blood settles in the body when the heart stops ... Maybe the cut was blood free."

She frowned at her bacon. "We don't *know* it was her, though ... Not for sure."

"Molls ..."

She continued eating in silence. I thought about all the things I could say, all the pearls of cynical wisdom I could shuck from my brain. But I could tell she was hurting for real, and not simply because of this latest macabre turn. Last night she had sought comfort in my arms, and my fear was that she had caught a whiff of the reaper. They always do, sooner or later. If it wasn't my wrists, it was my look. I was a man with one too many scars.

So, I waited until she finished her eggs, then tossed the folder I had brought. It whisked to a stop before her.

"What's this?"

"I want you to read to me." Truth is, I would have asked her to read it to me no matter what, but since she so obviously required some kind of distraction, I told myself this was the reason all along.

"Huh?"

"A copy of Anson Williams's statement to Nolen."

The Framer Compound looked like a Star Trek convention. About two dozen people milled about and beneath the giant willows out front, all of them dressed in variations of the same uniforms I had seen on my first visit. The women outnumbered the men by about two to one, which made me wonder whether Jennifer might have found herself on the wrong point of a love triangle. The ages were almost uniformly young, but the ethnic and racial diversity would have put an after-school special to shame.

I must have arrived between classes.

I cranked my stereo to garner attention—some vintage Iron Maiden. Most everyone paused mid-polite-conversation to glance at me as I rattled by. Smiling beneath my shades, I shot them the *live-long-and-prosper* hand sign.

I had called in advance, and had been greeted with the same air of formal, almost corporate compliance as on my last visit. Stevie stood waiting as I climbed out of my Golf into a haze of summer dust.

"Like the new suit," I called out as I approached the glass door. He was wearing the identical white uniform of course. He scowled but said nothing as I ducked past him into the air-conditioned interior.

"What's with the crowd out front?"

"Sometimes Xen likes to teach out of doors ..." He glanced at me with those cold, superior eyes of his. "Beneath the sun ... the *real* sun."

"Huh," I replied. "Tell me, can you get an invisible sunburn from an invisible sun?"

Stevie ignored the question. Rude prick.

"I suppose you have invisible sunscreen for that ..."

This time he led me around a bend and then down a long hallway that sported windows with melancholy glimpses of the far, shadowed side of the Compound, and a series of doors labelled Consultation Room 1 and so on. Expressionless, Stevie asked me to take a seat in Consultation Room 4.

"So the SPF must be, like, a million or something," I said.

He left, teeth clamped tight behind a phony smile. I sat humming a Whitesnake tune I heard on the drive, wondering where Baars found all his money ...

What's the overhead on New Age cults these days?

Anson Williams wasn't long in arriving.

"Is it true, what they say? That they've found one ... one of her fingers?"

Like pretty much everyone I had met so far, Anson defied my expectations. His face was broad, his gaze at once direct and friendly. He was tall, though somewhat pudgy through the middle, nerdy despite the cropped dreads twigging his head. After five minutes of listening to his meek and smoky voice I knew he had nothing to do with Jennifer's disappearance. He was the kind of guy who felt guilty cleaning out his friends in poker. One of those good-looking putzes.

"They've found a severed human finger," I replied, "most likely female. Otherwise, nothing's for sure."

"But ..." He trailed off, fixed me with a look I had seen twenty-seven times before, one peculiar to the bereaved: a kind of horrified-sorting-through-sensations look, as though trying to locate a bullet wound with your hands tied.

"Look, Anson, I've done this before. Sometimes things are straightforward. Sometimes they go sideways. The best way to move forward is to simply stay on course. Wait until the facts come in."

He bit his lip and nodded. I started with my questions, sensitivities be damned.

Like Jennifer, Anson had come to the Framers by way of the internet. At first he had laughed at the claims, but after listening to Baars's podcasts he became more and more intrigued. At any given point in time, he explained, some six or seven full members toured the country, meeting with long-distance associates, giving seminars to potential recruits, and offering, via hypnosis, a glimpse into the Frame—the world as it really was five billion years from the present. Outreachers, they called them. Evidently the Compound was more than a retreat; it was a base of operations as well.

Anson was hypnotized by an Outreacher named Cassie Guerin on January 11, 2005. Three days later he withdrew from all his courses at TSU and, to the enduring dismay of his parents (both of whom worked for NASA down in Huntsville, Alabama), moved into the Framer Compound to study with Baars.

"You all think we're fools," Anson said with an impressive lack of bitterness. "I know, and part of me doesn't really blame you. How can I, knowing what I know?"

"What do you mean?"

"The Frame. When the whole point is to keep consciousness caged, how can we condemn you for defending your prison cells?"

Something about the man glowed as he described those first, heady days living at the Compound. As the newcomers, he and Jennifer had become fast friends. Apparently they both loved to dance. And no, they had never been romantically involved.

When I asked him why, Anson simply shrugged and said, "She's with Xen."

I took the opportunity to probe him about Baars, hoping to mine the inevitable resentment women inspire in men. But if he harboured any ill will for the Counsellor, as they called him, he betrayed none of it. In fact his eyes, which had been sombre throughout his commentary on Jennifer, fairly lit up in admiration—adoration even.

"I saw several hotties driving in ..." I said.

"Are you asking me whether Xen sleeps with anyone else?"

I was starting to realize this was part of the deal, being a Framer. Where most people talk around delicate issues, or clam up altogether, these guys simply said it how it was. I would have found it refreshing if it hadn't made me feel like such a phony.

"No ... Actually, I was wondering whether any of them were, you know ... single."

He shot me the nerd's version of a *give-me-a-break* smile, like I had just asked him to explain the difference between an RPG and a first-person shooter. "This place isn't what you think, Mr. Manning. Xen doesn't seduce his students. Any of us can leave any time we want. It's *not* some ticking tabloid headline ..."

I thought about my conversation with Albert the previous night. If anyone could design a cult that didn't *smell* like a cult, I decided, it would be Xenophon Baars.

"Sure," I said with a shrug, "but certainly, as *Counsellor*, Xen possesses certain powers, certain privileges."

"And?" he asked. The question made him obviously uncomfortable, so I decided to hit him with another.

"And no one was closer to Xen than Jennifer, right?"

"Yeah—so what?"

"Seems like a recipe for jealousy and resentment to me. You can go on all you want about how egalitarian everything is here, but the bottom line, Anson, is that Xen is holding all the cards, and for whatever reason, he decided to deal Jennifer a special hand."

"They were *in love*! Who would resent that?"

"Well, how about Stevie? The guy pretty much oozes homoerotic rage, don't you think?"

"Stephen worships Xen. He would never do anything to hurt him."

"And that would hurt Xen, losing Jennifer?"

"Of course!"

My neck was stiff, so I bent my head from shoulder to shoulder.

"Well, the guy doesn't seem all that cut up about it," I said. "That doesn't spook you? The fact that they were so close, and yet Xen carries on business as usual?"

"Xen is the *first*," he explained. "Like Magellan—or Galileo, even more! Men like him don't stop for the sake of grief—especially when they *know what grief actually is*. He's the first to draw aside the curtain, to see what we *really* are ..."

"The truth, huh?"

"The *truth* of all truths!"

Did I forget to mention that Anson was as fucking crazy as the rest of them?

Thoroughly creeped out, I asked him to recount what happened the night of Jennifer's disappearance.

Nobody tells the same story twice.

One of the many memory researchers I've endured, a guy called Robert Kunitz, told me about a study where subjects were asked to write accounts of where they were and what they were doing when the space shuttle *Challenger* fizzled into smoke and debris. When they tracked these people down years later and asked them the same question, apparently a sizable minority of them had *completely* changed their stories. Some even went so far as to accuse the researchers of falsifying their previous accounts, right down to forging their handwriting.

"Unbelievable, huh?" Kunitz said in the strange-but-true tone that psychologists—perpetually tickled by the fact that they know people better than they know themselves—are prone to take. "It's really that bad."

I disagreed, told him that I knew, with utter certainty, that things were actually worse.

I could almost see the grant money reflected in his eyes.

See, unlike me, you *reconstitute* the events you "remember." Your whole life is quite literally a dramatization. You may be *based* on a true story, but you are not, by any sensible measure, true. You may earn an Oscar or two, but you will never snag a Pulitzer.

So when I say that inconsistency in a suspect's story is not necessarily a red flag for deception, understand that I speak from the standpoint of the sighted speaking to the blind. The sad fact is that variance between accounts doesn't necessarily tell you anything. Your suspect could be a premeditated liar—or fuckhead, to use the industry term of art—but odds are he's just another asshole.

The biggest complication I faced was that Anson's statement was paraphrased through the lens of Chief Nolen, whose skills at taking informal dictation were neither here nor there compared with the 161 other statements I've seen. The situation was even trickier because the statement was so recent. This meant Anson had *two* sets of coordinates to read from: his memory of the event itself and his memory of his official recounting of the event. The devil, if it were to be found anywhere, would be in the *consistencies.* This was the real reason I had asked Molly to read Anson's statement in the first place: to find evidence of rote and rehearsal, stuff that innocent people generally do not do, simply because they believe they don't *have* to, sweet fools that they are. If there's anything I've learned, it's that the truth will just as soon see you hanged as set you free.

Justice is just a fluke that occasions way too much art and backslapping.

He started with a discrepancy, a small one to be sure, in the time he and Jennifer had left the Compound to walk into Ruddick: 8:25, a number specific enough to prick my interest but round enough to preclude outright suspicion, had become 8:30 or so, which was far more in line with the haphazard way people keep time—gulps and swallows, not sips. This suggested not only the absence of rehearsal but the absence of guilt as well. Had Anson been involved in Jennifer's disappearance, he would have obsessed over the details of his story, since it was pretty much the only way for him to influence the outcome of events.

But the rest of his story followed Nolen's paraphrasing to the *letter.* Well, the imagined letter, to be more precise, since it takes more than a little imaginative reconstruction to see the actual phrasing through the paraphrasing. Either way, the problem was that I could see Nolen composing precisely the same statement given what Anson was telling me. But what did that mean?

Fucking hints and innuendoes, man. There's nothing to do but to file them and move on.

Besides, what could a kid like this, one who by all reports was Jennifer's dearest friend at the Compound, have to do with something that resulted in severed fingers?

I decided to press things in a different direction.

"What about Jennifer's parents?"

A hesitant pause. "What about them?"

I rubbed the back of my neck with a hooked paw. That motel bed was taking its toll. And here I thought the entire hospitality business had embraced the pillow-top mattress. Fawk.

"Did she ever talk about them?"

Anson shrugged. "Sure. Who doesn't talk about their parents?"

"You know what I mean. Did she ever *talk* about them?"

"Yuh."

By now my curiosity was piqued. "Why the reluctance, Anson?"

"Nah ... Just feels weird, you know."

"She swear you to secrecy?"

A stiff nod followed by, "Yuh."

"The circumstances have changed, don't you think?"

"Yuh."

"Things couldn't be any more radical."

He chewed on his lower lip for a moment, then said, "Suppose."

"So?"

He just gave me a blank, helpless look. Sometimes it doesn't matter how high you pile the reasons. To be honest, I already had that gnawing sense of doom that always accompanies moments like this ... moments of stumbling upon the Uglies, as I call them. The truths that no one wants to know.

"Anson, look. We have two different angles on this situation, you and I. The puzzles you see and the puzzles I see are completely different. You have a piece, a *fact*, that fits a certain way into a certain set of moral obligations. But here's the thing: when people swear you to secrecy—that's *almost* as real as it gets. The puzzle I'm working on ..." I watched him watch me.

"Is real," Anson said, nodding.

"As real as it gets. *Frame* real." I wince at recalling this because it was so *stupid*. In the course of impressing the tragic stakes of the situation on him, I had essentially reminded him it was all a video game.

Even still, he told me about a morning-light confession, about how Jennifer worried that she was failing Xen, failing the Framers, because she simply could not let go of this one night when she was thirteen, the night she could not sleep and happened upon her well-fed father in the basement—drinking and watching porno.

"Come here, sweetie ... It's nothing to be frightened of ... It's completely natural."

Anson talked, alternately staring at his palms and at the walls to either side of me. I watched him without expression because this is what I do: collect and interpret all the little atrocities we suffer and commit.

Then shelve them in the mad library that is my mind.

"You said she thought she was *failing* because of this?"

"Xen ..." Anson explained with an apologetic hitch of his shoulders. "He teaches us that we're here *to learn* from all these ..."—he swallowed—"things, you know? Sins, crimes ... What we suffer is secondary to the fact *that* we suffer, the meaning we take away from having endured. And because of this, he says we're supposed to *affirm*, to affirm our lives in their entirety, to realize that not a moment, not a breath, has been wasted ... And she ... Jennifer, just ... couldn't ... do this."

His long-lashed eyes finally fixed mine.

"Not with her fucking father, anyway."

Incest—the plugged toilet of the investigative world. *Christ*, I thought as Stevie led me away from the consultation room, *Christ Almighty*.

I sometimes think people have the same basic electrical service when it comes to their morals, that the real thing that distinguishes them is the way they *use* that power. Some people fritter away their moral amperage on all the little night lights and clock radios life offers: personal hygiene, sexual orientation, dinner table innuendo. You know, the *Who-does-that-bitch-think-she-is?* kind of bullshit. Others, the kind that join the Peace Corps or volunteer at their local women's shelter, channel their juice into big-ticket items, the stoves and central airs of the ethical universe. And me? Yeah, sure, my breaker box is all fucked up ...

My scruples are few and far between, I admit. But they draw a lot of power.

Too much for my line of work, truth be told.

Stevie's brisk stride carried me back to the same courtyard where Baars and I had taken tea on my previous visit. The table had been moved from the shadowed portico into the sunlight. Tea steamed from two freshly poured cups. Xenophon Baars sat on the far chair facing the entrance, his expression as avid as before, his white suit fairly incandescent in the sunlight, which also dazzled the assortment of porcelain across the tabletop.

"Ah, yes, Mr. Manning," Baars said, coming to his feet to greet me.

"I'd ask you to call me Disciple," I said, staring directly at Stevie, "but I'm afraid you would find it confusing."

Baars laughed—the guy always seemed to be laughing. "I would never confuse someone as singular as yourself, Mr. Manning. Not even in my dotage ... Come. Join me for some tea."

Stevie withdrew with a fluid, oriental air that I found menacing. I don't much care for imperturbable people—my job pretty much depends on rattling cages.

Baars had leaned back to sun his face. The lines of reflected light made him seem a plastic mould of himself. I wanted to say something clever or, failing that, something snide, but part of me was still humming the squalid notes Anson had struck just moments before ...

"He says we're supposed to affirm ..."

Rules. With belief come rules. But more on that later.

"Tell me, Mr. Manning. When you stare into the sky, what is it you see?"

"Sky."

He smiled a blind beach smile. "I see the sun."

I imagine he was hoping this would be a Zen moment, profound for its one-hand-clapping simplicity. I just thought it was stupid. I almost told him he should start a show on the local cable access channel, call it *Zen with Xen.*

I stuck to the stubborn point instead. "So I've been canvassing," I said. "Going door to door, looking for scraps regarding Jennifer. The Framers don't seem to be very popular ..."

"You don't take notes, do you?" Baars asked, eyes still closed.

This gave me pause. I decided to ignore it. I also decided to ignore the fact that no mention had been made of the severed finger Nolen had found.

"So that got me wondering whether there was anyone in Ruddick who didn't like you—I mean *really* didn't like you. You know, vandalism, threats, harassment in town, that sort of thing. I have it on good authority that cults ... or, ah, new religious movements like yours, experience their fair share of bigotry and, well ... discrimination."

I assumed from the way Baars lifted his head to regard me that I had garnered his attention. Most everyone likes to think they're persecuted. Almost everyone jumps at a *woe-is-me* opportunity ...

"Where do you think your remarkable memory comes from, Mr. Manning?"

For the first time, I revealed the hard eyes of my suspicion.

"Don't look so shocked," he said with a good-natured chuckle. "You googled *me*, didn't you?"

I shrugged. I had to admit, Xenophon Baars was a hard man not to like. All that *charisma.* I wondered if he was, like, the Obama of the cult world.

"Bet you thirty bucks my hit count is higher."

Baars laughed. "I'm sure it is! From the looks of it, there are more than a few researchers who would love to make a lab rat out of you."

"Yeah, well. Those days are over."

"But your memory remains the same, doesn't it? In the *New York Times* piece, one researcher described it as 'miraculous.' Is that what you think it is? A miracle?"

"No more than any other aberration."

"Ah, a happy deformity, then. Is that it?"

"I prefer to think of it as a 'joyous birth defect.'"

His sun forgotten, Xenophon Baars fixed me with a peculiar gaze. The shadow of his nose fell across his lips, and for the first time I realized how ridiculously small his mouth was.

"No system is perfect, Disciple. The law of unintended consequences applies as much to our future as it does to what you call 'now.' And with so many billions of people—"

"So ... I'm like in a pod or a vat, somewhere, is that it?"

A sad smile. "No. In point of fact, *you are a machine.* A kind of quantum computer, dreaming of its mammalian past."

"We're dreaming, huh."

I tried to imagine him eating a hamburger—couldn't do it.

"*Hallucinating* would be a more accurate term. This *is* the real world, only systematically skewed to simulate the way things were roughly five billion years ago. Think of the way schizophrenics incorporate elements of the real world into their psychotic delusions."

I blinked. How do you reply to something like that? Fawk. I reminded myself that Jennifer was the only point here, not Baars's whacked dogma. *Discipline, Disciple.*

"So what does this have to do with my miraculous memory?"

"Because sometimes, Disciple, our *true selves leak through*, shine as inexplicable gifts—gifts like your memory—given our ignorance otherwise. We see only *slivers* of the Frame, so like psychotics we continually *misinterpret*, claim to see ghosts or to remember past lives or to talk to God or to attain enlightenment. The list goes on, I assure you!"

That was the ninth time he had said, "I assure you."

I found myself wondering whether anyone had bothered to count up all the ways people can make stupid sound smart, when, like a bolt, I grasped the out-and-out *genius* of Baars's little story. It quite literally contained nothing *spooky*. Using it, he could pretty much rationalize anything paranormal, anything that seemed to signal some beyond, in *mundane* terms. A little technology and a lot of time was all it took ...

"Transcendence," I heard myself murmur. This old girlfriend of mine, a philosophy student named Sasha Lang, used to blab on and on about how humans hungered for transcendence, for something beyond the miserable circuit of their existence. I would just say something glib, like how Cheerios were more filling.

But Baars, the clever boy, had invented a way at once to feed that hunger and to explain it away.

The man fairly erupted in gleeful laughter. "Yes!" he cried. "Yes!" In an avid rush he explained how he used to teach classes on Transcendence back in his Berkeley days, how he even wrote a book on the topic before his "awakening." After pondering the issue for more than fifteen years, he apparently realized that the best way to understand paranormal experience was to look at normal experience, not as some kind of baseline, but as a *diminution* of a much broader spectrum of possibility. It was exploring this insight through hypnosis that led to his discovery of the Frame, the true present, where humanity had become indistinguishable from its technology.

It all came down to shrinkage.

"The world we see is but a sliver! But because it's all we know, we confuse it for the whole!"

I sat back and soaked in it: the stink of someone smoking his own ideas.

He must have caught a whiff of my disgust in my expression, because he caught himself, eventually. "You must forgive my enthusiasm," he said, beaming like someone who had asked for the letter E on *Wheel of Fortune.*

"No worries," I replied. "It's just us stoners."

The guy was a fucking first-class wanker, no doubt about it. The weird thing was that the more he talked, the more harmless he began to seem, the more my suspicion began to wane. Sure, I wanted to grab him, shake him, scream, *Are you fucking kidding me?*

But ...

He had convinced me *he was a believer.* Albert's drunken revelation from the previous night, that he had taught a course on cults at Berkeley and so knew too much about cults to honestly participate in one, had me convinced the whole Frame thing was nothing more than a self-serving fraud. So the enthusiasm which should have implicated him—the man, after all, had just learned that his missing lover was in fact dead—actually had the *opposite* effect. Xenophon Baars was a true, talk-you-blue-in-the-face *believer.*

And *if* he was a believer, then he *really* thought she had gone to a better place.

I was losing perspective. I could feel it. Leave it to Baars to give me a reality check ...

"I could *show* you," he said. "Hypnotize you ..."

"I was sexually assaulted by a hypnotist as a kid," I said, thinking of Jennifer and her father and not liking it one bit. "I'm sure you'll understand if I pass ..."

I've known more than my fair share of psychologists—certainly enough to know that *suggestion* is the cornerstone of hypnotic trances. Suspicion of murder aside, there was no way in hell I was letting Baars muck around with my head.

"Of course," he said, frowning, knowing that I was lying and not knowing how to deal with it. "Tell me, Disciple. What do you think about this? I mean, *really* think."

I studied him for a moment. Given my memory, I had become acutely aware over the years of all the small cues that establish hierarchies between individuals. I knew by now that Baars, for whatever reason, had accorded me the status of an equal. That he *respected* me.

What I couldn't figure out was why this made me feel *gratified.*

"She's with Xen ..."

"What do I *really* think?" I shrugged and made my favourite face: a crooked smirk that said *whatever*, and eyes that asked if it was bedtime yet. "Honestly? I think you're a fraud. I think you've used your talent for sincerity to hook these people, and your training as a philosopher to reel them in. Now you're living the high life, a miniature king of a miniature religion, filling young minds with ancient horseshit, and tender pussies with old cock—which is pretty much what this is all about, isn't it? Living out your guru-porn-star fantasies."

Baars leaned forward in his wicker chair as if winded. "Oh, my ..." he gasped.

"You asked," I said, leaning my face back to soak in the sun.

"You really think—"

"You say my memory's miraculous?" I snapped without looking at him. "Not half so miraculous as the consistency of old perverted pricks like you. You *all* invent a religion of some kind, don't you? Something to cover your horny old asses. A cult of misogyny. A cult of beauty. A cult of privilege. But somehow, magically, *miraculously*, it all comes back to fucking ..."

A smile creased the sun-hot skin of my face. The glare illuminated the backs of my eyelids. I realized I much preferred talking to him with my eyes closed. He unnerved me too much otherwise.

"You sound pretty certain of yourself," Baars said, his voice taut.

"Occam's razor, Professor. You know the drill. All things being equal, the simplest explanation is generally the best."

I could hear the breeze whisking through the willows in the near distance. Somewhere, a small radio piped the blues. The taint of driveway dust hung in the air.

"*If* all things are equal ..."

My smile broadened. I could feel the sun across my lips, close enough to kiss.

"So you tell me, Counsellor, how many initiates have you banged?"

I turned to appraise his answer and saw old-man horror—the signs of a body that had lost faith in its structural integrity. He seemed to shrink and to age at once. Fawk. You would think I had just kicked his dialysis machine or something.

"Only Jennifer," he said in a hollow voice.

Liar, I smiled.

I got up, made to show myself the way out. Amanda Bonjour came crashing up through my memory: *"The whole thing is a murderous con!"*

"Mr. Manning!" Baars cried. "Do you really think that this—what we have built, and more importantly *what we have discovered*—is as small and as *sordid* as ... as what? A libidinous *ego trip*?"

A Gallic shrug. "Isn't everything?" I replied.

I paused before rounding the courtyard threshold, spared him one final glance. I could see anger crawling into the gap his confidence had left behind. He even held one fist out, not in defiance. If anything, he seemed to be miming the act of seizing something—a bug, a coin, or even a wisp of smoke—from the open air.

"She's dead, Baars. You know that."

"No, Mr. Manning. Quite the contrary ... What I know—*know*, Mr. Manning—is that mankind conquered death long, long ago."

I lay on the hard board that was my motel bed, eyes fixed on the dust-furry blades of the ceiling fan above me. And I *also* sat carefully in my office chair, watching Amanda and Jonathan Bonjour struggle with what always should be a simple question and yet somehow never is.

"He wants to know whether the cult was just an excuse to escape us," Jonathan Bonjour said.

"Troubled," Amanda said stiffly. *"Troub—"*

"Not abusive," Jonathan Bonjour interrupted. *"There's troubled and then there—"*

"I'm sure Mr. Manning re—" Amanda began, her face slack with something—something.

"I just didn't want him to get the wrong idea!"

A pause directed at me. A request for confirmation, reassurance—certainly not more questions. *"And what idea would that be, Mr. Bonjour?"*

"Jon slapped her," Mrs. Bonjour said in a clear, broadcasting tone. *"The last ... fight we had. Jon slapped ... her."*

"I ... ah ..." A fat thumb wiping tears. *"I ... I don't know what to say."* A hand raised as a hood. A breath squeezed to the limit of manly self-restraint.

"Jonny blames himself," Amanda said.

That clinched it. Hearsay or not, Jonathan Bonjour was a lying fat fuck. And what choice did he have? Even the best of us are moral cowards at the best of times. And this guy was a lawyer, which meant he had cashed in his ethical chips a long, long time ago. He spent his every day wringing advantage out of ambiguity.

The only real question was how far would he go.

"I have one last question—for you specifically, Mr. Bonjour. Your law firm regularly contracts private investigators, does it not?"

A moment of shock. Not because I had guessed his profession—what I had thought originally—but because he suddenly understood that he had inadvertently grabbed a steak knife—me—when what he really wanted was to spread some more butter.

"I'm not sure I understand."

"Stuff like this ... personal stuff with consequences that are, well, as big as you can imagine ... such stuff requires trust. Why wouldn't you go to people you know?"

"This wasn't Jonny's idea," Amanda said. But it was his idea. He might have led her to it, rubbed the back of his neck and complained about how so-and-so had fucked up this-or-that, hemmed and hawed until, inevitably, she suggested they go with someone else.

"Even still ..."

Jonathan Bonjour literally squirmed. How could I have missed that?

"No offence, Mr. Manning, but my opinion of your profession is rather ... jaded ..."

Fucking lawyers.

"And?"

"Well, let's just say that I've come to that opinion through long experience."

"But it's not just that," Amanda quickly added. *"You see ... Jonny's already gone down there, asking questions and all, and the people are ... well, more like you."*

Fawk ... The implications of this were just beginning to soak through my deductive hide.

"Like me?" I replied, smiling. *"You mean socio-economically disadvantaged."*

"We thought that you might be able to talk their, uh, language."

"My ad in the Yellow Pages that bad, huh?"

They both laughed. Only one of them sincerely.

Had Bonjour hired me because I smelled like a reliable fuck-up? I could see it all. His wife was jamming him to do something, throw some of that morally dubious cash around. And I—apparent loser that I am—

was exactly what he thought he needed: a way to go through the motions of finding his daughter, all the while ensuring she would never be found ...

Because *he* had murdered her? His own daughter?

Now that was a big pill to swallow, even for a veteran popper like me.

The funny thing was, the longer I whiled away the afternoon poking and prodding everything I had seen and heard, the more Xenophon Baars returned to the fore. As impressive as he was in real time, he was proving to be a persistent fuck in my memory as well.

Again and again, no matter how hard I struggled to focus on the implications of this latest twist, *"Quite the contrary ... What I know—know, Mr. Manning—is that mankind conquered death long, long ago ..."* would rise into the thicket of possibilities ...

No such thing as death. Fawk.

But why would I find the idea so despicable? I mean, aside from the fact that it so obviously catered to human fear and vanity—like the things we're typically inclined to believe.

If you've ever been dumped by someone you loved, then you know the feeling, the tooth-tight, eye-alert, ear-pricking buzz of needing something to be true. Somehow Baars, as insane as he was, had managed to leave me with that beehive of sensations. For the first time in my life I realized that I needed death to be absolute—as final as video review, as irreversible as a frontal lobotomy. I needed it the way composers need silence.

I know it terrifies you, but then you're pretty much normal. This is me we're talking about. How could someone like me not look at it as a sanctuary, a promise?

Death ... The one thing that does not repeat.

Unnerved, I called the motel office and asked for Molly's room. I had heard her bumping around, so I knew she was back from whatever.

When she picked up, there was a curiosity in her voice: like me and most everyone else, she was accustomed to talking exclusively on her cell when on the road.

"The motel *phone?"*

"Ah," I said in a faux dismissive tone, "I was feeling old-fashioned ... You know, romantic."

"Don't you worry about germs? You know, phone germs?"

"I pulled a condom over the talking end."

She graced me with one of those drowsy, late afternoon laughs. *"What's up, Disciple? How was your day at the infamous Compound?"*

Something plucked me in the gut. I get caught like this all the time, striking inappropriate tones at inappropriate moments.

"A cataclysmic revelation."

"Woooo," she drawled. She was warming to my verbal game playing. *"Do tell."*

"Jennifer Bonjour was sexually abused by her father."

A pause, then, *"Ooof."* The thought occurred to me that her sunny New England upbringing hadn't been so sunny after all. Even people without skeletons have at least a bone or two in their closets. Erections have a way of fucking things up.

I gave her the quick skinny on what Anson had said regarding both his relationship with Jennifer and what had happened between her and her father. I also mentioned my previous suspicions: the fact that Bonjour, a lawyer with his own private investigative contacts, would turn to an outsider as dubious as myself.

"So what are you saying? That the man who hired you is a suspect?"

I was beginning to like this, the two of us lying on opposite sides of the same wall, staring off into multiple directions of nowhere, trading questions and observations to and fro. The fact that we were so close yet physically connected with a thousand looping miles of wire struck me as ... well, erotic.

But then, so does most everything.

"This is serious stuff, Molls, and serious stuff requires serious attention. At the very least, Amanda Bonjour needs to know her husband is a scumbag, don't you think?"

An even longer pause.

"Disciple ... You can't say anything."

I understood what she meant: there was a sense in which telling Amanda would simply multiply the number of victims. What was truth compared with the misery such a disclosure would cause? What was justice?

In the subsequent silence, I thought I glimpsed a small fraction of the genuine Molly Modano. The one who tidies herself in the mirror after crying ...

That means something, doesn't it? Glimpsing another's centre of emotional gravity?

"Don't, Disciple. Please don't say a word."

Track Nine
MR. DINKFINGERS

Saturday ...

Once, when I was eleven years old, my parents brought me to a pig-roast-slash-family-reunion hosted by my uncle Tony. Even though Mom and Dad were vegetarians, they allowed me to dig in with the rest of my cousins. They were already troubled—terrified would be the better term—by their little boy's peculiarities, so they were loath to do anything that might further segregate him from his peers. I remember that pork sandwich like it was yesterday. As the forbidden fruit, Meat simply *had* to be the best thing a boy of eleven could eat. Knowledge of grease and evil.

The hitch—and there's always a hitch where I'm concerned—was that Uncle Tony's nearest neighbour happened to be a *pig farmer*, which is why he got the pig dirt cheap, and why his property reeked whenever the breeze blew in from the south—as happened to be the case the day of the Manning family reunion.

As a result, every time I smell roasting pork, I quite literally smell pig shit—and salivate.

So when Molly and I found our way to the backyard of the humble white frame Church of the Third Resurrection, my nostrils flared even as my mouth watered.

"Do you smell anything?" I asked her.

"All stuffed up," she said, fluttering a hand around her small freckled nose. "Hay fever."

The church was situated just outside of town on a small lot fenced with trees and bracken. The lawn was redneck lumpy, but lush and green all the same. Around forty people or so threaded the expanse, forming a web of laughter and conversation. Groups of screaming children bobbed in and out of the fringes, some chasing balls, others chasing one another. The barbecue stood near the back, set perpendicular to a number of tables, most of which were covered in potluck delicacies. A keg of beer gleamed invitingly from one, accompanied by stacks of red plastic cups. The barbecue was one of those homemade jobs: metal drums cut in half then welded together end to end. The pig had been spitted whole. It gleamed and sizzled and smoked—and smelled like mouth-watering pig shit.

"The *head*?" Molly murmured beside me. "Who eats the head?"

"First pig roast, Molls?"

"They don't really *eat* it, do they?"

"Sure do. Actually, it's something of an honour to *eat the cheeks*. So if someone offers you the cheeks, whatever you do, make sure you act gracious and eat them ..."

"What?" She smiled, but with that furrow in her sunburnt brow that told me she worried I was serious. "Fuck that, Disciple. I'm not eating a pig's *face*."

"They'll take offence. Remember, we're *here* for Jennifer. *Jennifer*."

"Fuck that," she repeated, her tone more uncertain, more chastised.

I grinned and sorted through the crowd, the homely congregation of Reverend Nill's Church of the Third Resurrection. A good mix of men and women, old and young. A lot of fat-asses. Several butt-crack cowboys. A couple of so-so attractive women—I've always had a thing for chicks who dress sexy for church. I suppose Molly and I were conspicuous for our good looks, because I counted more than a few curious glances. I even recognized a couple of faces from our canvassing. Waved and smiled. Most everyone sported a red plastic beer cup, always a reassuring sight in a community of believers. I was also relieved to see a fair number of smokers blowing contrails into the motionless late afternoon air. So much so that I took the opportunity to spark a Winston of my own.

Number 99,933.

They were working people, by and large. *My* kind of people, truth be told. Construction workers. Retail employees. High school dropouts like me, with humble skills, warm laughs, and defensive hearts. Suddenly Jonathan Bonjour's choice of Manning Investigations didn't seem so out of sorts after all.

Did he know something I didn't?

I glimpsed a guy swearing and laughing, flicking liquid from his fingertips—beer, I realized. The spill had shrink-wrapped his red T around his gut, and I was just about to glance away when he pulled the shirt off in a single fat-armed motion.

A flash of winter-pale skin. I found myself blinking at the black arms of a tattoo *swastika* flexing across the flab of his gut ...

Uh-oh.

The guy mimed a striptease, swinging his shirt, wagging his hips, and slapping his ass to uproarious laughter. Apparently the Holocaust was no big deal around here.

"You gotta—" Molly began.

"Hey!" a voice shouted from our right. It was Tim. "Hey, Disciple!"

"Remember the cheeks," I muttered to Molly.

"I told you. Fuck that. No way. Besides, what the hell—"

I tuned her out. Tim jogged up to us wearing baggy blue jeans and a vintage Led Zeppelin T-shirt. His face was flushed with something akin to relief. He had been talking about me, I could tell.

I introduced him to Molly, who managed to be pleasant even though she was obviously distracted. Swastikas at church picnics tend to do that, I suppose. She tossed two *What-the-hell-Disciple?* glances in my direction as I made nice with Tim.

"There," the skinny young man said with a smile in his voice. "That's *him*. Reverend Nill."

I have this bad habit, a kind of *hmmpf* habit, where I immediately become skeptical of anyone described in glowing terms. At some level I think I actually *wanted* Reverend Nill to be an obvious putz, someone who would let me sling an arm around Tim's shoulders and say, "I hate to break it to you, kid ..." But if the swastika had spiked the pork punch, then Reverend Nill was a true-blue mickey. He looked unremarkable enough—you know, in that generic, doughy all-American way. Fit. Short dark hair. But his eyes, fawk. Even from a dozen yards away they fairly sparked Prussian blue. The first thing I literally thought was, *Rasputin.*

Rasputin. Have you ever seen pictures of that crazy fucker? A look that gropes you. Dead a century and still makes you feel your fly's undone.

Now, we all know how it works in the movies: the guy with the freaky eyes is *always* guilty. But this wasn't a movie, and as it so happened, I knew someone *else* with eyes like that, someone I would have died for had he not died for me first. Sean O'May.

One-hundred-and-sixty-pound frame. Thousand-pound gaze. Give you Alzheimer's trying to stare him down.

So I didn't jump to conclusions. I really didn't.

No, it was actually the chick glaring in ostrich fury at his side that sealed the deal. She was kind of hot, actually, only in a more mature way than Molly. High heels pricked into turf. Spray paint for blue jeans. A rack that would make strange babies cry.

"Who's the woman next to him?" I asked Tim.

"Uh, his wife, Sheila."

"Huh," I said, thinking, *Now that's one Angry Bitch ...*

"Well, *she* looks friendly," Molly muttered.

Gawd, I loved her when she was sarcastic.

Oh ya, I *know* angry bitches. They're pretty much my investigative bread and butter: nothing pries open the wallet quite as effectively as vindictiveness. A true, High Holy Angry Bitch would burn down the world just to see you scorched. She would sit beside you in the Burn Victims Unit filing her nails and then, when the nurses weren't looking, she would start wiping her—what is it called? emery board?—across your blistered skin.

In this instance, the most important thing to know about Angry Bitches is the *kind of men* who find themselves in their evil clutches. You see, typically, Angry Bitches sink their claws into the soft white souls of Nice Guys—you know the type, the kind who are blessedly happy to be relieved of command. A few Hapless Dudes fall into their clutches here and there—you never know where you're going to bounce on a bad rebound—but otherwise the main victim of the Angry Bitch is not a victim at all ... Far from it, in fact.

Sociopaths.

Given my own fears of falling under this category, I've actually spent quite some time pondering what it is that brings Angry Bitches and Sociopaths together. And I've come to the conclusion that, aside from the rigours of compulsive sexuality, Sociopaths are drawn to Angry Bitches because they, and they alone, *can make them feel.* I've often noticed in the Mexican soap opera I call my romantic life that it's painfully easy to confuse emotional violence with passion. So it strikes me that if you're generally passionless, if you belong to that not-as-small-as-you-think minority that has the same emotional response to words like "rape" as to words like "chair," then an Angry Bitch is bound to stick out in the long string of women you break and humiliate—to seem exceptional, even.

So there it was. I took one look at Reverend Nill's wife and pretty much instantly realized that Nill was more than just another evangelical, more than just another man whose vicious circles were exceedingly small.

He was a big fat Sociopath.

Which is to say, my new *prime suspect.*

In the absence of conscience, there's pretty much always some kind of crime. Nine out of ten Presidents agree.

So. Move on over, Baars. A new freak had come to Suspicion Town.

"Um, *Disciple* ..." Molly said, with the blank look of a babe soaking in a bad vibe.

"Thank you, Tim," I said with an air of gratitude I almost felt. "This is *awesome* ... Can't you smell it, Molly?" Of course all I could smell was pig shit. Don't ask me how memories can reek; all I know is that they do. "My mouth's watering already!"

The kid's grin fairly bubbled toothpaste, it was so raw and uncut.

Fawk.

"*Johnny's* the one," he explained in a rush. "The one responsible. He's an old buddy of the Rev's from seminary. Wait till you try his sauce, man. Positively. Kick. Ass."

"Who's he? The *biker* guy?"

There was actually a group of three *What's-wrong-with-this-picture?* types milling around a weather-worn picnic table behind and to the left of the good Reverend. Two looked like junkies, you know, with mean, hooded glares perched in beef-jerky bodies. But it was the guy who imperiously towered over them whom I had asked Tim about: auburn hair to his shoulders, a beard to his chest, and statuesque, a veritable museum exhibit of humanity ...

"Everyone calls him Dinkfingers," Tim laughed, "because of the size of his meathooks."

Even Molly had to chuckle at that.

"Scary-looking dude," I said.

"Yeah. Don't mind that—his looks, I mean. He's a fucking stand-up guy. Stand. Up."

And he was also an AB, I realized. A member of the Aryan Brotherhood. I could tell by his tatts, which were somewhat more subtle than Swastika-Gut's but just as clear. I found myself wondering about Reverend Nill's "seminary."

Another strike against the good Reverend. The future tends to resemble the past. Nobody knew this with quite the intimacy that I did. It was my fucking curse in a nutshell.

"Ah ... *Disciple*?" Molly said, nudging me with her elbow this time. "We should—"

"Well? Dutchie, my boy, aren't you going to introduce us?"

"—don't you think?" Molly finished.

I strolled across the lumpy grass with Tim to my left and Molly in wary tow.

Introductions were exchanged. Sheila Nill's smile made her look about as pleasant as a Klingon war cruiser. I almost shouted, *Shields up!* as I shook her clawed fingers. Reverend Nill folded my hand in two warm palms, positively beamed Christian welcome. Johnny Dinkfingers—that name still cracks me up, fawk—engulfed my little-boy hand in his banana-bunch grip. Smiling was beneath him, apparently.

"Disciple!" Nill exclaimed. "I *love* your name."

"My parents were nudists," I said. That got a laugh, even though I wasn't joking.

Tim explained that we were the canvassers he had told them about, and the good Reverend described his congregation's shock over Jennifer Bonjour's disappearance. "Would you please tell Amanda and Jonathan that our church is *praying* for them? Praying so hard."

Afterward, he excused himself with an apology—apparently he had a small sermon to make before Johnny began carving the "wonderful pig," as he put it.

Led by Tim, Molly and I retreated into the crowd of beer bellies and bra-strap-pinched shoulders that had gathered round the massive barbecue. Nill, looking dapper in his blue jeans and black button-up, began in the standard way. Community in Jesus. Salvation in Christ. All the usual bullshit, with meat sizzling and smoking behind him. But as he continued, the rhetoric became more and more heated, as did the response of the people surrounding us.

He told us all a little story. About how among the beasts that God created were the false men, created before the sixth day. About how Adam, whose name meant "shows blood in face" in ancient Hebrew, was the first *true* man, imbued with the sparks of divinity: conscience and shame. "Only the white man can blush," Nill cried over a ragged chorus of amens, "because only the white man is *human*! Because only the white man carries the Law of God in his heart!" The mud people live like animals, he went on to explain, because animals *are simply what they are*, subject to the dominion of White America.

"Does a man let his dog run wild in the streets?"

He talked about the serpent, Satan, and his seduction of Eve, which led to the birth of Cain, the first Jew. About how this "serpent race" was the *true* threat, the deceiver, spinning the lies of liberalism, convincing the sons and daughters of Adam to lie with the two-legged beasts ...

Fuck. Me. Gently.

You hear about these people, you hear about their whacked beliefs, and you think, *No ... Come on ...* Then your drunk cousin pulls you aside at Christmas, tells you he's afraid you're going to burn in hell. Black heart, black skin—what did it matter? Albert was right. People are capable of believing anything so long as it flatters them.

Soon Nill was railing about ZOG—the Zionist Occupied Government—and the coming Conflagration (pronounced Con-flag-*ray*-

shunnn), the racial Ragnarök that would see the righteous raised up out of the iniquity of liberal equity, redeemed, purified—and, of course, firmly in charge.

Funny how it all comes down to power, isn't it? You might almost think moral indignation was just another scam.

"Um, Disciple?" Molly began again—more discreetly than before, but still with the resentment of being stuck next to someone sick in the grocery checkout.

"Having fun?" I muttered back.

"Fun? *Fun?*"

"Yeah, you know, investigative *journalizing* ..."

She punched me in the arm for that—you know, the kind of smack that tells you what she really wants is to kick you in the nuts. But at least she stopped with the "Ums."

There was an organizational pause as the actual meal was laid out. Voices swelled, marbled with laughter and all the other sounds that soft people make no matter how vicious their beliefs. Molly kept nagging me—she had seen enough, it was time to go, she couldn't stand fatty foods anyway—but I was intent on watching Johnny Dinkfingers and his two junkie pals talking around the picnic table.

With Tim in tow, Reverend Nill came up to Johnny, who loomed over him, nodding. One of the junkies spit. Then the other, the one with the ashtray eye sockets, abruptly turned to me and grinned ...

Suddenly they were all walking toward Molly and me. The Church Elders, fawk. With the Angry Bitch not far behind.

"Just follow my lead," I muttered to Molly. She wanted to scream in exasperation, I could tell, but it was too late for any last-second commentary on her part. Reverend Nill was nearly on top of us, all good grooming habits and phony smiles.

"So!" he called out in ministerial tones. "Young Tim here has told me that you were posing some interesting questions. About ... *context,* was it?"

The fact that he brought Johnny Dinkfingers and the others told me he knew something was up.

"*Loved* the sermon," I replied.

"He's being sarcastic," Sheila said in that commenting-on-people-as-if-they-weren't-there tone. Another Angry Bitch thing. I'm always mildly amazed that racists have wives, as if part of me always assumes that women are too sensible for that racket.

"No-no," I laughed, holding my palms out in an *Easy-girl!* wave. "Don't get me wrong. I'm a *huge fan* of bigotry ..."

I'm not sure anything took a breath on that church lawn for a good second or two. Even the ants froze in their tracks. I could see Tim in my periphery, as pale as the Holy Ghost.

"We're not bigots," Reverend Nill said with a patient, parental air. "Just children of God."

"Now *me*," I continued, my gaze flat and friendly, "I hate stupid people. It's a little trickier than skin colour, so I guess I envy your set-up that way. Kind of like sorting beans, isn't it? White. Black. Yellow. With idiots you got to know what to look for. Things like simplistic, superficial thinking—you know, the tendency to look at things *skin* deep. And flattery—that's another big one. Idiots are always saying things like, *'Oh, me so special!'* and for the most fucking retarded reasons you could imagine. Like, because there's this dead guy who loves them or because they got pink nipples ..."

I swear I could hear Molly's watch go tick, tick, tick.

To his credit, Nill's endearing shepherd-among-his-flock smile never faltered in the slightest. But his crazy-ass eyes, oh my, did they *shine*. And Johnny Dinkfingers, he frowned like a cartoon Santa. Sheila I expected to de-cloak and launch a couple of photon torpedoes any instant.

"How do you guys think you would stack up?" I asked in an amiable, third-party tone. "If I were to give you IQ tests, I mean."

"What?" the towering biker asked.

My smile was pure ham and cheese. "Apparently not so well."

You see, in the movies it's always *Mom* who's sacred, the one thing people do not dare insult. But in the real world—and that includes Italians—people really don't get all that worked up about their moms. The Holy Grail of insults, if anything, is their *intelligence.*

This is just my way of saying that I was being deliberately provocative—in case the ball's bouncing a little too quickly for you to follow.

I have a simple, three-stage rule when actively working someone for information. The three Rs, I call them. First, reason. If not reason, then ridicule. If not ridicule, then a hard right hook. Since I was dealing with obvious, abject idiots, I decided to forgo stage one.

This is just one of many things that let me know I'm not normal: hitting people. I feel some kind of adrenalin spike, I suppose, just enough to make my pits ripe. Sometimes I fart. But otherwise it just feels like business, just another tool of persuasion.

An old girlfriend of mine put it best. "Always anxious, but never afraid," she said after a bad night at the bar. "You do realize that neurotics are supposed to be passive-aggressive."

Normal neurotics, that is ...

The fact that people respond the way they do says it all, really. We are born to violence. Our bodies react to it instinctively. I mean, some people piss themselves—literally. A fair fraction swing right back—I can appreciate that. Fair is fair. And who knows? Maybe *I'm the one* who needs a little persuading. Some scream like they've caught fire or something—I hate those fuckers. But most—a solid majority—go real quiet. Nothing like a smack to reacquaint you with your priorities.

I've seen the look enough to instantly recognize it by now. So I usually grin and pull a fin out of my wallet. Information becomes real cheap real quick after a smack or two.

Now I know you like to think you're like me, but you're not. Not if you're reading this you're not. If you met me, you would take the five, cough up your honour, and count your blessings. Nurse your wounded ego with a bag of Doritos or something.

Everyone but everyone knows that readers are pussies.

I had assumed Johnny Dinkfingers was my natural opponent, so I had squared my stance with reference to him. But Reverend Nill, perhaps seized by some instinct for initiative, beat me to the punch, so to speak.

He kind of *sidled* into my space, catching me off guard in a way that baffles me to this very day. His features became little more than a mob of angry extras about the leading role of his mad white glare. Somehow I knew things weren't going to deteriorate into violence—not *physical* violence. Not at this moment, anyway. Somehow I knew something stranger, something *worse*, was about to happen.

He leaned in close—smooch close. He was about four inches shorter than me, so he had to bend his face back to better wire his gaze into my own. And wire them together he did. An arc-welder look. A heartbeat had passed, less, and yet in that time the church backyard, the encircling fence of strangers, even the afternoon sky blew away like smoke.

Just Nill staring, leaning into me with chimpanzee rage.

Without warning, he raised his hands to his chest and began drumming—fucking *drumming*!—this primal beat. Then, his pupils soldered to the centre of my attention, the veins across his temple pulsing, he began to *chant*—a kind of rap, only infused with adrenalin and rage.

"God loves!" he began rasping. *"Those who hate!"*

His breath smelled like expensive cheese.

"Since Adam! Since Eve! Since the dawn of fate!"

And on it went. A litany of all the individuals and peoples cursed and destroyed in the Bible.

Cain. The heroes and monsters who brought about the Flood. Esau. Sodom and Gomorrah.

"As He rains fire on the Sodomite!

So He exterminates the Canaanite!"

The work of a vengeful God, a bloodthirsty God, one who punished virtue and rewarded deception. A God who *chose* some over others, and who delivered victims to the righteous in a pageant as long as history itself.

It was surreal. *Vicious* in a way that I really can't describe. His look, Maori wide and unflinching, seemed the very eyes of Judgment. His face, red with feral intensity, seemed a topographical map of hell. And his voice, scarcely human, a fist knotted about ten thousand strands of hatred.

On and on he went, to the staccato beat of palms against his chest ... *Boom-shicka-boom.*

Glaring at me like an evil hypnotist.

Describing all the poor bastards obliterated by the Christian God of Love.

It seemed I was next.

"You. Have got. To be fucking kidding me ..."

This was Molly. All this time she'd been as nervous as a lone hottie stranded in line with a bunch of hairy old truck drivers at the DMV. Now she stood there, her red hair aflame in the evening sunlight, staring at Nill with dumbfounded disgust. "What? Are you a *fucking psycho* or something, Reverend? Huh? I mean. Come. Fucking. On. What kind of goof *does that*?"

And somehow I just knew that pretty much every word she said was digestible ...

Except *goof.*

It's a prison thing.

"Goof?" Nill replied, twisting two fingers against his temple. "Psycho? What do you think happens when God—the *God Almighty*—lands in your brain? You think you stay sane? Read your Bible, bitch. All his vessels crack. All of 'em!"

"Some," Molly said, "apparently more than others."

"Manners," Nill grated. "Manners, Missy! The Good Lord has a way of teaching them!" He glanced at the hulking shadow of Johnny Dinkfingers, who almost instantly stepped forward, his hand drawn back for a bitch-slap ...

And my reflexes took over.

Johnny Dinkfingers was no pussy. He was big, surprisingly fit and fast, and, perhaps more importantly, he was *hard.* Prison teaches you that a straight line runs through every violent encounter. If you fail to find and to follow it, you will be maimed or dead. Ex-cons tend not to fuck around.

Mr. Dinkfingers was all these things and *mean* besides. But the sad truth was that he simply did not stand a chance.

Those of you with any long-standing involvement in sports know exactly what I'm talking about, even if you still fool yourself into thinking otherwise. I have heard no fewer than 3,687 fuckers claim, in this way or that, they were "ass-kickers." Of those, only 16 or so were credible: real ass-kickers tend not to talk about kicking ass all that much (though with all this MMA crap I seem to hear it more and more).

See, if you play a sport, you have an inkling of just how vast the difference in skill and strength can be between players. Now take that inkling and apply it to combat, and you have a sense of just how unlike the movies real fights are. Trust me: you do not ever—*ever*—want to find yourself in the ring with someone like me.

There was simply no way I could ever gain the trust of these fuckers the way things stood, even if I had five years and wept at the mere mention of Herr Hitler. I was too clever, too arrogant, and just too damn good-looking to ever really be trusted by men like these. So I had to reach for the next best tool in my tool box: *fear.* Not that these guys were going to go all wobbly in the knees when they saw me in the street—not by a long shot. But they had *done time,* which meant that *criminal paranoia* was stamped as deep as a sex change into them. Cops, you see, have procedures, all kinds of rules that make them fluffy and cute so long as you don't stumble into their sights—in which case they can bring the hammer down hard. But me? I was an *unknown.* And in a few moments I was about to become an unknown who could not be intimidated or otherwise bargained with—and who could kick some serious ass.

A *trained* unknown.

I was about to become the big *Who-the-fuck?* in the marrow of their little world. The *harbinger,* baby.

And I had come bearing a gift—a simple feeling, one that said, *I dunno but we gotta do something ...*

Something!

And something always leaves tracks.

I caught the arm swinging toward Molly—before she had even registered it, I think. I stepped into its lumbering arc, twisted and turned, drawing the big man around and down. He didn't really have much choice, given that he was simply following his own momentum—coaxed along arcs of my design, of course.

Afterward, I simply stood as relaxed as before, doing my best to appear as though I hadn't even moved. A little Jet Li drama never hurts, I've found, when the violence is secondary to the message.

"Now where I come from," I said in a toke-sharing voice, "you never—*never*—hit a white woman ..."

Tim gaped in abject horror. The other sheeple just stood blinking—a critical incident processing lag of some kind. Stupid Nazi fuckers. Even stunned, Johnny Dinkfingers rolled forward on his rump, reaching for his boot—a knife of some kind, I imagine. The world becomes a Yard when you're an ex-con. You always come armed.

Some woman screamed—a latecomer to the party.

Only Reverend Nill seemed unaffected. He held out a hand to stop Johnny mid-motion then turned to me with a mild expression of disappointment, placid while his Angry Bitch wife cackled in drunken laughter. It was pretty fucking hilarious, if you thought about it.

"I thank you for coming," the Good Reverend Nill said.

"Sure thing," I replied, drawing a shell-shocked Molly away from the crowd. "What time were Sunday services?"

He blinked those wild, freaky eyes.

"Ten," he replied. "In the *A.M.*"

Molly started crying on the drive back to the motel. I apologized—*for real* for a change. Told her some nonsense about provocation, the perfect balance of aggression and intelligence.

I sometimes forget what it's like ...

Being normal.

She should have been furious with me for putting her in a situation like that. Instead, she was embarrassed. She was young, eager to hammer pitons into the sheer cliffs of print fame and fortune. Her head was stuffed with almost as many ideals as romantic notions. Everyone knows that investigative journalists are fearless hard-asses, capable of staring down civil wars in illiterate nations, and here she was, getting all weepy about a little jiu-jitsu at a church picnic. She kept her face averted, pretended to stare at the setting sun through the passenger window. From time to time she wiped her eyes with fluttering fingers.

I could even hear her curse herself as she marched to her room.

"They were *Nazis!*" I cried out in encouragement.

That was something, wasn't it?

* * *

Once in my room, I called Albert, left a message on his machine or wherever the hell it is you leave messages nowadays—the nowhere of the Web probably. I needed to find out as much as I could about the Church of the Third Resurrection as soon as possible. There was piss all about them on the Web.

Say you were in a bind, a really, really tight bind, like the mob was out to hit you or something. Now, most men pretend they've stepped out of a movie, make believe they're ready, willing, even *eager* to do what it takes, no matter what that involves. Most men pretend to be capable of calculated murder. But press them, and when the time comes I guarantee you they'll find some bullshit way of backing out. Everyone postures in a vacuum, but when circumstances take hold, the sorting happens real quick.

Now, you can call this cowardice if you want. But let's face it, murder is stupid, particularly if you have any personal connection to the dude you intend to murder. So I'm more inclined to call this intelligence rather than cowardice—the brave ones are the ones who shatter lives and go to prison.

Reverend Nill understood this all too well. He knew what it took to get people to kill for him.

The key is to get them young, when peer group pressures are well-nigh irresistible. Then you start small: graffiti, other kinds of petty vandalism. Then you do something *for* them, something low-risk but illegal all the same. Like so many things human, trust is the foundation of co-operative crime, and few things inspire trust like someone breaking the law for you—actually risking his neck. Then you ask them to commit some crime in return—to reciprocate. Once their cherry is popped, once they get away with something *bad*, it becomes oh so easy, even addictive for some types.

You don't need to be a chromosomal mutant to enjoy hurting people. You just need to believe that your victims *deserve* their pain. And we're wired to think that already.

No. Reverend Nill was no fool.

This was the realization I kept in mind as I lay on my bed, boots and all: that I was dealing with a sociopath in the full manipulative sense of the term. If Reverend Nill was behind Jennifer Bonjour's disappearance, then he was "behind the scenes" in every sense of the word. Not only would he have a herd of complimentary character witnesses, he would have an ironclad alibi.

Which meant the place to start would be his *tools.*

The moment came to me as it always does, the one most pertinent to my questions and concerns. Johnny Dinkfingers and his two junkie cohorts, sitting at the crooked picnic table. They were both as skinny as marathon runners, but the one was older, sporting a grey mullet, while the other, the younger, had short-cropped hair dyed an artificial black. They were having a long conversation without jokes, eyes fixed then wandering. Looking down and bored, then matching gazes.

A single nod from Johnny, eyes closing as the mouth said, *"Okay. I see."*

The older junkie sucked in his lips. *"Sheesh. Too much."*

Fists clenched to mime blows given and received.

A face raised to offer bruised evidence. The younger one had a shiner.

Laughter, but reserved, as if they talked on the corner of a major thoroughfare.

Johnny shot them a look over his shades. His eyes darted up and out, then down again. A knuckle glanced his nose. Weight shifted from foot to foot. A string of inaudible, unreadable words. From beneath his sunglasses his lips said, *"Give me a fucking break."*

An impassive look from the younger one. *"So?"*

A sour stretch of Johnny's lips.

And the sentence I swear that I saw. *"She's dead."*

Johnny shrugged and spat. The old junkie turned to me and grinned.

* * *

A hard knock at the door startled me from my reverie. It was a wet-haired Molly, her freckled face scrubbed of makeup, staring up at me with wide and hungry eyes. Suddenly I understood what it was she wanted from me. She wanted my cynicism, my numbness ... She wanted my *disease.*

Because she thought they would make her strong. Stupid twit.

"I know ..." she began, breaking eye contact and hesitating. "I know you said you wanted to ... work ... or whatever the hell it is you do."

"Recollect. Remember. I kick back, sort and sift and interpret."

"If you say so."

"I say so."

I breathed deep. Gawd, how I love the smell of a woman fresh out of the shower.

"Well, I just wanted to *thank* you, you know, for what happened back there."

"No thanks necessary. Getting hot young stringers into life-threatening situations is just what I do."

She laughed, looked at the finger she had raised to pick at her hair. "Yeah? What were you thinking?" she asked, cross-eyed.

"Just doing what I do best, Molls."

"Which is?"

A strange pang accompanied the question. Hard to explain, actually, like doing a somersault without moving, a kind of figure-field inversion of the soul. I could tell from her eyes that she could see it on my face, all that past crashing in. I reached for her hand, retreated with her into the orange of my room's tacky light.

"Screwing with people."

Oh, I got *laid* that night.

Ladies, you can deny it all you want, talk about how violence makes you ill—whatever. Weird as it is, a good number of you *like* it, not as a spectator sport—more like an Olympic demonstration. For whatever reason, a man's hands tingle all that much more when they're scabbed with another man's blood.

You see, we're savages together, you and I.

Children of Reverend Nill.

Track Ten
FORTY THINGS WE SHARE

Saturday night ...

One man's dog is another woman's pig. I get that. But I like to think that I'm a dog in a *deeper* sense.

Did you know that the word *cynic* comes from the ancient Greek for *dog*?

Apparently the Roman Cynics were actually *evangelical*—some to the point of burning themselves alive to make their point. They went around preaching virtue and screaming hypocrite everywhere they went—kind of like Jesus. Fuck that. No, give me the ancient Greek version. Give me good old Diogenes, living in a stone tub, tossing the odd load in the agora, and searching, endlessly searching, for a single honest man. The dude that Alexander the Great said he wanted to be were he not Alexander. The guy that Plato called Socrates gone mad.

Even better, give me Diogenes *as he should have been.* Doglike in every sense of the word. Gnawing on his leash. Chewing up his master's shoes. Crapping on the neighbour's putting-green lawn.

And, of course, humping everything that moved.

Rules, brother. That's the real difference between you and me. Every-fucking-where you turn: admonishments, tickets, citations, not to mention out-and-out convictions. Judgments, endless condemnations, raised on the clay brick of half-baked belief. You can't see them because you can't *remember*, because the million ways you repeat continually topple into the bottomless abyss of five minutes ago. Over and over, the same way, the same time. Even your flaws and foibles—*even your sins*—follow ironclad commandments. Again and again.

Rules. *This* is how you remember. Rules are what binds you to your past. The content of your life shrivels into a wicker cage of imperatives, where mine is trucked to the landfill.

It's a paradox, really. Your inability to remember dooms you to repeat things—and here's the kicker—*for the first time.* You are imprisoned and utterly convinced you are free. While here I stand, soaked in an awareness of everything I've done, totally able to step sideways, to walk perpendicularly to you and your pantomime world—able at any instant to do something radical, something genuinely *new* ...

And knowing, because you're so fucking predictable, that I would simply run afoul of your rules. That first you would tag me, lest you lose track of me in the absent-minded scrum, call me "crazy" or "troubled" or "pathologically self-centred." And then you would bag me, dump me into some Secure Housing Unit, or give me one of those jackets with armholes but no cuffs.

So, I *try* to be a "good boy," even if I shit on the carpet from time to time. Begging for treats, barking at strangers, not so much feeling shame as cocking my head and watching it.

Whatever it takes to keep the feed bowl full.

Take the Holocaust, for instance. I mean, seriously. How, after the greatest, most thoroughly chronicled tragedy in the history of the human race, could a cadre of *Nazis* take root and blossom in a town like Ruddick, PA?

Fawk. Kind of says it all, doesn't it?

This is generally what I do when I can't sleep—rant to the congregation of me. I usually try to take advantage of my insomnia, use the time to relive the particulars of whatever case I happen to be working on. But for some reason I found myself batted back and forth between Reverend Nill and his surreal God Plays Favourites rap session, and Baars saying, *"What if cynicism and self-righteousness were one and the same thing?"* I understood the comment this time around: the self-righteous prick was calling me a self-righteous prick—an irony I could appreciate. Condemning others becomes a trifle when you stand condemned in your own eyes. I got it.

Even still. Fuck. Him.

I stared at Molly in the gloom. She lay on her side facing me, her hand out as though braced against the possibility of the mattress tipping. Her hair had been swept back in some accident of restless sleep so that her face lay bared in the dim illumination. Feminine yet strong in an impish, Julia Roberts kind of way. Full lips that I could still taste on my own. I slowly drew the sheet from her freckled shoulder down the line of her arm and along the curve of her waist. Her brow furrowed in dream perplexity. Her top leg was drawn forward, concealing her pussy like a Renaissance nude. Lines of white etched her horizons, from the arc of her shoulders to the long curve of her buttock.

I could see her breathe.

Sasha Lang, that old philosopher girlfriend I told you about, once claimed I was the kind of guy who knew the price of everything and the value of nothing. That was January 20, 2001, another bad day, as it so happened. The description struck me as apt enough. Sasha loved to theorize, and I loved to tease—not a great combination given that teasing is so much easier. She had figured it out—Christ, she had an IQ that would make most physicists blush. She understood that a cynic is just someone who believes nothing to better judge everything.

So was *that* what I was? Just one more pious prick?

Take Molly, nude and unconscious, her skin pimpling in the air-conditioned cool. I understood what made my gaze so ancient, so lecherous. I understood what made her so ideal, so desirable that whole industries had been raised around her. There was promise in her youth, strength in her morals, glory in her naïveté ...

I understood all that—even as the hour hand crawled along my belly toward the high noon of my navel.

I could see, even appreciate, the value of things apart from all our tacky self-aggrandizing.

And that's the *point*, now, isn't it, Doctor? Here I was, poised on the threshold of something breathless and profound, peering into the mists, straining to make lucid my epiphany ...

And all I really wanted to do was fuck.

That was about when my cellphone spanked out its riff and Molly's eyes popped open. She blinked, curled into a shivering ball. Her gaze faltered then focused, first on me, then on my sheet-tenting boner.

"Disciple? What the fuck?"

I leaned back to grab my cell.

She flopped like a fish to her side of the bed, snapped on the bedside light.

I held my hand out against the glare, concentrated on the voice murmuring through the receiver. *"Disciple. This is Nolen here. I just wanted to give you a heads-up before I arrived."*

Arrived?

"You ... You ..." she said, sitting up with the sheets clutched tight to her neck, squinting and scowling beneath a dishevelled pile of hair. "Ugh! You're such a fucking *creep*!"

"Yeah," I said to the Chief in a rough voice. "Do you know what time it is?"

"Sorry," Nolen said in an entirely genuine tone. *"But I'm kind of in over my head with this one."*

"What?" Molly continued ranting. "Were you ... like ... *beating off* or something?"

I clubbed her in the head with a pillow.

"You found something?" I asked.

"Another one. We found another one."

Molly was talking to herself now, her hands raised in *Why-me-God?* exasperation, her expression one of abject, mystified disgust. "While I was *sleeping*? Ah! *Ah!*"

"What?" I said into the receiver. "Another finger?"

That shut her up.

"No," Nolen said. *"A toe. This time we found a baby toe."*

We were scarcely dressed when Nolen's headlights panned across the room's curtained windows. Molly had spared me a couple of scowls but otherwise pulled on her clothes—a white button-up and blue jeans—with her eyes unfocused in that unfinished-business way.

"Look," I finally said as the headlights flashed out, "I *wasn't* whacking off, okay. I was just ... admiring ..."

"Not now, Disciple."

"I'd be a liar if I said I didn't *want* to ..." I added as I strode to the door in anticipation of Nolen's knock. I pulled the chain—the church picnic had left my nerves a little peckish.

"I'm supposed to be flattered, huh."

"You make me fat, baby. What can I say? Hi, Caleb."

Policemen typically look intimidating when they darken your door, but Nolen had too much of a Barney Fife aura. He was drawn, taut in voice and manner. "Um, would you mind coming with me to the station?"

He looked like a kid, standing as he did, awkward in the irregular parking lot light, a high school senior suddenly tapped to play lead man in his community's first bona fide disaster. He had that overmatched mien, face and eyes disconnected lest the fear shine through. Like Bush on the day after 9/11, before prayer fooled him into thinking he was equal to the trap fate had set for him.

"The finger belonged ..." he began, "or, ah ... *belongs* to Jennifer. And now with the toe ..." He grabbed the back of his neck, blinked skyward. "... we're almost certainly dealing with a homicide ..." he said, letting his voice trail away.

Homicide! his eyes repeated.

I understood—or thought I understood—what he was driving at. "It's okay, Caleb. I'll call the Bonjours first thing in the morning." The guy had enough on his plate as it was. Besides, I had given too many people too much bad news in my life. Practice makes perfect.

And as any private dick will tell you, it pays to collect markers from The Authorities.

Caleb's relief was obvious and immediate. "Thanks, Disciple ... I would really appreciate that. I mean, I know I'll have to talk to them ... eventually. B-but I'm, ah ..." His voice pinched about a sob. Apparently he had bigger terrors on his list. "I'm, ah, not so good at, ah, you know, *failure* ..."

Why was I the only person who had assumed she was dead all along?

Nolen raised thumb and forefinger to the bridge of his nose. "It's, ah ... It's, ah ..."

He was crying—crying!

Fawk. Me.

I blame it on Hollywood. Christ, I blame it on our whole fucking *Just-believe-in-yourself* culture. The problem wasn't that Caleb Nolen possessed the sensitivities of an interpretative dancer; the problem was that he had been fooled into thinking he could be *anything he wanted*, if only he were to try-try-try. He had been an imaginative little boy, I'm sure, one captivated by blazing images of justice and domination, when he should have been practising how to stand on his tippytoes.

"Just, the stress, ya know?" he exhaled. He tried to smile, grimaced instead.

"Go slow, Caleb," I said with a reassuring smile. Iraq—the old one, fought for the old Bush—had taught me how to fake crisis-compassion. "Remember, the freak show is just getting started. Everything works better if you tune out the noise and take things one step at a time."

"One step at a time," he repeated, breathing as though preparing for a dive. He did his best to avoid Molly's gaze, which condemned all the more because of its obvious pity.

He swallowed, nodded to himself as if remembering some original purpose. "Sorry, Disciple. Stupid, huh? A chief of police who loses it over a baby toe!" He flinched from this line of observation, realizing that it was making things worse. What was important was that he pretend ... That was the human answer.

He copped an artificially relaxed pose, hand on hip, something an underwear model might practise in a mirror. "Um, hey, Disciple? Have you ever worked a case ... I mean, I was wondering, if you had ever worked a case involving, ah ... you know"—a quick swallow—"ritualistic murder."

That was how Molly and I found ourselves in the back of Nolen's cruiser, whisking beneath a long necklace of street lights. Nothing was said for a minute or two. Molly and I just sat stewing in our embarrassment for Nolen. I could almost feel him grinding his teeth in shame.

I was actually relieved when my cell riffed for the second time that night.

"Hi, Disciple. Albert." I could tell from his tone that he was embarrassed about his previous call on Thursday night. *"I know it's late, but I thought I should take a chance anyway—leave you a message at least. Did I catch you at a bad time?"*

"Kind of. Hospital emergency room, actually."

"Oh ... *Is everything okay?*"

"Don't have much time, Albert. I think I see the proctologist waving to me now." Molly punched me in the arm for saying that.

"The Church of the Third Resurrection ..." he said with an air of hesitation. *"I actually came across them researching my last book. They're what's called a Christian Identity sect."*

I knew a thing or two about identity politics and several things more about evangelical Christianity, enough to know that any love child of theirs was bound to be a homely bastard.

"Lemme guess. White supremacists, right?"

An appreciative pause. *"You do know why it's called the third resurrection, don't you?"*

It was a good question—one of those obvious things I keep overlooking. "I don't know, Albert. They all seem to have some kooky name. I just assumed they used it to differentiate their racist brand, you know. It's a crowded market out there."

"Well, they call it the third resurrection because they think the Second Coming's already happened ..."

"You mean Jesus has *already* come back?"

"Oh yeah. Only this time around he went by the name Adolf Hitler *..."*

Ever get that wet-your-mental-pants feeling? I always knew I was swimming in the deep end—that I was investigating a *murder*—but this was where I realized I had forgotten my water wings.

"You gotta be kidding."

"Shit you not. Just watch yourself, okay? These people may seem silly, but

they have their fair share of dedicated fanatics. From what I can tell, they spend most of their time whacking each other, but ..."

I just love the way civilians throw words like *whacking* around. Fucking HBO, man.

"Life just wouldn't be the same without me, huh, Albert?"

"Don't underestimate them, Disciple. There's a good reason we can't stamp this lunacy out. Just look at the nearest school playground. We're born little fascists."

I've always thought that kids are overrated—even as a kid. Can't hold their liquor worth shit.

"Hitler as Jesus, huh?"

"I told you, man. Nothing's quite so cheap as belief."

Sometimes insights hit you so hard, so fully and completely, that your IQ drops through the bottom of your boots. How could I be such an idiot?

"And let me guess," I said, my scalp prickling. "Their cardinal sin is ..."

Albert said all he needed to say. *"Miscegenation."*

People get all fucked up about purity. I dated this chick, Brenda Okposo, who was a social psychology professor teaching religion at New York University. Bitter and beautiful—my kind of girl. A "sessional," she called herself, which led me to crack innumerable jokes about our "sessions" together. Anyway, she said that humans have specialized regions of the brain dedicated to avoiding contaminants. Apparently even before we knew about germs, we had evolved instinctive aversions that helped us avoid them. Then along comes culture, and the ability to train children to attach aversions to this or that, so that we can be utterly revolted, out-and-out nauseated, by pretty much anything.

We get all fucked up about purity.

The ironic thing was that it was a small disagreement about condoms that festered into the blowout that ended—or "Brended" as I joked to my buddies at the time—my relationship with Dr. Okposo. She got it in her head that condoms were simply another expression of our culture's pathological addiction to purity. So, of course, the best way to slip this obsessive noose was to submit to a battery of clinicians and blood tests and throw the rubbers out the window. I was busted at the time, flat-fucking-broke, and too proud to take her up on her offer to pay.

The last words I heard were literally, "I can't believe you're choosing cock balloons over me!"

That was October 3, 2002—what should have been a bad day, but was just too weird to be anything ... really.

"Caleb," I said, leaning forward to talk through the slot in the safety glass. I fixed his eyes in the rear-view mirror. "I just have a couple questions." He was enough of a nervous Nellie that I could tell he knew what I was about to ask him. He had caught my conversation with Albert—or as much as he needed, anyway.

"Shoot."

"Why didn't you say anything about the Church of the Third Resurrection?"

When he failed to answer, I glanced at Molly, saw the twinge of sudden apprehension.

"Yeah ..." he finally said, his eyes bouncing back and forth from the street in the windshield to me in the mirror. "What about them?"

Evasion. Plain and simple. This was when it dawned on me that Molly and I were pretty much *trapped* in the back of his cruiser ...

I blinked and saw him sitting behind his desk—our first meeting. *"I know how it sounds. But you live here long enough and you begin to take a dim view of things, you know? There was just something about her that made you think she was, well,* in danger. *Like she was an endangered species or something."*

You would think double takes would be part and parcel of a career like mine, but the fact is, they're not. I mean, I didn't simply get into the business because I was tough, charming, and didn't need to take notes. Thanks to all the retards in Hollywood, I also thought private investigating would be filled with surprises. Wrong. Like I said, people repeat, even when they're busy fucking each other over.

I had been had. Despite all the goofy precautions I take, all the little anti-social gimmicks I use to remind myself there's always more than meets the eye, I had willingly jumped into the jaws of what could be a lethal trap. People take things at face value, especially when those things gratify the old ego. So when a cop calls you at 11:38 P.M. to say that he needs your help with the latest twist in your case, what do you do? Apparently you leap to your feet like the stooge you are, shout, "Hurry, Watson!" and jump into the back of his police cruiser.

Motherfucker.

"That wasn't my question, Caleb. I asked you why you never said anything *about them*?"

But the fact was, he *had*, only in ways that had made me think he was soft in the head.

Shit. Shit. Shit.

I had purposefully antagonized Reverend Nill in the hope of goading him into action. And then, true to form, I had let the prospect of getting laid derail everything. As bad as James fucking Bond, only minus all the class. I mean, with all those references that Nolen had made to bigotry in our first talk ... All I had to do was rehearse that conversation and all the obvious questions would have asked themselves. And now here I was, trapped in the back seat of Nolan's cruiser, with every reason to believe that the turd *actually belonged* to the Church of the Third Resurrection.

Why else would he have worked so hard to put verbal distance between himself and bigotry that first meeting?

"I don't understand," Nolen replied with an oh so phony smile. He braked at one of Ruddick's few stop lights. I could see Molly covertly trying her door. Locked, of course.

"Well, Caleb, let me put it this way, then. You have this beautiful *white* girl, named Jennifer, who likes going out dancing with her best friend, who happens to be a handsome *black* man, at a bar that happens to be frequented by several fanatic members of a *white supremacist religion*, which is not only run by a cadre of ex-cons but also happens to be actively recruiting in *your* jurisdiction, and then suddenly, *poof*, this beautiful white girl disappears, vanishes ..."

While I was saying this, I pulled my cell out of my belt clip and handed it to Molly, who snapped it up like a fat kid with chicken nuggets. Caleb didn't reply at first, so the sound of Molly leaving a "detailed message" for her editor at the *Post-Gazette* seemed to grate with sham intent ...

"Yeah," she was saying, "so I'm, like, with Chief Nolen right now, Chief *Caleb Nolen*, and we're heading to the station ..."

I glared into the rear-view mirror with violent intensity, watched Nolen's face from the angle of out-of-body experiences and guardian angels. His eyes clicked to meet mine once—twice ...

"I have a daughter," he fairly blurted. "Cynthia. She's seven, more beautiful than ... I don't know. About eight months ago I get this call, an anonymous prowler tip ... over on Ross and Maitland. Turned out to be nothing ... except that I was almost forty-five minutes late picking Cynthi up from her swimming classes. When I finally arrived at the school, I find out that someone's already driven her home ... her coach's assistant, a woman who just happens to belong to Nill's church ..."

His eyes flash up to the mirror, and for the first time I glimpsed real fury. "Thirds," he says, staring at me for a heartbeat. "We call them Thirds ..."

His gaze bored on down the road.

"They own this town."

* * *

He pulled up in front of the white-glowing station, dropped the cruiser in park. A call crackled across his radio—some small-town nonsense that he completely ignored. My hackles had smoothed somewhat, but I wouldn't breathe easy until he cracked the fucking back doors. He had fairly admitted that Nill had leverage, that he was frightened for his family. Maybe *that* explained his emotional outburst at the motel.

Nolen turned in his seat, continued explaining in a more apologetic tone. After the incident with his daughter he had researched Nill, discovered that he was in fact an ordained minister. Nolen had toyed with the thought of discrediting him before his congregation. But he was a former convict as well, one with connections that ran deep into the Aryan Brotherhood and the Hells Angels. This was why the man leapt to the top of his list when Jennifer went missing.

"I went and talked to him," Nolen said in defensive tones. "To Nill. He was pious ... furious ... Said that there's no one in his church who would *dare* cross his word. And his word was to keep everything quiet, to express nothing but Christian charity, to do everything they could to see the Thirds *grow* ..."

He turned his face to the white gleam of his station, hesitant and brooding.

"Maybe I was afraid. Hell, I *know* that I was afraid ... And why shouldn't I be, when both you and I know I'm just a grocery clerk playing cops and robbers." Even without seeing his expression, I knew that this admission cut him deep.

The upholstery creaked. He turned his face back, glanced at Molly then at me through the slot. "But I *believed* him, Disciple. I just thought ... I just hoped that I could have it, like, *both ways*, you know? So I believed the lunatic."

And for my part, I believed Nolen. Well, to be more precise, I believed that *he believed* what he was saying—which is about as good as it gets with someone like me.

I mulled his words for a moment, thought about how Baars had avoided my question of whether they had any enemies in Ruddick. "And what about the Framers?" I asked. "They would know about the Thirds, wouldn't they?"

"You would think so," Nolen said. He stared down into his palms, frowned as if seeing a stain he thought he'd washed away. "But the town they live in is five billion years away."

The Ruddick police force was about the size you would expect for a town of around four thousand souls: a chief, a deputy chief, two sergeants, and about twelve PFCs. But since Ruddick had once been a small manufacturing hub of some twenty thousand, the police station was almost ludicrously oversized—it was like Nolen and his people had set up shop in the corner of an abandoned warehouse.

Nolen waved us past his unblinking duty sergeant and ushered us into a conference room adjacent to his office. I had popped the cork on my memory and was reciting details of every similar ritualistic murder I had seen on A&E, Discovery Channel, and so on. The truth was, I had never worked a case remotely like this one before. Murders like this, ones involving intentional as opposed to inadvertent clues, are a bona fide rarity. The vast majority are either simple crimes of passion or involve money and property. If anything, murderers are even more allergic to symbolic abstractions than the general population. There's nothing quite so literal as blood.

It really is a miracle when you think about it: that there could be so *many* brains—billions of them buzzing out there—and that so *few* of them would suffer this kind of glitch. Thank God for natural selection, I say.

It was Molly who asked Nolen if he could pinpoint the locations of the two fingers and the baby toe on a map. He left the two of us blinking in the fluorescent glare for several moments, then returned to spread a large map of Ruddick across the veneer-topped boardroom table.

"So ..." Nolen said, scratching his head with a pencil while he found his bearings. It took him several moments peering at street names, but soon he had marked the map with three little-girl-neat Xs. Dancer, I thought. The guy was a dancer.

I tried to make a show of being hard-boiled and wise, but all I could really think about was how gay Nolen's Xs looked. He should be politicking behind the scenes on the latest Britney Spears tour, not policing.

"What if ..." Molly began.

I knew her well enough by now to take her thoughtful tones seriously. "What if what?"

"Nothing."

"Spit it out."

"It's just so ... cheesy," she said.

"Nothing original about murder, Molls."

"Well," she said, leaning over the map, "what if the fingers have been arranged, you know, in *order* ..." Nolen answered her questioning hand with his pencil. "So that if you draw a line ..."—she connected the two Xs marking the locations of Dead Jennifer's index and bird fingers—"between these locations ... and extended it ..."

I laughed. She was right, it *was* cheesy, but then so was the bulk of the American public. Hell, even I had a weakness for skulls and eagles. Odds were the killer was cheesy as well.

"A *cross*," I said. "Fuck me."

"What?" Nolen asked with the anxious air of a keener struggling to keep pace with his more witty peers.

Molly handed me the pencil so that I could show him. "See," I said. "If you join the location of the baby toe at right angles to the finger line ..."

"And if you take the interval between the fingers ..." Molly added.

I eyeballed several more Xs along the length of both lines. There it was,

Ruddick dissected into quadrants, the stick-thin shadow of the cross, with the intersection matching Molly's hypothetical intervals perfectly.

"If Molly's right," I said, pointing to the crossing, "that's where we'll find her ... what? Thumbs and big toes, I suppose."

"Or her, ah ... her body," Nolen said, his voice as thin as his face was white.

The lines were hand-drawn and inexact, but they nevertheless intersected in a shaded region containing grey blocks instead of the orange the map-makers had used to represent other large buildings.

"What is that?" Molly asked, peering for a title of some kind. "Another factory?"

"Nashron," Nolen said, frowning and nodding. "The deadest of the dead. Packed up before there even was a China."

The Nashron plant was old, positively ancient by industrial standards, built at the turn of the nineteenth century, long before zoning had become a going concern. A chain-link fence that had been skinned with scrap sheets of siding ran around the perimeter. The main structures loomed above, brick walls so stained and chapped they looked Roman, their monumental monotony broken only by the long rows of what had once been windows but were now empty frames, lattices of rotted wood about blackness—utter blackness.

"You gotta be kidding me ..." Molly said as Nolen pulled the cruiser across the turf and scrub thronging about the gate. The headlights flashed across an old rust-scabbed sign with red lettering—something about legalities. A large commercial real estate sign had been planted to the right, shiny new even in the dark.

"Think of the *story,* Molls," I said as Caleb cracked the door.

She glanced at me in her wry, endearing way. "Yeah, hey ... I might even end up with, like, an in-depth special report."

I grinned and winked. "I was thinking obituary."

Not the best joke, I admit, given that we were hunting for Dead Jennifer's thumbs and toes, but it kept me chuckling while Nolen sorted through keys for the lock—a land mine–sized thing hanging from a heavy-duty chain. Apparently Nolen and his deputies periodically accessed the grounds to check things out. "Tracking itinerants," he explained, which I took to mean rousting bums.

I helped him yank back the gate, which was quite heavy thanks to the sheets of corrugated aluminum. Our flashlights probed the grounds: pale ovals revealing sumac, sundry weeds, and humps of rusted iron—old train parts by the look of them. We followed the remains of a concrete walkway. The night soared about us, painted the aural world behind the crickets and cicadas with utter silence.

We paused before a battered entrance: a heavy, metal-skinned door that had been smashed from its tracks. Our flashlights chased the shadows of weeds and debris deep into the structure's interior.

"Eew," Molly said with the bubbling beginnings of panic. "What's that smell?"

I raised my flashlight to my chin, made a campsite face. "Me ... I always fart before battle."

"You eat potato chips or something?" Nolen asked without the whisper of a smile. He seemed remarkably at ease, given the circumstances. This raised my hackles once again. I much prefer weak people *stay* weak, if you know what I mean. The idea had occurred to me that pretty much *anything* could happen on this nocturnal expedition, and that the world would be captive to the facts as the *survivors* told them. Just where were Nolen's patrolmen anyway?

I thought of my revolver stuffed in the bottom of my bag in my room. Fawk.

"Follow me," I said, striding over the low heaps of junk and over the threshold. The factory interior was at once cavernous and cramped with ruin, like a mine shaft and an airplane hangar all in one. Another stinker slipped loose as I picked my way forward; it felt like a hot marble between my butt cheeks.

The building was largely open, broken only by the ruins of stairs that led to a series of hanging offices above. Debris had been scattered like flotsam, leaving patches of floor bare. Sweeping my light back and forth, I glimpsed graffiti, stick imitations of the baroque stuff I was used to seeing in Jersey. I saw the same *FUCK UP NOT DOWN* as earlier. Numerous metal posts stumped the floor, the remains of long-dead workstations. The air reeked of water damage and industrial squalor. In the sea-wreck distance you could make out blackened presses, machinery that had been too ancient to auction, or so I imagined, when the factory had closed.

Nolen and Molly seemed content to follow me. We creaked forward together.

My memory, as always, continued to torment me. This time with a Tragically Hip tune about fingers and toes. I did a mental version of blocking my ears and singing, "Na-na-na." If Molly was right, if we did find Dead Jennifer's thumbs—or her corpse—I would rather attach the experience to something more emotionally appropriate, like some old Sabbath tune. My memories, remember, cling to their original emotional charge. Mashing together recollections from opposite ends of the emotional colour wheel often jars me to the point of becoming nauseous. Imagine a mouthful of shellfish and ice cream.

I'm not sure what drew my eye the first time my flashlight scrolled over the work table. The relative cleanliness, perhaps. Whatever the reason, I found myself turning toward it, stepping across the wobbly backs of several smashed cinder blocks. The table was one of those old metal jobbies you used to find in high school shop classes, the kind designed to protect ducking and covering students in the event of a Commie nuclear attack. The thing was about as big as a snooker table, and probably just as heavy.

The message on its back lent a whine of horror to the silence. Molly's *"Oh, God ..."* were the only words spoken. Several moments passed before I breathed.

There it was: a cross in the plain fundamentalist style, made of some kind of wood ... only turned into a swastika with two thumbs and two toes set at right angles.

We just stood there dumbfounded. I found myself at once knowing they were real and thinking they looked like dollar-store fakes. The nails, especially—like something dripped from a candle.

"He *is* insane ..." Molly finally said, her face as ashen as the digits it regarded.

We all knew who she was talking about.

"No ..." I said. "Nill didn't do this." I'm not sure where this insight came from, the sudden realization that I knew him—or his type anyway. Nill had taken a long haul from the crack pipe of power. Like Nolen said, the Thirds owned this town. Why remortgage with a risk like this?

"*Who* then?" Molly cried.

"Someone who thinks he's selling out."

That's the thing about power: it ropes in rationalizations the way shit draws flies. And Albert himself had said white supremacist types had a weakness for whacking each other ...

"Caleb?" I asked. Poor bastard. He was one of those guys: no matter where you aimed, you could be sure as shit that he would come stumbling into your sights. I thought of his daughter squirming and kicking in the pool. I thought of the Bonjours' daughter doing the same in the open air ...

"Caleb?" I repeated.

He just stood there, terror in uniform. Molly, who had been aghast moments earlier, now had a covert, concentrated look, like the bitch who had won bingo yet again but was too wary of resentment to openly celebrate.

"I know what we need to fight these guys," she said in response to my questioning gaze.

"And what's that?" Nolen asked in a voice that was more than a little panicked. Was he thinking about his daughter swimming beneath Reverend Nill and his crazed eyes? To this day, I wonder.

"Publicity," she said, and I could see the triumph shining bright in the cracks of her sombre expression. She had found her break and she knew it. Poor Dead Jennifer.

"The national spotlight."

Even for a cynic like me, that was a new one. The National Spotlight. A phrase from salacious crime shows and pompous cultural studies seminars come to the real world—and sounding almost normal.

What a rich and absurd life I lead. Chock full of nuts.

Molly said this and *poof,* the tension was gone. It's funny how it works, the way we think in stories even when we find ourselves beyond the narrative pale. Complication had piled onto complication, and we had climbed the crisis summit. Here we were, stranded in the dead of night with assorted body parts in the wrecked heart of an old foundry, and suddenly it all seemed downhill. If it hadn't been for Nolen and his uniform, I probably would have sparked a joint.

The only wrinkle remaining was that we had *accompanied* Nolen on this little adventure.

"It would be better," he said with the blank face of a brain running successive worst-case scenarios, "if you two, ah ... *let me* handle this."

He was speaking the international language of in-over-their-head amateurs now, a lingo I had learned from my commanding officers during the war.

"Yeah," I said with a sage nod. "It would probably be better if you discovered this *after* you dropped us off at the motel."

Molly had that squint women get when they smell masculine-scented bullshit. Motes of dust settled through the random wag of our flashlight beams. "What are you saying?"

We all get pinched by circumstances like this, times when saving face and necessity collide. Me? I embrace the embarrassment. Say *Yeah, so I'm a dickhead—tell me something new.* But Nolen was one of those guys who lived in perpetual terror of his weaknesses. The most he could do was stare at Molly with a kind of chagrined helplessness, as if wanting to point out that *he* was the one dispensing favours here ... at first ... but ...

I decided to spare myself the spectacle. "This Scooby-Doo stuff isn't what you would call standard operating procedure, Molls. Caleb did us a solid, so now we're going to do a solid for him in return."

Nolen shot me a gratified glance.

"But I get to *write* about this, right?" She had aimed her light directly at Nolen as she said this. Skewered the poor guy.

"Of course, Molls. Only this time *you'll* be the anonymous source you quote."

I knew she would warm to this, and by all appearances she was. The wheels were turning, anyway ... maybe a little too much.

We began picking our way back across the factory floor, each of us mortified in our own way, not simply by what we had seen but by how the competing demands of our lives had, well, clouded things. Jennifer Bonjour was dead, for sure this time, and here we stood, negotiating self-promoting details.

Truth be told, I really didn't have a problem with this. People die. It sucks. It hurts like all hell. And sometimes, when you're a cop or a journalist or a private dick, it *helps.* Profiteering is just the nature of the beast.

Life.

We picked our way through dark industrial cavities, each of us muzzled by our own petty concerns. Then something, a sound, scraped out in the blackness. Our heads jerked toward the sound—off to our right. A shadow lurched. Our flashlights caught the rim of some ragged human form ...

And Nolen's automatic cracked through the hollows.

Or something like that happened. Even though I pretty much remember everything I *experience* of the events I participate in, the truth is, my mind wanders sometimes. If my attention is sketchy, then my memory is sketchy as well.

Fact is, I was wondering whether I could lure Molly away from her laptop and into my bed. I wish I could say I was pondering the origin of multicellular organisms or the tragedy of the atom bomb, but no, it was Molly's ass, plain and simple.

"No!" Nolen cried out in bad-acid-trip tones. "No-no-no-no—"

I stumbled forward, searching for the source of the rattle and gurgle in the dark before me. My shadow danced in the erratic light thrown by Nolen's flashlight. My own light swayed and dipped, painting distant brick walls in dim watercolours, striking the jumbled confusion of the floor with electric detail. For some reason I remember the blood as black. I mean, I *know* it was red—the way blood should be—but I remember it as black.

The guy was laid out on his back doing a kind of tap dance across an ethereal floor. I understood instantly that it had been a head shot, that the poor bastard was dead, and that Chief Caleb Nolen was fucked—not murder fucked, but manslaughter fucked ...

Fucked enough.

I knelt into the old bum's smell. He had one of those faces you've seen a thousand times, on street corners, staring out sidelong from alleys, asking for change, pinched around the light of a shining cigarette butt. Except that his left eye socket kept spilling blood.

With our flashlights converged, the bum glowed like an angel in the dark. We all gaped at him, stupefied. He was dead, as dead as dead can be. His body just needed some time to come to grips with the proposition.

"He had a gun!" Nolen shrieked from my side. He was the marksman. He knew his target was doomed. "Look for it! It's gotta be here somewhere!"

Somebody always chokes in cases like this. Better the home team.

I stood and turned to Molly, who was little more than an apparition beyond the glare of her flashlight. I wondered what I must look like, frozen against the contrast of my shadow. Pale as an escaped con, I supposed. Blank as a bereaved comedian. I thought of all the others who had seen me in similar light.

Nolen was tripping and scrambling, searching for his magical gun. He had the look of a man stumped down to his bones. I almost laughed. And here he'd thought *Jennifer* was a mystery.

"C'mon," I said to Molly as I walked toward her. "I'll call us a cab."

"You g-guys *saw* it, didn't you?" Nolen cried. He was bawling now—pretty much. Weeping. Sobbing. It was all gone. He had trusted to his hopes, and instead his worst fears had come crashing through ... *I'm innocent!* his expression cried. Apparently innocents didn't kill innocents.

Molly simply gazed up at me in numb horror. "*Disciple* ... You gotta do something!"

I looked at her and shrugged. It was *way* past my bedtime.

Track Eleven

THE THREE IMMOBILITIES

Things were getting weird.

Sometimes working a case is like being the parent of a large family: controlling the direction of the avalanche is the most you can hope for. Well, the avalanche had started, and things weren't looking so good. If the Dead Jennifer Case had been a family, Junior would be smoking crack, Missy would be shooting amateur porno, and little Bobby would have been busted shoplifting panties at Walmart.

Needless to say, Molly politely declined my invitation to spend the night. "Let me get this straight," she said in the no man's land between our two motel room doors. "A girl is dead. A good cop's career has been ruined. Some poor homeless guy took a bullet in the head. And you were thinking you *might get laid* a second time, huh?"

"We all grieve in our own way, Molls."

She gave me a look I had seen 138 times before ... Funny, the way old dope smokers grow suspicion like fur.

"You actually *scare* me," she said in the flat tone women reserve for utterly honest comments. "You know that, Disciple?"

She was exhausted, bewildered, and now she was hurt.

Even still, I said, "Yeah ... I suppose you have your fifteen hundred words to write ..."

Her tears took me by surprise. She started to say something but literally caught her mouth in her hands. She darted to her door without a word, but I knew what she had wanted to say.

Poison, Disciple. Why do you turn everything into poison?

I schlepped into my room, absorbed the chaotic landscape of tangled sheets, pocket trash, and tossed clothes. What a slob I was.

Tired. So tired.

I smoked a joint.

Jerked off.

Bed.

Sunday ...

I slept like the dead. Cruel hearts always sleep soundly, I suppose. It was almost noon before I awoke.

I had no idea how police shootings were investigated in Pennsylvania, so I thought it would probably be a good idea if I stashed my bag of weed for the time being. I went to Odd-Jobs for a solo breakfast, hid my Baggie in the dropped ceiling of their washroom.

They had this ancient TV in the dining area, one of those fat-screen jobbies that had looked futuristic back in the Clinton days. A little electric window on the world, and a safe haven when Brittany, the waitress, caught you checking out her cleavage. There it was, live as live can be, electromagnetically speaking.

Ruddick was being televised. I could tell by the courthouse facade rising behind the saccharine beauty of the reporter's face. Some local channel by the looks of her—too much asymmetry in her face for the big time. Too much nose. The volume was muted, or maybe broken, but the title glowing beneath the painted woman confirmed what I already knew ...

POLICE CHIEF ALLEGEDLY SHOOTS HOMELESS MAN

Molly had been busy. I felt a flare of pride for her, and no small amount of regret. Up to that point I had been anticipating some vigorous make-up sex ...

Celebrity has a way of booking people solid.

I returned to my room all perked on coffee and finally sat on the end of my bed with my cell. The time had come to call Mandy—Mrs. Bonjour. My brain was buzzing: it had yet to process the consequences of last night, let alone wrap itself around this latest twist in circumstances.

There was the Church of the Third Resurrection situation for one. It seemed to me that I was looking at one of two possibilities: either Reverend Nill was even crazier than I thought and he was the one responsible for Jennifer's murder, or someone was trying to bring him down. My gut told me that it was the latter, but unlike the rest of the human race, I have no faith whatsoever in my gut. It does a fair to middling job processing my dinner into shit, but other than that, it clearly does not know shit.

I know that *you* buy into all that "go with your gut" or "follow your heart" bullshit simply because I see versions of it everywhere, from tampon commercials to Palme d'Or–winning cinema. But I *remember* all the instances where my instincts have been dead wrong, not to mention the instincts of those around me. Given that your bean is a cherry-picking machine, you remember only what confirms your assumptions. So of course you think your gut is a pretty good one, *especially* when you're full of shit.

No. I wasn't going to listen to my instincts on this one. I'd spent too much time with my thumb up my ass as it was. When it came to the Thirds, I needed to review things, maybe talk to Tim ... Dutchie.

I imagined he was pretty pissed.

As for Nolen, well, I supposed he was pretty much out of the picture. The Bonjour investigation would be handed to Jeff Hamilton, his deputy chief, and it would probably take a day or two to re-wrangle things. I probably couldn't count on the kind of assistance I had enjoyed so far: he struck me as a hard nut. Since I was the Bonjours' man in the field, he would have to extend me certain courtesies—regular updates, the odd heads-up here and there—but copies of official statements? Fat chance. He would be too bent on proving himself.

The gathering media storm could change all that, of course. The positive was that it could turn Dead Jennifer into a national celebrity, and so enhance the chances of catching a break from someone who knew something without realizing they knew anything. The biggest negative was that it would slowly starve the Bonjours of emotional oxygen. The second drawback was that it would *politicize* the investigation. The simultaneous promise and threat of optics would bring in the Attorney General, state law enforcement, the FBI—as sure as shit.

Sooner or later, the heavy hitters would roll into town, and the "courtesies" they extended me would become more and more ornamental. Backslaps and grins tend to make me especially prickish.

Besides, I wasn't sure how much "media scrutiny" a tarnished fuck-up like Disciple Manning could bear. I would look good on TV—that much was certain. For that reason alone I would probably be forgiven quite a bit, at first anyway. The world really is that super-fucking-ficial. But if they started *digging* ...

Yup. I would be well and truly fucked.

There was a real issue here. An animal's habitat is defined by the range of environments that allow it to squeak by. Feed and fuck, basically. So far I had been able to do both quite nicely. But things had changed radically, and were about to change even more radically still. The media sun was about to burn very hot and very close. The question was whether I could continue playing a role in the environmental collapse to come. Whether I could be a plus. For the case. For the drug-and-bimbo-binging travesty I call my life ...

Would it be possible for me to run a *clean* private investigation?

Not bloody likely.

In any event, it was already too late. At the time I had thought myself pretty clever, gathering both "donations" and information with the toss of a single fraudulent stone. Vegas, baby. Now I wasn't so sure. I could even see the news caption:

PRIVATE DETECTIVE DEFRAUDS RUDDICK RESIDENTS OF THOUSANDS

Yeesh. What was I thinking?

Certainly not about CNN—that's for damn sure.

The dismay came across me slowly—catastrophic realizations may outrun their emotional implications, but they never outdistance them.

Unless something decisive fell into my lap, and soon, I was going to have to cut and run ...

Fawk.

"Amanda ... It's me, Disciple Manning. I'm afr—"

"I know ... I h-heard ... It's on the news ..."

Owich.

God hates me. That's gotta be it. God hates me because I don't believe in him.

"My baby." She started weeping. *"M-m-my ..."*

"Amanda," I said sternly. "I know this is the worst of possible times, but we have to discuss *money*. I'm running out of dough down here."

I know what you're thinking. You bastard. The woman has just discovered her daughter is dead, that her daughter's fingers and toes have been turning up across an obscure industrial burnout of a town, and you're asking her to cut you a cheque—when you're already flush with the cash you scammed!

But that's not it at all. I would cash the cheque, eventually, but that's not the reason I brought up money. Money is cold, and more importantly, money is *routine*. Like I said earlier, that's what makes money *talk* such a great way to throw cold water across overheated or overwrought clients: it reminds them of the *reason* they came to me in the first place.

Amanda Bonjour had an important decision to make. I may have known that I was investigating a murder all along, but as far as she was concerned, I was hired to find a missing person. That missing person—or parts of her, anyway—had just turned up dead. Amanda had to decide whether she wanted to keep me or to cut me loose. Bringing up money was just a way to calm her down so that she could make that decision rationally, *responsibly*. I was charging her my highest rate, after all.

And it *worked*. So fuck you.

Her voice seemed to waver from a wire. *"Um"*—a viscous swallow—*"c-could you tell me what you know?"*

And you know what? I told her pretty much everything I've told you—everything short of her husband, her daughter, the basement, and the bottle of bourbon. At some point the memory of her tying her shoe in my office entrance just rose and stuck in my mind's eye, until it seemed that was who I was talking to, Mandy silently crying while tying her shoe. It wasn't so much that I couldn't *lie* to that image as I couldn't hurt it ... couldn't cheapen or demean.

Whatever dignity truth does possess comes from tragedy. It's all bullshit otherwise, without pain to do the sorting.

* * *

She wasn't worried about money, she said. She just wanted to know what had happened to her daughter. She understood if I wanted to fold my hand and clear out of town—she didn't want me to do anything that could endanger my future—but until then, she wanted me to keep asking questions.

"And Disciple?"

"Yeah ..."

"I wa-want you ... want you to ... If you find whoever did it, I mean ... could—"

"Don't worry about that, Amanda."

She was crying again—this time in fury. *"Call me Mandy,"* she said.

Afterward I just sat there in the wallpaper silence, just ... absorbing emptiness, it seemed. I honestly didn't have a fucking clue as to what I should do next. Put the thumbscrews to Baars about the Thirds? Find out more about Nill's biker cronies, maybe pay them a visit? Hit all the residences around Nashron to see if anyone had seen anything suspicious? Go to the police station, check on Nolen, reintroduce myself to Deputy Chief Hamilton, and lay the groundwork for the inevitable ass-kissing to come?

Instead, I scampered across the street so that I could get my dope back from the ceiling in the Odd-Jobs restaurant. I almost got clipped by a Lexus (where do people get all their fucking money?) scampering back to my room. I sat at the small, cluttered table and rolled a joint while watching TV. I needed *perspective*, I decided, a wide-angle, psychedelic lens. I surfed through the channels and there it was, as sure as shit ...

Dead Jennifer hadn't simply made the tube, she had made CNN. I just sat there blinking in amazement. Christ, things were moving fast. Especially for a dope-smoking chronic like me.

"I have a story for you here, Soledad—interesting story. In the course of investigating a grisly ritual murder, a Pennsylvania police officer accidentally

shoots and kills a homeless man. We'll be sure to keep you up to date on what promises to be a tragic ... *and* extraordinary ... *story."*

Nolen. Poor bastard. People always make at least two mistakes in judging the actions of others. The first is confusing what they would do with what someone else *should* do. The fucking hubris of this is staggering, given that we only have our pinhole perspectives to work with—pinholes we continually confuse with the sky. The second is thinking they actually would do what they *think* they would. The ugly fact is that we rarely live up to our good intentions, that it's a combination of wilful blindness and strategic amnesia that lets us continue duping ourselves otherwise. It's not just that we judge people by the yardstick of ourselves, our lives, but by the yardstick of idealized selves—a self-congratulatory *fantasy.*

The yardstick you're using to judge me, in fact.

Oh yeah. Nolen was fucked. The only thing Molly and I could do for him—literally—was keep him company on his tumble down. She would realize this sooner or later. Then she would forgive me ...

By around seven or eight at the latest, I figured.

The question was whether she would have time for a quick hummer.

I got a little more fried than I expected, though I should have known: the bud I picked had been especially frosty. CNN kept coming back to Ruddick every half an hour or so, displaying an assortment of shots of Jennifer that I recognized from her Facebook page—the ones that made her look particularly wholesome and fuckable, of course. It was kind of fun watching them cobble together a story arc from what few details they possessed. They used every opportunity they could to repeat the words "young," "attractive," "severed," and "cult." I found myself wondering whether they had a formula for this, or whether they still "went with their gut" when it came to pushing verbal buttons.

Even still, the piling on of inanities got very stale very quick. I tried to imagine having sex with the flat-chested blonde who was anchoring. Ah, yes, Linda. When that didn't work, I clicked off the tube, stretched out fully clothed across the bed. Closed my eyes.

The Third's pig roast leapt into the breach—I mean, like, *immediately.* Hard to believe that it was just yesterday.

"Disciple!" the Reverend called out. *"I* love *your name."*

"My parents were nudists," I said.

People laughed even though I wasn't joking.

I lay there, my mind swinging in vulture-slow circles. Usually the memories come at the behest of some kind of suspicion, conscious or unconscious, when I allow them to free-associate. But sometimes emotional ferocity alone seems to drive them. The louder the shout, the more persistent the echo, I suppose.

I was staring across the ceiling, at the gossamer webs in the corners, listening to Nill's crazed rap session, seeing the spectre of his reddening face, his eyes like clenched teeth. God hates, he was saying, therefore to hate *is godly.*

"What kind of fucking goof does that*?"* Molly cried in disbelief. She was a classic "face-tripper," one of those chicks with no inclination whatsoever to conceal her feelings behind a neutral expression.

"Goof?" Nill spat. *"Psycho? What do you think happens when God—the God Almighty—lands in your brain? You think you stay sane? Read your Bible, bitch. All his vessels crack. All of 'em!"*

"Some apparently more than others."

"Manners! *Manners, Missy! The Good Lord has a way of teaching them!"*

The looming shadow of Johnny Dinkfingers. The moment of movement and violence. And I saw them without seeing, the faces of the Third congregation tucked in the corners of my attention.

I raised a thumb and forefinger to my eyes, tried to focus my thoughts. I reminded myself of my theory, that Nill, despite his Charlie Manson gaze, was too wedded to his power to be behind Jennifer's disappearance. That he was being framed ...

And then I saw them, or *remembered* seeing them, which is altogether different. Johnny Dinkfingers and the two characters I had pegged as junkies, bent in counsel about the rickety-rotted picnic table.

A long conversation without jokes, eyes fixed then wandering. Looking down and bored, then matching gazes.

"Okay. I see," Johnny mouthed.

"Sheesh. Too much," the older junkie said.

The younger junkie mimed blows, raised his face to boast a black eye.

Caged laughter, a set of sideways glances. An exchange of inaudible words.

Johnny watched. He seemed nervous, twitchy. *"Please,"* he said. *"Give me a fucking break ..."*

The younger junkie looked at him as if to say, *So?*

Johnny smiled, then mouthed, *"She's dead."*

He shrugged and spat. The older junkie turned to me and grinned.

I sat up in bed, blinking. This happens to me sometimes. It's almost as if my memories possess a variable amplitude. The past concentrates, gathers valence, and assaults the *now*—to the point where it seems like I'm dreaming more than remembering. Sometimes the breakers overload and my brain snaps me out, like a reality fail-safe or something.

If there's one thing my career path—as sketchy as it's been—has taught me, it's that things tend to be pretty obvious in the world of humans fucking over humans. Like I said, people *repeat.* This isn't to say that every murderer is a serial murderer, only that a murderer will typically have a *history* of some kind. Why do you think cops and courts are so fixated on rap sheets? Events in our psychological future tend to resemble events in our psychological past.

So the presence of *cons* in Nill's congregation fairly screamed for attention. I've been to prison, I know first-hand the vicious cunning that characterizes prison-gang power struggles, the way bloody shivs seem to float from cell to cell until they find the person-to-be-fingered-by-the-bulls.

Kill a man. Send another to the SHU. Two birds with one shiv.

Was that what this was? Was Dead Jennifer's murder simply a higher-order weapon? A way for strung-out foot soldiers to take down their crazy Reverend? Albert even said these groups are far more likely to go gunning for one another.

I mulled these questions, considered the different angles from which these memories of mine could be interpreted. At some point a fragment of Nill's initial sermon struck me. *"Does a man let his dog run wild in the streets?"* I had to laugh at that, it was so sad: fucking fortune-cookie racism.

I smoked another J.

Had a nappy-nap.

It was a classic summer evening: a charcoal sky leaning low over the silhouetted town, contrails soaring violet to black. Molly still hadn't come by to forgive me, so I drove by the police station. The plan had been to check in on Nolen, see if he was still in action, and if he was, see if I couldn't sweet-talk a rap sheet on Nill out of him. Soon as I turned the corner onto Curtis Street, I realized that things were not going to go as planned. Vans packed the curbs and sidewalks adjacent to the station's corner lot, all glossy in the dying light, festooned with decals on their sides and satellite dishes on their rooftops.

Something was going on. I drove by slow and more than a little paranoid. It's hard to appreciate the power these Barbie-doll people have until you run into them in real life. It's like a stage light follows them everywhere they go. They just seem brighter, cleaner than the rest of the world. Besides, I was well and truly stoned.

A crowd of ridiculously well-dressed people had assembled beneath a podium set before the station entrance. Portable lights glared, cut everything with brilliant clarity and pitch shadow. I crept along, hoping the rattle of my ancient diesel wouldn't attract any undue attention. I parked illegally farther down the street. Resolved to become a terrorist if I got a ticket.

The air was warm and still, and I squelched the urge to buy a case of beer and party. When I was a kid, we used to play Ping-Pong in our driveway on nights like this.

I pretty much crept to the back of the scrum—slunk all incognito-like, you might say. Everybody smelled like air freshener. Made me think of McDonald's bathrooms. Nobody paid me any attention because I wasn't paying anybody's bills. They were used to rubbing elbows with scalliwags, I supposed, what with all the loser journalists from the internet. Things had already started. Someone I didn't know, one of those guys who looked like he had been born wearing a suit, was making a statement of some kind. Nolen was standing beside him, one pace back.

"—repeat: a firearm *was found* in the possession of the victim. Of course, the investigation is only in its preliminary stages, but I remain confident that the facts will bear out Chief Nolen's version of events, and that he will be able to return to his duties, which, as you all know, are of the utmost priority ..."

A firearm, huh? Clever boy.

Nolen's gaze was too steely not to be medicated in some way. He saw me almost immediately. Even in a crowd of news models, my looks are quite striking. I could see the panic sputter beneath whatever wet chemical cloth he had thrown over his terror.

I shrugged and winked, hoped that was enough to let him know it was all okay. More than okay, really: co-operation was now a foregone conclusion. I almost convinced myself that it had been my plan all along, clearing out so that he could plant his evidence. Forensics could fuck it all up for him, of course, but forensics tended to confirm whatever it was the cops or the screenwriters wanted it to confirm.

No. Molly was the real question. She was still a *believer*, not a player like me.

I was surprised she wasn't there.

Her car was parked, so I knew she was in. One low light brightened the curtained corner of her window. I found myself staring at the 17 on her motel room door.

It was a capitulation, I know, but I couldn't stop thinking of her heart-shaped ass. Dope makes me horny sometimes. The idea was to apologize *first*, then to let her know, not only that Nolen had saved his own bacon, but that we had actually made that possible by fading to black.

The real challenge, the real argument, would turn on the bum, whom CNN had identified as Alex Radulov.

Does a bum deserve justice? I certainly hope so, given that I've been a borderline hobo myself. I've had one foot in the gutter for a long, long time. And I've had many a friend who's shrunk from the street lights, preferring to spark their pipe in the alley.

But let's face it: there's injustice and then there's just bad fucking luck.

Maybe you think things are black and white, that we live in a do-the-crime-do-the-time world. But what about Nolen's *daughter*? What about her swimming lessons? What about the rich soil of her life? Should we dry it out, parch it by putting away her father? Should we say "Tough fucking luck, kid," to *her*? Or should we say it to Alex Radulov? Let him take one last hit for the human team?

I'm not saying I know the answer. All I knew was that I liked Nolen almost as much as I liked what he could do for me. Yep. I said it. Erring on the side of Nolen was convenient as all hell. If you find that odious, then ask yourself why the world needs judges and independent arbitrators. Mistaking self-interest for truth is just part of the human floor plan. Fact is, I was just doing something consciously that you do *unconsciously* all the time: believing what I needed to cover my own ass. Remortgage your house to buy a hybrid lately? No? Let me guess. You have a bunch of excuses ...

And maybe that's not so bad, considering how principles are as liable to get you a Hitler as a Gandhi.

This was what I had to impress upon Molly to get her to play bally. The virtue of hypocrisy.

I really had no idea how she would respond, aside from knowing she would be shocked that I could think such a thing. Unlike men, women possess an almost infinite capacity for *moral* surprise. No matter how many times the office sociopath burns them, they are hurt and mystified.

I reached out and knocked. The door swung wide as if she had been expecting me.

Except she hadn't been expecting me. All that was left of her was a small puddle of blood.

Fawk.

It had been quite some time since I had last experienced genuine terror. I had forgotten not so much the tenor as the *immediacy*. Wow. Bummer.

Her laptop was still up and running on the small table. The lamp next to her bed glowered with dim indifference. I could see *DISCIPLE* scrawled across a sheet of paper folded on the pillow. I sat on her bed, took comfort in the fact that her mattress was at least as hard as my own. I snapped the sheet up in tingling fingers. Opened it.

Hydradyne Assembly Plant

NO COPS

I dropped the sheet on the floor, gazed at my palms and fingers. Hands are miraculous things. Placed thumb to thumb, they're perfectly designed for wringing necks ...

I gazed around for several moments, looking from this to that, just to be sure it would all be there if I needed it. In my skull.

Nazi, I decided. The room smelled like Nazi.

I drove through the centre of the town. Dark business fronts. Stretches of deserted sidewalk, freckled with gum. The street lights crawled over the lip of my windshield. Shadow and light dropped like water across me. The gleam of my Volkswagen struck me as alien, made me feel as though I were the squishy insides of a bug.

Ruddick. Fawk. If it had been a city, I could have romanticized things. I could have waxed wise about the scum, squalor. I could have mythologized the ethos of the parasite, or even the out-and-out killer. Lots of people deserved to die in the city. Lots of people brought on what they suffered.

But Ruddick was a small town. There was no anonymity to round off the hard edges, no background clamour to lift the music out of human screams. Everything was stark, real.

With no cracks to fall between, the dead made themselves noticed.

The light of the Kwik-Pik fanned across the small asphalt parking lot. I parked next to the car I recognized from that first meeting, back when Molly and I were still knocking on doors. I sat and waited for the paying customers to leave. Then I cracked my door, breathed deep the oily smell of summer leaking from brick and concrete. For a moment Ruddick almost tasted like a city. My heels made no sound across the tarvey.

I pressed open the glass door.

I walked into the white-baked interior, floated past all the pretty plastic colours. I reached back and tugged my automatic from my belt, held it directly in front of me. Tim stared in abject horror.

"A guy pulls a gun," I said.

Track Twelve

THE WHATEVER FACTORY

Sometimes I see myself through the scope of a sniper's rifle. Crosshairs parse me into sliding quadrants, pin me to the centre of the packed parking lot, the variety store foyer, the entrance to the motel office—whatever. I am oblivious. My gaze roams every angle except the one belonging to the lens.

Everything I do is soundless.

Tim was only too happy to help me. He fairly fell over himself in his rush to betray his friends.

I was right about Nill and his techniques, the way he progressively implicated his recruits in various crimes, nurturing a sense of impunity even as he forged a sense of belonging—always invoking the false blood of gang-family ties. Tim was supposed to meet the others at the abandoned Hydradyne plant after his shift—to relieve one of the others if I failed to turn up in a timely fashion. God's work never ends.

I told him this was precisely what he would do. Only forty minutes to go, as it turned out. The Kwik-Pik closed early on Sundays.

Another car pulled into the lot, so I took his cell and retreated to the magazine section, whiled away the time with *Maxim, FHM,* and finally the skin mags proper.

I was still staring at pussy when he locked up.

His Honda Civic was three years older than my Volkswagen Golf. Even still, I suffered a pang of shame driving a car in the same status range as that of a punk racist high school dropout.

Gave me second thoughts about poor Radulov.

I worked off my sense of material inadequacy by leaning forward and describing—in excruciating detail—the fates of those who had crossed me in the past. Two Baathists skinned in the desert. An unscrupulous coke dealer found hanged in his apartment. A mob hit man discovered in three different counties.

"You will wave hello," I grated, "even though you're shitting your pants in terror. You will smile, even though you're shitting your pants in terror. *You will do everything I tell you to do ...*" I reached forward to pinch his trachea. "Because if you fail, Dutchie my boy, you will die *convulsing,* you will gasp your final breath *gnawing dirt.* Do you copy?"

He blinked tears, blubbered something I understood as an affirmative.

Tim drove down Highway 3—toward the Framer Compound, suggestively—before turning off on an unpaved service road. The little car rocked to the dip of parched potholes. Weeds and scrub scratched and brushed the fenders and underbody. Tim sat rigid, gazing out at the bobbing fan of illumination before him. Skeins of dried grasses. Tracks in the cool dust. Shadows in the dark.

We drove past an opened chain-link gate then turned down a slope. Sumac and other scrub fenced the lane. A wall of corrugated siding resolved out of the black, windowless and nondescript. Tim slowed, and I saw the gleam of a pickup truck and the hindquarters of another car flash through the headlights. He parked beside the two vehicles. I glimpsed a figure with a flashlight walking toward us. "Stay in the car until he comes," I barked, pressing the muzzle of my gun against the side of his eye. "Leave it running ..."

Then I slipped out into the night. The surrounding terrain leapt into view: swales of brownlands beginning a long regression to pre-Columbian forest. The factory's main structure, I realized, was effectively shielded from the neighbouring subdivisions, which was why, no doubt, the Thirds had chosen it out of all the abandoned shells on offer in the industrial park.

Tim had parked to the left of the pickup and car. I couldn't duck in front of the Civic because of the headlights, and I couldn't bolt behind because that was the figure's direction of approach. My only alternative was to huddle in the overgrowth, risk the approaching flashlight. I fell prone behind a hump of grasses, peered between shredded threads ...

"Heeeeey, Dutcheee-boy!" the figure called, kicking the dust tracks. Fucknut, I decided to call him.

He was one of the two guys from the picnic table. Junkie thin. Beard trimmed to the craggy contours of his face. Older, with a grey mullet dropping in strings around his shoulders. He looked like George Carlin at the wrong end of a hunger strike.

His flashlight swayed negligently, missed me altogether.

"Hey? Everything okay?" he said, sauntering around the Civic. "You remember to grab me a pack of Camels?"

He leaned into the driver's-side window. "You forgot aga—" He heard my rush, but too late to do anything but grunt in abbreviated alarm. I clipped him as he turned, catching him on the notch in his orbital—just above his left eye. He dropped like a rolled carpet.

I retrieved the flashlight to inspect Tim. He sat there, as ashen as a heart attack, his hands clamped on the wheel. His Kwik-Pik name tag gleamed in the white.

"Drive home, Tim," I said. "You weren't made for this. You weren't made to *hate* ..."

There's something about tears in flashlight illumination, the way they sparkle like rhinestones. Like something apparently precious.

"Do you understand?"

"Yuh," he said, swallowing.

"Then go, kid. Get the hell out of here."

Surprise. We like it the way we like our pets—small and slavishly dependent.

Every heartbeat is an ambush, if you think about it. The key to success in combat is merely to remind your opponent of this fact at opportune times. To make weapons of his routines and his assumptions.

This was why I simply strolled toward the factory in the wake of Tim's car, dandling the flashlight in an offhand manner. I suppose I could have done a bunch of Navy SEAL shit, diving and rolling through the shadows. But why take the scenic route?

I followed the side of the factory, kicking my feet through the weeds and grasses the same as Fucknut. I found myself glancing up along the looming plane of the wall—a relic of a time when I despised rooftops, I imagine. That's the thing about war days: they never stop being yesterday.

The stars lent a chill to the air.

I saw Fucknut's partner, Dipshit, little more than a silhouette leaning against the wall next to an opened door. He was blowing smoke and watching it, which meant he was either bored or scared shitless. The spark of his cigarette floated along an arc anchored to his elbow. I watched it swing up to his lips, burn bright, then swing down to his thigh, and *flick* ...

I held the flashlight high enough to discourage any peering. Dipshit, I could see, was another chain-on-his-wallet fucker, just as skinny as Fucknut but with more of a Sid Vicious look. Anger as fashion.

"Where the hell did Dutchie go?" Dipshit said, finally turning toward me. "He forget your smokes or something?"

I raised the lamp to his face. He cursed, actually swatted at the glare. Then about a pace away, I tossed the light at him, kicked him square in the nuts. I tagged him with a strike on the temple as he doubled over. In all honesty, I'm not sure he was breathing when he hit the ground. The convulsions suggested a direct hit.

What can I say? They don't make Nazis the way they used to, I guess.

With both Fucknut and Dipshit tucked in for bed, I figured it was time to draw my gun. I stood in the darkness of the door opening, ears pricked. I heard the drone of a masculine voice reflected off hanging metal surfaces. Reverend Nill, I decided.

This was about when the farting started. What was it about these dead factories?

I stepped across the cracked concrete of the threshold. I paused, my senses tingling at their limits. The air smelled of dust and the trademark Manning-family reek: shit and potato chips. Details of the interior resolved as my eyes adjusted to the absence of the flashlight: a strewn floor, the hint of cavernous walls, and a dim subterranean glow emanating from around a corner. I heard laughter sucked hollow by open space.

I was standing in what looked like a warehousing annex. You would like to think you could step into an abandoned factory and easily guess what it once manufactured, but the fact is, everything has become voodoo in this world. Precious little makes sense to the untrained eye anymore. Hydradyne, I knew, would be as much a riddle to me in broad daylight as in the pitch of night. Some shelving had crashed to my right—that was pretty much the best I could do, identification-wise. It made an obstacle course of my way forward, or so I imagined, because I couldn't see jack shit.

With one hand out to paw the spaces before me, I moved to the left. I followed a track of rollers—like the kind they use to feed your groceries out to your car—along the wall, toward the truncated glow. My breathing was even, my steps measured, and except for the low, doggish whine of a second fart, I moved without making a sound.

The voice was clearer now.

"Can you talk now? Huh, bitch? Do you think you can talk like a sane, rational, *fucking bitch?"*

A moment of *ain't-no-such-thing* laughter. Definitely Nill, but more winded—almost breathless.

A feminine cry pierced the dark, shrill with rage and terror.

Molls ...

I would like to say that I remained professional at this point, that I behaved with cold, consumer detachment, but the fact is, I began running. Only dumb luck saved me from making a noise kicking or slamming into something, because I could see little more than the gleam of the roller track next to me. I whisked through the black, felt the aura of unseen obstructions fall away harmlessly.

I slowed to a creep as I approached the corner. The illumination was bright enough to airbrush the lines of my automatic. I always feel better when I can see my gun, for some reason. Never had much stomach for abstract instruments of murder.

A second or two passed before my eyes digested the complexity of the scene. It was a receiving bay of some kind. A series of catwalks and grilled floor platforms caged the air above the cluttered floor immediately before me. A single kerosene lantern on one of these platforms was the only source of light, casting fishnet shadows across the bare floor and rubbish below. I could hear its hiss hardening the silence. The greater factory fell into darkness beyond, another derelict arena blasted hollow by unfathomable economic forces.

I saw Molly, bound and gagged with tape, kneeling, burnt white in the glare of the lantern.

And I saw him, stripped to the waist, covered with a sweat-shiny array of comic-book tatts. Reverend Nill, the post-industrial demagogue. I imagine Brenda, my old sociologist girlfriend, would have some kind of interpretative paradigm to explain him. A kind of psycho-social parasite feeding off the resentment of the uneducated service castes. Something like that. You can only reform the economy for the sake of numbers instead of people for so long, I suppose.

That was when I wondered about Johnny ...

My eyes clicked down, around. I noticed the unattended shotgun leaning against three stacked pallets.

Something scuffed something behind me.

The bat chipped the back of my skull, but I was already diving—an old mortar-attack reflex. Even still, it rang my bell hard enough to send my automatic skidding into the black. I crashed face first into debris. There was a bag of something in there, probably concrete mix or something, powdery soft and hard all at once. A jutting nail ripped the meat of my left palm, but I wouldn't realize this until afterward.

I kick-rolled onto my back just in time to catch the next bat swing in the shin—a fucking stinger. But better than catching it with my face like the batter intended.

Johnny Dinkfingers loomed above me, graphed by lattices of light. A giant man out for giant revenge.

I had caught him pissing or something—away from his weapon, which was why he was still alive. Now, with me down in a crab defending myself with my legs, the best thing he could have done was simply leap for his weapon. He had the drop on me, plain and simple. But the thing was, he *already* thought he had the drop on me. After all, he had the *bat* and I was down on my ass. And more importantly, after his humiliation at the pig roast, he had something to prove to himself. The cheapest way to save face is to scar another.

So he came at me, swinging the bat wildly. Teeth clenched, eyes wild and exultant, he looked like something out of a Viking nightmare. I scrambled back, fending his strikes as best I could, but largely taking it on the shins, retreating into the gloom ... to the point where I hoped I would find my gun.

We have this psychic connection, you see, me and my government-model Colt. One second I was clawing the floor blindly, then, *Why hello there, little buddy ...*

I was up on my feet, depressing the trigger, plugging him in the face.

Bam-bam-bam. One-two-three ... He teetered, held up by some residual brain stem activity, then crashed forward to the floor. Petals of blood bloomed across the dust.

Score.

He looked like a drunk licking up a spilled Caesar.

"Johnny?" Nill called from immediately above. "Sound off, brother!" With the light next to him, I imagine we must have looked like rats battling in shadows.

"He tripped," I replied, my automatic still tingling in my hand. "Fell on three bullets."

If you haven't noticed, I tend to talk too much.

Rubbing the back of my head, I slowly backed out from under the platform to where Nill could see me pointing my Colt directly at him. He reflexively pulled Molly tight, using her as a shield. I have to admit, she looked hot, her mouth taped, her arms bound behind her, as sweaty as a cold beer on a humid day, wearing only a tank top and boxers—like something out of those boner detective mags I used to "read" when I was a kid.

Nill, on the other hand, looked positively desperado. I understood instantly: he was one of those guys with only two gears in his emotional transmission. Challenge him a little and he seems utterly invincible;

challenge him more than a little and he starts putting with his driver.

"Who hired you?" he croaked with what was left of his voice. "Was it Leighton? Or the Mexicans, huh? Who're *you working for*?"

"Jonathan and Amanda Bonjour."

Crazed laughter, dry, as if coughed through ropes rather than vocal cords. "And here I thought *I* was cold!" he chortled. "Look. I know, man, so you can drop the fucking act!"

Ah, I thought. So *this* was where it was hiding. The Law of Unintended Consequences always rears its hoary head at some point, and here it was, bright and shiny and as deep up my ass as always.

"Un. Fucking. Believable," I said in disgust.

I had decided to be aggressive at the pig roast to provoke some kind of incriminating response from the mad Reverend. Well, I certainly succeeded in provoking a response. Unfortunately, it didn't seem all that incriminating ...

"You're *framing* us!" the Nazi cried. "We know you were at Nashron with that pussy Nolen! We know that you're pushing his buttons!"

"Huh?"

He laughed and cried and sneered all at once. "Wh-what kind of fucking fool do you take me for, man? If you're not the one who planted all that shit, then *who else* could it fucking be?"

"That's what the Bonjours are paying me to find out."

"No! Bullshit! Bullshit!"

I paused at this. One of the worst things you can do to some people—apart from being wronged by them—is to witness them in a moment of abject weakness. Nill was pretty much a human craps table at this point. I had to be sure I had all my bets covered before rolling.

"Listen up, Reverend," I said with a marvelling smile. "We have three ways we can play this. In the first, you shoot Molly and I shoot you in a place where it takes a long time to die, because afterward, I shit you not, I will make you scream enough to shame the entire white race. In the second, I simply shoot you, in the mouth if I can manage it, in the hope of knocking out your motor cortex, and so save Molly. In the third, you simply set the gun down, and me and Molly here leave ..."

"Yeah?" He cried. His screech echoed through the tin-pot hollows. It's always embarrassing when men cover weak hearts with crazed voices. "How—how can I trust you?"

I shrugged. "Because I'm a chronic weed smoker ... I'm too much of a slacker to dig graves. And I get too paranoid to cope with all the police bullshit. Afraid that I'll fuck up. Afraid they'll find my weed."

All true.

"Buh-because *you smoke weed*?"

So far we had exchanged all these words around the fact of my gun pointed at his face and his gun held to Molly's cheek. I've lived a good chunk of my life in the company of guns, and yet I will never get over the way they seem to *vanish* in the course of this or that. Here's this *thing*, this tool that has been exquisitely designed and manufactured to bring about brain death in large mammals, and in the course of joking or negotiating or simply pissing away the time, we completely forget this mortal truth, wave them around like fucking Xbox controllers.

"Look," I said, allowing more than a little impatience to leak into my tone. I realized that I had simply *assumed* all of Nill's cronies were dead. "If we both fold our hands, split the pot, then we both get to rewind the clock. I don't have to answer for your dead buddies. You don't have to answer for abducting Molls here. We leave, you bury your flock, tell the rest of the congregation that they left to avoid the media attention, whatever. Sometimes people move away. Sometimes you never hear from them again ..."

Especially junkies. Hard to keep tabs on junkies. But I didn't need to say this because Nill was telling himself the same thing already. His balls had slipped out of his boxers—no doubt about that. He was dangling.

Debating.

"Hard to shoot a porno with good intentions," I said. "Show us some wood, brother."

Everyone breathed real hard.

You spend your whole life building this persona, this no-shit-no-way-no-how illusion that you somehow manage to cling to even as you talk Jesus or push those grocery carts across the parking lot. Then you bump into me. There's nothing like someone who *really* doesn't give a fuck to remind you how dearly—how *desperately*—you love your skin.

His crazy-ass eyes wide and shining, Reverend Nill stepped back from Molls.

He stood naked at that instant, in his own eyes as much as mine. I have no doubt the spin-doctoring would be quick in coming, that he would mythologize everything that had happened this night, that he would remind himself he had buried dead men in secret places. But for the moment, he stood utterly revealed: a fool clinging to all he genuinely owned, his skin colour and his hate. I would be lying if I said I didn't think of tagging him.

Molly slumped to her knees.

We left him there, alone and shirtless in the pale fire of his one light. Molly held me, held me tight, as we stumbled through the dark. She did not cry. At some point Nill began ranting behind us, or reciting actually, crying out a guttural German I'm sure he didn't understand—some old speech I remembered from the History Channel. Hitler at Nuremberg.

The empty factory roared in reply, roared with the absence of collective will. Hydradyne. Makers of whatever.

He was still shouting as we stepped out into the night.

We had no wheels, so we had no choice but to walk the ruined service road to Highway 3.

At some point my legs failed me. I skidded to the weeded dirt, to my knees.

I could hear her voice. Despite the tsunami of crashing memory ...

Like calls to like, you see, when it comes to the mind. I had killed three men tonight—bad enough. But over the years I had killed others, and so there I was, killing them, *killing all of them*, all over again. Fawk.

"Disciple? Are you *crying*? Disciple? It's okay. *I'm okay!*"

She didn't understand.

It ain't easy, being an abattoir.

Once we reached the highway, I called a cab and we began walking back toward town to meet it. The thought that Dead Jennifer had walked precisely these steps occurred to me, but the noise of recent events made the observation inaudible. The cabbie, some local fat-ass, said nothing, though I'm pretty sure he noticed everything—the gash on Molly's forehead, certainly. But I wasn't worried. Cabbies have a way of saying nothing. Too jaded to be surprised, just like me.

Our argument didn't start until we found ourselves at the motel.

"Look," I finally said. "The question you need to ask is whether you want to send *me* to the can for fifteen to twenty ..." I have some pretty savage instincts when it comes to self-preservation. I admit I suffered a dark thought or two for a moment, watching her balance my future against her sense of violation.

"But Nill—"

"Didn't. Harm. A soul."

"But—"

"You're thinking in *common sense* terms: I saved your life, so I gotta be good. But the authorities won't give a flying fuck why I killed those guys. All they'll care about is the *who*. As far as they're concerned, *I'm the murderer*. How? How? Because I'm the one who violated the state's monopoly on deadly force."

It all came down to turf.

She gawked at me with a look halfway between astonishment and indigestion. "What *happened* to you?" she cried. The stress had caught up to her by now, and she was crying freely. "How does someone get so, so ... fucking *cynical*?"

The blood had started to flow from the cut on her forehead.

"They remember," I said, daubing her brow with a tissue. "We need to get you to a doctor."

As it turned out, the nearest hospital was forty-five minutes away, in a town called Innis. We took my Golf because she said she wasn't sure if her car insurance would cover me. Can you believe it?

I took a roundabout way, stopped on one of the bridges, tossed my beloved Colt into the river. What a pisser.

"Why do you drive this piece of shit?" she asked as I climbed back in.

"Because I'm a loser," I snapped back. "Ruly-truly."

I get prickly about my car.

I began talking about the case, as a distraction as much as anything else—the way couples with rotten relationships find common purpose in slagging the friends they both despise. In a sense, the two of us found ourselves on opposite ends of the incentive spectrum. Everything had gone swimmingly for Molly—even her abduction would find its lucrative way into print somehow, I imagined. In the space of a weekend she had become the go-to girl for what was becoming America's latest media crime fetish. I thought of the economic consequences. A million bottles of shampoo sold. Ten thousand Toyotas. Wild swings of market share ... one, maybe even two points—who knew? Enough for Buffett to start unloading shares of Gillette ...

The more I considered it, the more it seemed that everybody was making out like a bandit except me. I was even out my gun. Do you know how much of a pain in the ass it is finding an unregistered .45 automatic? How fucking expensive?

Her elbow propped against the door, Molly leaned into the towel she held pressed against her head. She had that struggling-to-stay-awake look you see on the faces of so many critical incident survivors.

"So if it isn't Nill ..." she said, gazing into nowhere.

"Who knows. Could have been one of his cronies, like I said." This was my secret hope, but I was dubious.

"But then why would they help him abduct me?" she asked. "I mean, if the idea was to get Nill to self-destruct, you'd think they would've found some way to bail ..."

I glimpsed Tim, his tears blue-green with reflected dashboard light. Did he have a role to play in all of this?

Nah.

"Maybe it *was* this Leighton guy he mentioned," I said. "Or the Mexicans."

Always easy to blame the Mexicans.

"Or Baars," she said.

"Or someone who thinks they're *helping* Baars."

I glimpsed Stevie, watching me from behind the world reflected across plate glass.

"What do you mean?" she said, turning to study my profile.

"Tim told me that Nill and Baars had a sit-down. Well, what if one of the Framers thinks Baars *made a mistake* giving Ruddick to the Thirds? You know, like a Starfleet versus the Klingons thing ..."

She almost laughed.

We tunnelled through the Pennsylvania dark. I found myself hating my poor little Golf. I hated the look of it. I hated the sour-milk smell of it. No power steering. No air conditioning. It even had *manual windows*, for fuck's sake. I hated the fact that I was embarrassed that Molly had to sit in it. Tin fucking can.

Fucking *Nazi* car, that's what it was.

So that pretty much summed up my situation. No leads. No *gun.*

Three more souls on my conscience (I had this fucked-up image of Nill braining Fucknut and Dipshit to make sure they were dead-dead). And a total shit-box for a car.

God hated me, the thin-skinned prick.

Oh well ... At least I had saved the babe.

Finding the hospital took some doing. I navigated the maze, wondering how heart-attack sufferers ever made it to the Emergency doors alive.

"I'll just drop you off here," I said, braking in front.

"It's okay," she replied, in the thoughtless way of couples, actually. "I'm quite capable of walking from the parking lot."

She looked at me in vague alarm when I didn't release the brake.

"Sorry, Molls. Disciple doesn't do health care facilities."

Feminine Dismay slackened her expression. Another old friend.

"But ... but how am I supposed to get home?"

"You have a credit card, don't you?"

"Yeah ..."

"I'll catch you back at the motel, then."

Cold, huh? But like I told Molly, me and hospitals do not mix. I got my reasons—*specific* reasons. But even in general, they're anathema to people like me. Delivering babies on the top floor, stacking bodies in the basement. Hospitals are the one place where death and birth meet, where the human circuit, you might say, is closed.

Where only earnest voices have the wind to speak.

Track Thirteen
THE BUZZ KILLERS

Monday ...

Knuckles on aluminum. Knocking. *Persistent* knocking, wandering into consciousness from the edges.

If I hadn't known it was her, I probably would've just rolled over to the other side of the bed, planted my face in the cool pillow. Only cops were prick enough to roust you out of bed this early in the morning.

But it was Molls, of course, looking at once perky and exhausted in the morning light. Traffic roared behind her. "They kept me overnight for observation."

"Perverts," I replied, grinning.

It took her a moment, but she got the joke. So much had happened that it seemed weeks ago, that night she caught me staring at her in the dark.

"I should be pissed," she said. "I kept asking myself what kind of guy saves the girl just to dump her off at Emergency."

"And?" I said, rubbing sleep from my eyes.

"And I decided ... well ... I don't know what I decided."

"Good."

"Good?"

"As soon as you grow a backbone, I'm through."

A breath of laughing air. She stepped across the threshold, no longer needing to be invited. Her arms clung. Her kisses came hot and hard.

We lay in bed, beneath the warm glow of the sun smouldering through the discoloured curtains. Our smell filled the room, salty and mellow. Her head on my shoulder, she had been describing her short stay in the Meaford County Hospital, and the enormous 1,342-dollar-and-61-cent bill she had charged against her MasterCard—just to find out she hadn't suffered a concussion. When I asked her whether she still wanted to press charges against Nill, she waved the thought away, saying that it would give her a stake in her story, compromise her journalistic independence.

Not because it could land me in the can or anything.

"Things are ramping up, Disciple ... *seriously* ramping up. As big as the JonBenét Ramsey circus ..."

"So what are you doing here with me?"

Something crept into her eyes. "Because we need to figure ... to figure this out."

"We have plenty of time to sort things, Molls."

She bent her face down, away from my scrutiny. "What if we don't have time?" she said strangely. "What if ..."

"What do you mean?" I asked. She was little more than a mop of red hair against my shoulder.

She turned, climbed my chest to better match my gaze, let go an *oh-my* sigh. "I think ... I think I'm falling for you."

Fawk ...

I tried not to swallow, but it was too late. "Don't say that."

"Say what? That I've never met a man like you? That I ... I *love* you?"

Owich. Can you believe this shit?

"No. *No*, Molls. You can't love me."

"And why's that?"

"Because *I'm not safe* ..." I tend to become vague in exchanges like these. To leave room for future bullshit rationales, I suspect.

"But isn't love about risks?"

"No. Not at all. If you can't feel safe with the person you love, you spend your whole life on the run."

Can you believe it? Instead of pulling out a can of whup-ass, I opened a club pack of Oprah.

Why do I do this? Why do I always make things so hard? For me. For them. Lying is always so much easier—so much safer. And yet I really only do it when things *don't* matter.

What the fuck's my problem?

"But I *feel* safe," she said. "I really do." A goofy little laugh, as short as a hiccup. Her left hand had settled on my chest. The pad of her ring finger pressed across my right nipple. "I'm not sure I've ever felt safer."

"That's because you only see a sliver of me," I said. "The part that resembles something human."

The whole of life, it sometimes seems, is just one long slow pan out, watching the details we're born to slowly shrink into an ever-expanding vista. More, always more, scrolling in from unseen edges of our ...

Frame. Huh.

"Well," she said, "I *like* what I see."

I licked my lips. Did my best to hold her gaze. "That'll change. Believe me. You'll glimpse the monster soon enough ..."

My dick lay as cold as a fish fillet against my thigh. Man, I hate that.

"Disciple ... You're *not* a monster."

Oh yes I am.

"You should get going," I said brusquely. Fucked-up word, *brusquely*. Makes you want to clear your throat.

I paused—hesitated, more like. She felt so warm, so inviting, a gold-windowed cottage stranded in a winter world. I *needed* her at that moment. I needed the sanctuary men find in feminine pity, the safety of retreating into angelic intentions. I can be such a suck sometimes.

Suddenly I was up, sweeping my gauchies up to my waist.

Love.

What a buzz kill.

I suppose she would have left either way: the Framers had scheduled a press conference at 2 p.m. that afternoon, something she simply could not miss. But it was better that she left hurt.

I lied, told her I would mosey on by later. And this brought back her words from several minutes before.

"What if we don't have time? What if ..."

I ignored them, banished them with a blink. I'm continually doing that, it seems, brushing away flakes of the past. I kissed her longer and deeper than I intended.

The click of the door behind her delivered her words again, this time with even fiercer clarity.

"What if we don't have time? What if ..."

Fear, I realized. She had spoken these words, not with the anxiety of uncertain relationships, but with real *mortal* fear ...

Epiphanies are fucked-up things. I had this friend, Cochrane, whom I used to train with a few years back. We called him Three-Ball because he busted so many nuts at the gym we figured he had to have a spare. Anyway, he comes in this one afternoon saying that he had an "epiphany" the previous night, that he had—you guessed it—found Jesus. So I argued with him, pointed out how people the world over have these profound, life-changing experiences, finding whatever, everything from Krishna to Elvis. "I know you feel all special, all saved and shit, but feeling that way is common as dirt, Three-Ball. It's *you*, not Jesus. You've saved yourself."

"But I *know*," he replied, saying what they all say. "I *know* that I know!"

Sad story, really. He suffered from bipolar depression, stopped taking his medication. "There's no pill for the devil," he told me. He electrocuted himself in his bathtub on October 4, 2005. Another shitty day.

That's when I realized: the insights or revelations that make you feel like you *know* are simply not to be trusted.

Epiphanies—*true* epiphanies—leave you sucking on the tailpipe of your own stupidity.

And I could feel it, my mental retardation, buzzing like a palpable thing. I lay there in my boxers, pinned to the mattress, my arms and legs stretched out, while I leaned back in my chair in Consultation Room 4 listening to Anson Williams say, *"Sure. Who doesn't talk about their parents?"*

"You know what I mean," I replied. *"Did she ever talk about them?"*

"Yuh," he said.

Why? When he seemed relatively calm when it came to discussing Jennifer's disappearance, why the hell was he so nervous about this?

"Why the reluctance, Anson?"

"Nah ... Just feels weird, you know."

"She swear you to secrecy?"

"Yuh," he said, nodding.

"The circumstances have changed, don't you think?"

"Yuh."

"Things couldn't be any more radical."

He chewed on his lower lip. *"Suppose."*

Suppose? What the hell? At the time I assumed he had been filtering events through some Framer bullshit.

"Xen ..." Anson explained moments later. "*He teaches us that we're here to learn from all these ...*"—a reflexive swallow—"*things, you know?*

Sins, crimes ... What we suffer is secondary to the fact that we suffer, the meaning we take away from having endured. And because of this, he says we're supposed to affirm, to affirm our lives in their entirety, to realize that not a moment, not a breath has been wasted ... And she ... Jennifer, just ... couldn't ... do this."

Couldn't ... That wasn't what he had been about to say. He had hesitated because he had caught himself ... Because he had almost said *can't.* Jennifer just can't affirm what her father did to her.

Was he still holding out hope that she was alive?

"Nah ... Just feels weird, you know."

Or did he somehow know she was alive? ... More life-after-death Framer bullshit?

I lay motionless across sex-tangled sheets, the centre of a slow-twisting pinwheel world. In the Compound courtyard I heard myself say, *"She's dead, Baars. You know that."*

"No, Mr. Manning. Quite the contrary ... What I know—know, Mr. Manning—is that mankind conquered death long, long ago."

This time I focused on his eyes ... And there it was, the twinkling look of an inside joke.

He was playing me. He had been playing me all along. He knew all right, and not the way Three-Ball knew Jesus. He knew the way I knew my gun was at the bottom of the river ...

That was the joke.

Then it hit me. The crushing sense of failure and stupidity ...

The epiphany.

Dead Jennifer wasn't dead. Christ, she wasn't even fucking missing ... That was why Anson had been so reluctant to say anything about her being molested by her father: because he found himself pinched between theatrical and *living* obligations.

Because Jennifer Bonjour was in the next room.

The sun burned white through the curtains. The smoke from my cigarette piled like hair toward the ceiling. A pang clawed into my throat. Even though I lay on my back, I hung there, hooked through the trachea.

Then, click. The puzzle came together.

All of it. The fingers and toes. The Thirds. The papers. Even fucking CNN ...

Which was to say, Molly.

I lay in bed with a sheet sprawled across my midsection, and laughed long and hard. I laughed at my stupidity, at my heartbreak ...

I laughed at the sense of doom sponging through my veins.

He's weak, sometimes, Disciple Manning.

He has his buttons like everyone else, triggers that get pulled now and again, by women, by failure, and by bad fucking news most of all. The clicks they make are the same, but the booms tend to be bigger.

So he has this kit stashed in the upholstery of his shitty car. Not much really. A Slurpee straw. A fold of tinfoil pouched by a few crystalline flakes. Rocks.

He sits hunched like a little boy on the corner of his bed. Kicks his Zippo with his thumb. Draws deep on the sizzling of joy and relief ...

Score.

Fuck it, he tells himself, grinning as he sinks back. The mattress doesn't seem so hard anymore.

Fuck it, he tells himself, smiling his famous sneering smile, laughing at his thoughts.

Look at Holmes ...

He fucking injected that shit.

So there I sat soaking in relief and gratitude—transcendental gratitude. Renewed—I felt renewed, even if it was a drug-induced crock of shit. The biggest misconception squares have about drugs is that the highs have this poisonous taint, like the faint odour of rot in frying bacon. Not so.

Dopamine is dopamine, whether the brain has forgotten how to recycle it or not.

I studied the charcoal reflections in the television screen. A bulbous man sitting on the corner of a bed. A fish-eye motel room. Funny, I thought, all the ways reality reproduces itself. Monotonous, really.

I don't remember picking up the remote control—sometimes my attention wanders, as I said. I thumbed my way through the gaudy parade of channels—ShamWow! and Obama commemorative coins and sports utility vehicles—and there it was, the ticker tag line of the minute, as real as CNN ...

JENNIFER BONJOUR: VICTIM OF CULT WAR?

Quickly replaced by,

LOCAL WHITE SUPREMACIST "CHURCH" IMPLICATED

And Baars's smiling face, serene and centre-screen. From the willows slowly heaving in the breeze behind him, I knew he was standing in front of the Framer Compound. The sunlight played off his glasses in an eerie way, making them flash utterly white from time to time ...

Or was it crimson?

"You said you have a message for the American people?" the off-frame reporter asked.

"Yes," Baars replied, so much humility compressed into his smile it could only be called smug. "Yes, I do. They need to know that these are the Final Days."

"You mean that the world is about to end?"

"Yes, but not in the way you might think."

The unseen reporter was on him in a click. "You think the sun is about to swallow up the world. That the world is billions of years older than it appears."

This seemed to surprise him—an *informed* interviewer, imagine—but a quick blink was all he needed to reclaim his Vedic composure. His smile broadened as a chorus of shouts climbed in the sunlit background. Someone close cried out loud enough to be picked up on the interviewer's microphone.

"It's her! Jesus! It's really her!"

I chortled in front of the little screen. This was news?

I saw her even before the cameraman had the presence of mind to redirect his shot. Even before her granular image found its way to the centre of the nation's perspective, I knew. Slight and beautiful even in a wheelchair. Her hands and feet bound into bloody paws. Buddha smiling and heavy-lidded. Stevie pushed her into the photo-op sweet spot fairly glowing in his white uniform ...

Dead Jennifer.

A girl fucked up by a father fucked up by a bottle of bourbon—and the list goes on.

I couldn't tear my eyes from her bandaged hands and feet. Now that was taking one for the team. Positively hardcore. They had the medical facilities at the Compound—the little episode with the dying stroke patient, Agatha, had demonstrated that. The only thing that confused me was what Nolen had said earlier: that the coroner thought the digits had been severed *post mortem.* And then I realized: they had been cut *twice.*

Remove them, leave them overnight, then cut them again closer to the knuckle.

Everything was pixilated madness on the screen. Voices shouted and battled. Only her name was intelligible, repeated over and over and over. A new tag line popped onto the bottom of the screen.

Man, they had this breaking news thing down to a *science.*

And the world watches—why? Because the *world* is watching.

So please don't tell me the media are sane.

I thought of Molly. I thought of Mandy. I wanted to weep, but all I could do was laugh. But my room, the prick, swallowed my hilarity whole. It was too shoddy not to be mean-spirited. A Holiday Inn would have joined in.

Someone—I couldn't see who—had imposed some kind of order on the scrum. Baars had moved to Jennifer's side. Now he spoke into at least a dozen microphones. You could just see her in the corner of the screen, gazing up with the adoration of a Republican's wife.

"Your *whole* life," he said in an evangelist's tones, only sadder, wiser. "Your whole life you've been dogged by this feeling, this baseless faith that somehow, someway, *you are more* ... More than a grocery clerk, line worker, tax auditor, stonemason. More than your children, your husband or your wife. More than the slapstick you watch night after night parading across your TV. At some level, *you already know* what I am about to tell you."

"And what might that be?" The CNN reporter's voice rose above the fray of questions.

But Baars had moved beyond interviews and into the realm of religious calling. He was staring into *my* eyes now, peering through the fog of all the intervening cameras and transmissions—through the fog that was me. "I have lived ten thousand lives ten thousand times," he explained. "I have dreamed across the ages, and so have you. I have been emperors and I have been slaves ...

"I have endured far more suffering than joy."

A sad smile. A recognition.

"And so have you."

Was this some kind of trick? I turned to make sure he wasn't sitting beside me. When I glanced back, a new tag line gleamed below his erudite image ...

XENOPHON BAARS MAKES STATEMENT

That was when he pulled the gun from beneath his white jacket. A Glock.

Cool.

Now *that* was a statement.

The cameraman fell backward in his scramble to escape the gun, but to his credit he managed to capture Baars, who suddenly seemed statuesque stretched across the open summer sky. The Glad Garbage Bag Man about to reveal *the* truth of human existence: certainty and stupidity are one and the same.

He moved with the grace of milk—it was quite remarkable really. He stretched out his left hand to the camera, as though holding back the ethereal hordes, while swinging the automatic in his right laterally, toward Jennifer's joyous face.

They were on something, I realized. Some kind of drug—no different than me. Drugs have a way of recognizing each other.

The cameraman managed a haphazard zoom on the gun and the girl. I saw her lips move: "Elephant sh—"

I couldn't hear the report because screams had overloaded the mike. But I saw it all, one thumping heartbeat: the flash, the puncture, the blowback of blood, even the shock wave rippling through her lips—all of it CGI-seamless.

I saw Xenophon Baars shoot his lover in the face.

Dead Jennifer.

* * *

Baars raised the automatic to his temple.

"All of us are here because we have chosen to stay," he said, his voice background-noise thin yet somehow dreadfully clear against the ambient shouting. Everyone hears the man holding the gun. "All of us have chosen to die with our world ..."

The frame wobbled as the cameraman shimmied backward on his ass. You could hear the correspondent gasp, *"You getting this?"* followed by a gravelly grunt in the affirmative.

"But some of us ..." Baars said with a beatific smile. And there was nothing frantic, nothing strained about his tone. He spoke the just-the-facts way cops do when they find themselves dragged onto the witness stand yet again. "Some of us do not want to die in our *sleep*."

The weapon popped—a pathetic sound, really. The screaming came through real clear, though.

Even still, the sound guy should have been canned.

The end was nigh, the eons-old machines preserving earth from its bloated sun were giving out, and Baars simply wanted to give everyone a chance to make peace with their existence. From his standpoint, he had done nothing more than take a surprise messianic turn in a video game ... A first-person shooter.

A part of me wanted to slip into the morgue that night and shake his dead hand. I mean, there was the Frame and then there was the frame. Brilliant, utterly insane, Xenophon Baars had managed to turn the *world* into his fucking bullhorn.

It was nothing short of ingenious. A missing hottie? A cult cold war?

Rock for the great media pipe. Pure. Uncut. This was Jim Jones without the body count. Heaven's Gate on a hundred live feeds ...

I could see them plotting, Baars and a select group of his followers. I could hear Baars chastise the others for taking pleasure in the destruction of the Thirds at their enlightened hands. "They are simply exploring a different life," he would say—some bullshit like that. I could see Jennifer cutting across the brownlands, sneaking into the Compound from the rear. And I could see that fucker Stevie, ever faithful, driving through town with his collection of little cages, a single wooden cross, and of course a zip-lock bag filled with Jennifer's fingers and toes.

With material this sexy, all Baars needed was to catch the attention of a single editor to start his conflagration. All he needed was Molly Modano ...

"At the very least," I had said, *"Amanda Bonjour needs to know her husband is a scumbag, don't you think?"*

She said nothing at first. Managing the truth required consideration.

"Disciple ... You can't say anything."

Because Jennifer was more than her "big break." Jennifer was her friend. Her fellow Framer. And you don't screw with the personal lives of your friends, do you? Not even at the end of the world.

"What if we don't have time? What if ..."

And me?

Well, Judge, you see, it was like this ...

I was framed.

I retrieved the photograph that Mandy had given me that day in my office: young Jennifer, innocent and sun-smiling, thumbs and fingers spread wide in a ta-da pose. I wedged it in the corner of the television screen, my own boxed insert—the only headline that mattered. I hit the mute button, listened to the traffic shivering through the walls. We stared at each other for a while. She did not blink.

"Dead," I whispered, saying the word the way kids say "bad" to household pets.

Dead Jennifer.

Track Fourteen

ONE MORE ATROCITY TALE

The thing to remember about me is that I don't forget ...

Anything.

Ever.

It all comes back, endlessly repeating, circumstances soaked in passion. Love. Terror. Disgust. A life crushed in the wheels of perpetual reliving.

Write about it, my therapist says. Writing gives you "distance."

Distance. Fawk.

A great thing, not forgetting. Makes writing real easy.

Almost as easy as going crazy.

I get this sense sometimes, typically when things get real weird, that I remember the *future* as vividly as I remember the past. In Iraq I swear I once dove before the mortar round landed. Good for me. Bad for two other absent-minded fools. Either way, I know that I looked at my cellphone where it sat artfully poised in relation to spilled change and crumpled receipts the instant *before* it began buzzing.

I'm sure Baars would have had an explanation.

"Disciple! Where are you?"

It was Molly, sounding as shrill as her skin had been smooth.

"Already at the airport, baby. Getting as far away from you crazy fuckers as I can."

A strange noise, a kind of coughing, sobbing ... A sharp intake of breath.

"Disciple! Disciple, please! I know you're lying. I know you're still at the motel. Puh-pleaase! It—it's horrible! I didn't know! I swear I didn't know! There—there's no way I would've ... there's just no fucking way! This is crazy! Please, Disciple. You have to tell me what's going on. What's going on?"

I believed her, instantly and utterly. Baars had only told her enough, nothing more, nothing less. "A media hoax," he called it. A way to wring *enlightenment* out of the instruments of mass delusion. Molly had been a conspirator, sure, but she had also been the biggest dupe of all.

It was a genuine moment of wonder for me. How long had it been since my ears had been so simple?

"Sorry, Molly. Big security guy, telling me to shut down my phone. You know how they are when it comes to security."

"No! Disciple! Dis—"

I snapped my cell shut, set it across the loose change and coffee mug rings. I'm really not sure why I hung up. Just seemed safer that way.

Besides, back in my day, when you burned your ass, you sat on the blister.

I left the door slightly ajar so that it would simply swing open when she came knocking.

"I've been there," she said, sobbing. "You have to believe me, Disciple! I've been there!"

The Occluded Frame.

"There's no such thing, Molly."

Her eyes are swollen and so am I.

"No. No. I've seen it with my own eyes!"

Rather than speak, I encircled her in my arms, brought her in from the summer cold. We made love because that was the basis of our relationship, our HQ, the place you retreat to when the mission goes wrong. *I will relive this,* I thought as she dipped and heaved above me, searching for a bliss that was long in coming. *I will relive this a thousand times.*

"You have to believe me, Disciple."

She whispered this to me, as though armed patrols scoured the streets, as if floodlights streamed through the room's windows.

"Baars," I said. "He made you into a blank tablet. You know how hypnosis works ..."

But I knew my words were useless. She *believed,* just like you—like everybody.

It's an instinct. Like fucking.

Afterward, we simply lay breathing, me on my back, her on her stomach. There was this sense that we had done all that could be done, here, in the shadow of a setting world. I imagined this was what critters do when their habitat collapses around them. Indulge and impregnate. Another litter to pick through the trash.

She wept.

And somehow I understood that I had become a memory for her, a trigger for that clutch in her stomach, that cold wave of horror that stopped her halfway through whatever. Somehow I knew she was already in the process of forgetting ...

Healing.

We talked for a couple of hours in that naked, languorous way. There was a heaviness between us, and a sorrow, as if we were a divorced couple who had wavered in our resolution to seek different genitals.

She had been recruited out of Berkeley. Like Anson had, she went on and on about her initial skepticism. She had laughed out loud at first, but her Outreacher, Mohammed Kadri, had been so nice and so persistent. She really had no choice but to listen, and the more she listened ...

It's like we have this hand within us, a hundred million neurons shaped like a palm and clutching fingers. *Something,* it cries. *Give me something to grasp. You mean nothing until my palm is full.*

Any old bullshit will do.

She was first hypnotized, and first experienced the Frame, on November 27, 2006. Apparently they celebrated the date like a second birthday.

"You have no idea, Disciple. No idea what it's like. To have no body. To think at the speed of light. To remember everything ..."

Like being an angel, she said.

Apparently Baars himself had called her about a month ago. The Framers had been on red alert for quite some time, preparing for the earth's imminent demise, so when the call came, she had dropped everything. He told her that they were planning to stage Jennifer's disappearance, but that he could say no more because it was imperative that no one know Molly was one of them. It would compromise her credibility, he said. All she was supposed to do was keep working the story. The hook would catch soon enough. He said the media had a fetish for cults, that they packaged them into something called "atrocity tales," stories that all cultures use to define themselves against outsiders.

He should know: he used to teach the shit.

"He told me not to waver," she said, wiping her eyes with the bedsheets. "He said everything that happened, no matter how shocking or how bizarre, was simply part of the plan."

But believers always waver. Crisis is inevitable, which is why belief systems squander so much energy defining doubt—the hard road, and certainly the one less travelled—as a kind of weakness. God's greatest trick was convincing the world that belief was hard. For Molly, the crisis came in the form of Jennifer's fingers. That was when she caught her first real whiff of madman.

"I almost told you, Disciple. I should have told you!"

"But I thought you said the Frame was real."

She cried for a time. I talked the stupid talk I always rely on when I don't know what to say. Gambling stories, mostly. A couple run-ins with the law.

Her breathing was growing thick, so I asked before it was too late.

"When is it supposed to happen? The end, I mean."

Just for curiosity's sake.

"Friday," she said numbly, her lips moving behind a violet netting of hair. Her eyes did not open. "The world always ends on Friday."

Fawk. Vegas is so much more fun on the weekend.

I wake up in the middle of the night. There's a young woman beside me, red hair askew, pale and naked in tangled sheets. Her breath is deep and crisp and even.

A crimson glow taints the windows. I get up, walk nude to the curtains, which I pull wide with hands that have ended lives. Red paints me, but for once it's not blood. I shiver despite the heat.

I stand motionless with patience. I so rarely see the sunrise, what with the weed and the women and the good times. I want to meet this goof they call the Dawn. I want to greet him with a knowing grin and an enigmatic wink. Say, *"Some forms of life flourish in the absence of sunlight ..."*

But even as I dream these thoughts, I know something's wrong. The frequency. The geometry, maybe.

The sun's arc burns through the paper horizon, an incandescent wire that grows and grows, swelling with ruby brilliance, becoming a scimitar, a crescent smouldering with retina-burning wavelengths. It scores the horizon from end to end, drawing the sky away like a curtain, burning higher and higher above a mountain range of atmospheric processors, a heaven-wide holocaust that would have boiled away the atmosphere, made slush of the continental plates, had the earth not been transformed into a machine.

A sky that was a sun. A sun that was a sky. Like staring up at a beach ball perched on the tip of your nose.

And it seemed *so obvious*, standing there, cooking in my illusory skin. It seemed so obvious why so many of us would stay here, die here, rather than flee to the stars with the others. The Gods were long dead. All we had was emptiness, twisted into Möbius convolutions. And monotony.

In the absence of any destination, why not worship our origins?

Simulate the twenty-first century. Make a flag of our skin.

She was gone when I awoke. I'm not sure what bummed me out more: the fact of her escape or the fact of my slumbering through it. Usually I'm such a twitchy sleeper. Makes me feel safe, the belief that I can be unconscious and alert.

I sat naked on the corner of the bed and smoked a Winston, reflected on the difference between quiet and lonely. Smoke one hundred thousand and *one*, I realized with no little dismay. I hate missing milestones.

I shaved to the image of my face floating behind *SORRY* scrawled in cherry red lipstick. I pondered my age, wondered how many more Mollys would love and leave me. The only things wrinkles flatter are poets and their plots. I packed up my shit and loaded my Golf. I could already feel the buzz building on the horizon, the scramble of souls ducking for cover beneath the sweep of the National Spotlight. The media clowns would be out in force, cramming Ruddick into as many small-town clichés as they could think of, and searching for inside angles, for material witnesses they could lionize or implicate.

Either way, me and my bag of weed were no longer welcome in this town.

There's a profound peace in the monotony of a road already travelled, a *been-there-done-that* security that lets the mind wander paths not quite of its own making. Novelty, I had decided, forces you to fucking *think*, and I had had enough of that. The summer roared hot through my open windows. I daydreamed to the rattle of my diesel, pondered taking the first exit to Atlantic City and to the inexhaustible allure of dice, booze, and poon.

Instead, I found myself popping open my cell and calling Kimberley.

"Hi, babe," I said with phony cheer.

"Where are you?"

"Arrivals at JFK."

"You don't say. Where did the crime take you this time?"

"Tahiti, baby."

A snort, packed with amusement and exasperation, as only a woman is capable. *"I watch TV, you know, Disciple. Every once in a while my thumb slips and oops! there's CNN."*

"Yeah, well, you know me. Plugging the toilet no matter where I go."

Something in my tone must have tagged her, because she paused. *"Is everything okay, Disciple?"*

No.

"Sure. But I was thinking ..."

"Uh-oh."

"I was thinking I haven't been so ... good ... to you. You know?"

That wasn't entirely true. At the strip club where I first met her, I was the guy holding twenties in my teeth when everyone else chewed dollars or fives. But still, true enough.

"Something's wrong. I can hear it in your voice."

"No. Not at all. I just ... ah ... thought it might be nice if we went out on a ... you know, *date* or something."

"Date?" She fairly barked with laughter. I could almost see the smoke blowing out her nose. *"Weed's pretty good in Ruddick, huh?"*

"No. Seriously, Kim. I want to take you out. Seriously."

A long and wary pause. Strippers tend to be at once cautious and confident when dealing with men—kind of like animal trainers that way. *"Okay ..."* she said with a heavy *What-the-hell* sigh. *"I actually have Friday night off for a fucking change. You know, I told Jimmy. I sa—"*

"Make it Saturday," I interrupted, savouring the sluice of hot air over my face and scalp. Maybe it wasn't so bad, driving a car without an air conditioner.

That was Tuesday, August 18, 2009. Good. Bad. Another day to be remembered ...

Whether I wanted to or not.

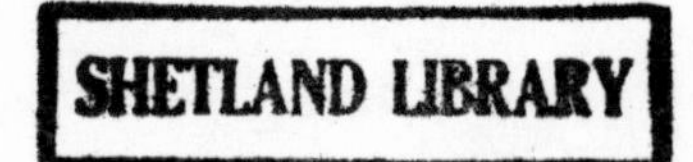

Acknowledgments

As a writer I spend my days swapping souls, imagining this or that perspective, deciding who gets sharpened and who gets dulled when they scrape up against one another.

Which is just to say that I bullshit for a living.

The best way to bullshit, of course, is to surround yourself with bullshitters, so I've gradually become one of those coffee shop writers. *Disciple of the Dog* was almost entirely written in a wonderful little place called The Black Walnut. If you've been there, then I owe you my thanks, one bullshitter to another.

Specifically, I need to thank Michele Lenhardt, Roy Cook, and Rhia Baines, for putting up with me and my geeky sense of humour, and for brewing the best damn coffee south of Toronto. I especially need to thank Ashlan Potts, for being one of those exceptional people who forge families wherever they go.

I need to thank the usual suspects, Adrienne Kerr at Penguin, Eric Raab at Tor, Jon Wood at Orion, and of course, my agent, Chris Lotts, who I'm convinced has a better sense of character and story than the bulk of his clients, me included. I should also thank Dan Mellamphy for our conversations on the ways memory impacts experience, my brother,

Bryan Bakker, for carrying the tune when I sang out of key, and my brother-in-law, Rick O'Brien, for innumerable drunken, dirty-minded gems.

This has been a big year for my wife Sharron and I. After almost twenty years of student living, we have finally settled down, and welcomed a little baby girl into our life ...

Ruby.

The one soul I've made, but did not imagine. My first *true* creation, and far and away the most beautiful.

Thank you, Sharron.